THE SNOW WAS THEIR UNDOING

By the same author:

The Battle of El Alamein and Beyond,
　　　　　　The Book Guild, 1993

To The Wars, The Book Guild, 1997

Sun and Shadows, The Book Guild, 1999

THE SNOW WAS THEIR UNDOING

G.A. Morris

The Book Guild Ltd
Sussex, England

This book is a work of fiction. The characters and situations in this story are imaginary. No resemblance is intended between these characters and any real persons, either living or dead.

This book is sold subject to the condition that it shall not by way of trade or otherwise, be lent, re-sold, hired out, photocopied or held in any retrieval system or otherwise circulated without the publisher's prior consent in any form of binding or cover other than that in which this is published and without a similar condition including this condition being imposed on the subsequent purchaser.

The Book Guild Ltd
25 High Street
Lewes, Sussex

First published 2000
© G.A. Morris 2000
Set in Baskerville
Typesetting by
Southern Reproductions (Sussex)
Crowborough
Printed in Great Britain by
Athenæum Press Ltd, Gateshead

A catalogue reference for this book is
available from the British Library

ISBN 1 85776 446 3

To some survivors of Hitler's Russian Campaign whom I knew very well: Petr, a Cossack, a Guards' tank regiment officer; Dr. Med. Paul Bideau, a front line doctor; and Josef Schramm, infantry officer of the Brandenburgers.
Also Madam Oudinot, a friend I knew in Baghdad, a direct descendant of the Marshal.

CHAPTERS

1	France	1
2	Spain	8
3	France	17
4	Prussia	29
5	Into Russia	35
6	Smolensk	41
7	Borodino and Moscow	45
8	The Retreat	56
9	Paris	59
10	Germany	66
11	The Crimea	72
12	Germany	81
13	America	86
14	Germany	111
15	Into France	123
16	Germany	132
17	Europe on Fire	138
18	Hell on Earth	147

19	The Final Act	164
20	A Fragile Peace	173
21	Into France	180
22	Operation Barbarossa	189
23	Objective Moscow	201
24	*Vorwärts Wir Gehen Zurück*	215
25	Stalingrad	220
26	Kursk	231
27	*Nocheinmal Vorwärts Wir Gehen Zurück*	237
28	The Western Front	244

PRINCIPAL CHARACTERS

Pierre Flamand	Marries Collette Armand, killed in action 1812.
François Flamand	Their son. Collette remarries Kurt von Winterstein.
François becomes	François von Winterstein and marries Marlene Detterling. Killed in Crimea at Balaclava.
Otto von Winterstein	Their son. Marries Heide von Richtman. Assassinated Paris 1870.
Erika von Winterstein	Their daughter. Marries Paul von Ritter.
Karl von Ritter	Their son. Marries Eva von Brausch.
Kurt von Ritter	Their son. Marries Sasha Grudzyn. Killed in France 1944.

FOREWORD

Both Napoleon and Hitler invaded Russia with the conviction that the Russians would be defeated in a matter of weeks. Instead, stubborn resistance by the Russians, the vast inhospitable terrain and poor communications discounted any quick victory. Both were caught unprepared for the savage winter. The German army crossed the border in summer uniforms and six months later were caught in the freezing snow and ice of the appalling winter. Hitler should have learned from Napoleon's bitter experience. Unfortunately for him, Hitler, like Napoleon, was obliged to attack Russia to remove the threat to his territorial ambitions. As with Napoleon, the snow was their undoing.

1

France

Pierre Flamand, child of the Revolution, born in 1789, of landowner parents dwelling in a modest chateau near Caen in Normandy, now in 1811 passed out from the French Military Academy and was going home for a short leave. He was glad to be riding through the verdant Normandy countryside, land of Camembert cheese and calvados, astride a fine horse and wearing his new officers uniform, and especially looking forward to once again being in the company of his fiancée, a neighbour's daughter, Collette Armand whom he had grown up with, both he and she being very happy to be betrothed.

His parents were overjoyed to see him, their only son. They were also blessed with two older daughters, both married, but their pleasure was blunted by the everpresent war which Napoleon was waging in Spain and knowing that inevitably Pierre would be involved in the fighting. After their evening repast Pierre and his parents sat comfortably round the fire with the brandy, when Pierre decided to broach the subject of the conflict raging against the British and their allies, Portugal and Spain, in the Peninsular, not so far distant.

'When my leave is up, I am posted to a Hussar regiment which is in the south with Soult's army, a quiet part of the country, near Seville, far away from the action.'

His mother was immediately upset and asked, 'Why must you go, my only son? What shall we do without you? Napoleon should end this horrible war, the English are devils and their Wellington a monster.'

'Mother, I am sorry but I have to go, it is my duty. I propose to marry Collette before I leave, provided all agree.'

Pierre's parents were happy for him to go ahead, and his father said, 'You arrange with Collette and we will discuss the wedding arrangements with her mother and father.'

That same evening Pierre went over to see Collette, who greeted him lovingly.

'Let us walk in the garden,' said Pierre. 'I have something very important to talk about.'

They came to a gazebo away from the house which they had often used during their courtship, when they discovered each other, but had not gone the whole way.

As they sat on the chaise longue which was there to provide a comfortable snoozing place for warm summer afternoons, he said, 'Chérie, I am now commissioned and after my leave I will be going to Spain. Let us get married before I go. My parents agree and will speak to yours.'

Collette was overcome with joy.

'Of course, I will, Pierre, I have waited since we were children, it was always in my thoughts. My mother and father will certainly agree. Let us tell them. Before we go shall we love a while? We can be free to go further than before.' Nothing loath, Pierre laid her on the chaise longue and took her in his arms, caressing her breasts, which were half-exposed as was the fashion. He then lifted her dress and under her shift she was drawerless as was the custom, ladies' underclothes being not yet the fashion in France. He had on previous occasions indulged in love play but not all the way. With the skill which seems to be an inherent part of French men, he entered her. She cried a little as her opening was breached and then clasped his body to pull him further in. Pierre, not very experienced, however, understood what was necessary to give a woman satisfaction and worked steadily until he could restrain himself no longer, thrusting vigorously to a climax.

Collette screamed, '*Mon dieu, je vien, je vien, ooh, aah*' and was still.

When they recovered, she said, 'Oh, Pierre, that was wonderful, why have we waited so long?'

When they returned to the house they were a little dishevelled and flushed so the wise parents, who were all waiting for them, suspected that they had been up to something. All were in agreement to the proposed marriage and at once began discussing the details. If there had been sufficient time, it was possible for the ceremony to have been held in Caen Cathedral, but under the circumstances it would have to be held in the church which the families habitually used. The prospective bride and groom were to see the curé on the morrow.

The curé was delighted, he knew them both since they were born and had been christened by him. It was arranged for the wedding to take place in three days' time, giving sufficient time to invite relatives, friends and neighbours, all of whom lived near enough in Normandy. The reception was to be held at the chateau, which was more commodious than Collette's house.

The wedding was well attended and the church filled, the overflow of villagers outside. The bride was ravishing, as they always are, in a borrowed wedding dress, there being insufficient time to make a new one. Pierre was very handsome in his Hussar's uniform and a guard of honour was mounted by the local militia. After the reception the newly-weds set off for a short honeymoon in nearby Deauville, on the coast. They stayed at an hotel well known to them, looking across *La Manche*, which the English called the English Channel, towards the hated enemy. Daily they walked along the fashionable promenade, but above all they made love, a newly discovered joy, especially for Collette, who was, to say the least, enthusiastic.

All too soon it was time to leave so, sadly, they left the coast for home, Collette radiant-looking and Pierre a trifle tattered. It would be a miracle if Collette were not pregnant. On the day following they said a heart-rending farewell and Pierre set out for the depôt of the regiment at Lyons, where the remnants remained, the regiment being in Spain.

Pierre reported to the adjutant who informed him that he would be leaving in charge of a party of twenty replacements with an old sergeant who was returning after recovering from wounds received with the regiment at Torres Vedras the previous year.

The next day Pierre paraded his replacements with their mounts. Pierre had his own fine charger which he had specially selected at Caen. The sergeant, an old sweat, greeted Pierre with a practised salute and an air of, 'Well here is another useless young officer, God help him.' However, he was not unimpressed by the efficient manner in which he checked the men, their equipment and horses.

Pierre, when he was satisfied with the turnout of men and horses, addressed them.

'Tomorrow we leave for Toulon and Spain.' (The journey over the southern part of the Pyrenees was too arduous and beset by Spanish partisans.) *'Nous marchons à la gloire, pour la belle France,'* he said, adding, *'bon chance, soyez brave, à la victoire.'*

He discussed the move with the sergeant after dismissing the parade and they decided to stop for the night at Valence and Avignon where there were military barracks. The sergeant remarked that a close watch must be kept to prevent desertion.

The journey was accompanied without incident, the ride through lovely country in the warm spring weather of early April an invigorating send-off to war, and all were in high spirits. At Toulon they went to the barracks near the harbour, where Pierre reported to the embarkation officer and was told that they would be leaving with a convoy of transports the next day at nightfall, embarkation at noon. Pierre decided to risk letting the men out and as they had behaved well so far, let them have a last night in town, their last opportunity for a fling on French soil.

Pierre tidied himself up in preparation for an evening out, a good dinner and wine, and then, who knows? He had recovered his vitality and appetite, impaired after the honeymoon, and his desires were whetted by the experience. Along the waterfront, with its many bars, he came to a restaurant of a good appearance, obviously used by officers, so he went in and was shown to a table where another young officer was seated.

The maitre said, 'If you do not mind, sir, the tables are rather full. Perhaps this gentleman would allow you to join him.'

They introduced themselves.

'Jean, I am probably, like yourself, leaving tomorrow. Please join me. We should enjoy tonight.'

'I am Pierre, I am pleased to join you. We will see what happens after dinner. A little fun would not come amiss.'

After a good dinner with the best of available wines, Jean said, 'I know of a brothel nearby where we can drink, gamble and, above all find some charming girls. It is expensive but after all it may be our last night in France.'

They walked to the house and were admitted by the burly doorkeeper and found themselves in a large well-furnished salon where the madam greeted them.

'Well, you young officers, I am sure you want some nice young ladies.' She called a maid. 'Order your drinks and I will send some nice girls. You may think we are not busy, but the gentlemen are all upstairs.'

They sat with their drinks and soon two girls arrived, one not so young, but very charming.

Pierre thought, that's the one for me, and so it was and they went upstairs.

The room was sparsely furnished with a bed and two chairs and in a corner a washstand and a bidet on metal legs. She undressed, revealing a good ample body, something to get hold of. Squatting on the bidet, she washed herself between her legs and then called for Pierre, who was also naked.

'Come, chéri, let me wash you also, then you can go inside me nice and clean.'

After the wash they lost no time and coupled on the bed.

It was soon over and Pierre said, *Ça c'etait bon, je suis trés méchant, ma pauvre femme, mais . . . !'*

Jean was already downstairs. They paid madam and left for the nearest bar.

Later, parting, Pierre said, 'I have enjoyed our evening but maybe we shall not meet again.'

In the morning the troop rode down to the docks, some of the men hung-over and looking far from well. At the entrance they were given a guide who took them to their allotted transport. Loading the horses, as always, was a problem; some were resigned and docile, but a few caused a terrific rumpus as they were swung on board by canvas harness round their bellies, lashing out with all four legs and landing on the dock kicking furiously until tethered and calmed down.

The six transports formed up outside the harbour and in the late afternoon set sail escorted by two frigates of the French navy bound for Cartagena, some 500 miles to the south-west. (Cartagena, a Spanish naval base, was once sacked by Sir Francis Drake in a daring raid in 1585.) Due to Royal Navy activity around the Straits of Gibraltar it was unwise to go further along the coast to say, Malaga. The weather was fine, the wind moderate from the north, a fair tack in a calm sea, the Mediterranean, a fickle inland sea, could at times be rough and stormy. The voyage was expected to take about a week and all went well, the soldiers and horses unaffected by seasickness. Happily, they would arrive in good shape.

On the fifth day out, nearing their goal, a lone sail was sighted on the horizon to the south, judged to be on a course that would intercept the convoy. As the afternoon wore on, it became clear to the frigates that it was a British man-of-war, a lone figure, intending to intercept them. The French commander ordered the transports to turn on a course towards the land and the two frigates proceeded on a bearing to close with the enemy ship. Soon they could identify the ship as a Royal Navy frigate, with its battle ensign flying.

The three warships drew together and the enemy commenced firing at extreme range ineffectively. By superior seamanship, the British frigate managed to manoeuvre between the two French ships and, within range, discharged furious broadsides into them. The French returned the fire and the three vessels were being seriously knocked about. Marines in the topmast platforms fired their muskets continuously and the decks were blood-soaked, littered with dead and wounded sailors. The odds were evened in the enemy's favour. A chance shot penetrated into the powder magazine of one of the French ships which exploded with a roar like thunder and rapidly sank. A few men could be seen, survivors clinging to debris. The two remaining frigates battered away at each other until the French ship was reduced to a hulk, masts down and on fire, and was compelled to surrender. Both vessels set about picking up men in the sea and finally the enemy took the French frigate in tow with a prize crew on board.

Meanwhile, it was getting dark and the transports were out of sight, proceeding to their destination hugging the coast. Soon after dawn they reached the great harbour of Cartagena where there was consternation over the loss of the frigates to Nelson's navy, but relief at the safe arrival of the much needed reinforcements.

2

Spain

Pierre gathered his troop on the dockside and was directed by a transport officer to a transit camp on the outskirts of Cartagena. Reporting to the adjutant, he was told that the Hussar regiment he would be joining was near Seville, some 300 miles away, as the crow flies, to the west.

'Before you leave, in three days, you will attend a situation report which will be given by myself to the new officers tomorrow. Meanwhile, rest your men and horses. The journey to Seville is somewhat trying, the roads are sometimes ambushed by the Spanish irregulars.'

The following day the officers gathered in a large tent where above a dais was a map of Spain indicating the situation of the French and the enemy.

'Now,' said the adjutant, 'you will see that Wellington is firmly entrenched inside Spain before Ciudad Rodrigo on the vital road to Madrid. He is now looking for another door into Spain from the south, to develop a pincer thrust towards the capital, from north and south, dividing the French armies.'

He went on to say that General Beresford, Wellington's commander in the south, had made an assault on Badajos but gave up after a few days, having failed to reduce the great fortress of San Christobal. Meanwhile, Marshal Soult was advancing with an army of some 25,000 men and in response Beresford was moving down towards Albura to counter the threat, a composite allied force of British, Spanish, Portuguese and some German and Polish mercenaries.

'You will all join Soult on the Seville road towards Albura, leaving tomorrow and making all speed.'

The reinforcements from the transports travelled in a composite force, commanded by a Colonel who was going to join Soult's staff. As they were a numerous body of troops they were not attacked on the way and arrived to join the army on the road from Seville to Albura. Pierre was directed to the cavalry division and located the Hussar regiment, reporting to the adjutant.

The adjutant said, 'Well it is good to see you, we need reinforcements. You will report to Chef de Escadron Benoit, who will find a place for you.'

Pierre reported to the chef with his sergeant and 20 cavaliers and the chef said, 'You are very welcome. You will take over a troop which is at present commanded by a sergeant, a very experienced man who will help you in the short time we have before the coming battle.'

When Soult was a few miles from Albura he ordered the Hussars to carry out a reconnaissance as close as possible to observe the enemy positions. The Hussar colonel briefed Benoit to carry out the task, with his Escadron. Chef Benoit held an officers' and sergeants' order group and at first light the following day they set off. Pierre was not quite orientated and when they reached the high ground above the Albura River, at first could see nothing. His sergeant pointed out to him what was to be seen of the enemy.

'Look sir, at the left front, cavalry, probably Spanish as they are careless and exposing themselves unnecessarily.' He pointed to the right along a ridge. 'You can see smoke from cooking fires and some enemy soldiers moving about, British Infantry.'

And so he went on, past Albura where Portuguese cavalry were visible.

Pierre was still confused and at least two hours passed before he began to get the picture: signs of a whole army deployed a mere two miles distant. In the afternoon Chef Benoit sent for Pierre and his sergeant.

'Flamand, I want you to make a recce on foot over the river you can see below and work your way along the enemy side towards the town. You may encounter the odd soldier near the river. Be very careful, it would be a wasted effort if you were killed or captured. Take the sergeant and three men, leave at dusk. You are to look at the going, any pitfalls and anything you can deduce about the enemy.' He added, 'So learn to see and not be seen.'

They slipped away down the slope towards the tributary, carrying only pistols and long knives. The men picked by the sergeant were very likely lads, one a particularly large, strong-looking fellow, a good man in a scrap, thought Pierre. They waded across the shallow river, barely knee deep, no obstacle to man or horse and made their way towards what they had observed to be the Spanish cavalry camp on Beresford's right flank. It was now dark and cooking fires were visible over the area and considerable noise of talking and shouting could be heard. The area was largely scrub land, with some trees and cleared cultivated fields: plenty of cover. As they walked a soldier came out of the camp towards them, obviously to relieve himself. As he squatted, the sergeant motioned to the strong man and pointed to the Spaniard.

'Get him,' he whispered.

The poor fellow did not stand a chance.

A large hand clamped over his mouth and a voice warned him, 'Be still or else.'

It was important for them to take prisoners, so Pierre sent the captive back with one of the men, hands tied and led on a rope: a very cowed and frightened Spaniard, who would obviously tell all he knew, without much persuasion.

They continued cautiously along the British front, noting anything they could deduce from activity among the enemy. Nearing Albura about two miles from their starting point, they heard voices and, creeping towards them, spotted two figures sitting against a tree, smoking. Pierre signed to the big man to take the one on the left and he and the sergeant would deal with the other. Simultaneously they approached from behind the cover of the tree and silently overpowered the two. Unfortunately, one struggled violently and, overexerting himself, was awarded a broken neck and was dead.

Pierre said to the other in passable English, 'Be quiet or you will follow your friend.'

Pierre decided to cross back over the river and return to the regiment, the mission completed successfully. The second prisoner turned out to be a lieutenant of infantry. At least they could identify his unit and probably he would talk, under 'rigorous' interrogation.

Pierre reported to Chef Benoit, who was pleased.

'Well done, Flamand, especially bringing back the prisoner. Write your report and I will give it to the colonel for forwarding to the marshal's staff. Things are getting warmer and we should see some action soon.'

The forthcoming battle was very critical. If the French caused Beresford to retreat, the way was impeded by the river Guardiana, where one crossing was under the guns of Badajos, and the other exposed to the French advance. Beresford believed Soult's main effort would come along the main Seville road and consequently had established his divisions there, the British infantry and the German Legion. His right was held by the numerous but ineffective Spanish, brave individually but lacking proper training as a force and undecided and left-footed when opposed by the enemy.

It was mid-May, a still morning, when Soult attacked before daybreak. An infantry brigade crossed the stream in front of Albura and fired at the German Legion in front of the town. However, this was a feint. French cavalry and infantry moved down across the river following the route of Pierre's reconnaissance and surprised the Spanish, who were messing around in a disorganised way. Two brigades of cuirassiers were joined by the two brigades of Hussars, a formidable cavalry force which advanced on the hapless Spanish, throwing them into a piecemeal retreat. The French infantry moved behind the enemy cavalry, Soult's intention being to roll up Beresford's flank.

The Hussar brigade led the way down the slope and over the river.

Pierre remarked to his sergeant riding by his side, 'It looks as though our journey was not wasted, we are following the same route that we looked at.'

Over the river in front of the Spaniards, the two divisions of cavalry, a formidable force, formed up, three brigades out front and one in reserve. As they cantered towards the Spanish, they could see considerable confusion, some mounted but milling around uncertainly. When the French cavalry were almost upon them, there was some musketry and a few cannons were firing – too late and ineffective. The French were into them, sabres slashing and thrusting, Spaniards falling all around. Pierre exulted at the first taste of battle, competently cut down a cavalry officer who opposed him, pressing on to hack away at some infantry who were still firing their muskets, brought to a semblance of disciplined order by a redoubtable senior officer. Finally, the Spanish army was plunged into confusion and did not take further part in the action.

Behind the cavalry the massed battalions of Soult's army were advancing towards Beresford's flank, all of his forces except for one brigade in front of Albura. The British divisions concentrated at the centre, where it was assumed most likely that the attack would come, were hurriedly marched along the ridge towards the Spanish position. The French cavalry division were striving to extricate themselves from the Spaniards who, no longer a threat, were simply a hindrance. The Hussar brigade was clear and reforming out in front when it was attacked by a British cavalry division and a brigade of infantry were coming up behind them. In the ensuing mêlée the Hussars were savaged by the charge of the cavalry which passed on through the Spanish to attack the oncoming French infantry. Hampered by the Spanish and unable to reform, the Hussars suffered many casualties and then it rained, very heavily, mixed with hail, obliterating the scene. When it cleared a little, Soult's brigade of Polish lancers appeared on the left, sweeping away the British cavalry. The artillery on both sides were firing grapeshot at close range, but with little effect on the forward troops. The battle was now a fight between two stubborn contestants, slugging away through the rain. The British slowly advanced towards the French, both sides firing furiously, men falling dead in swaths. The Hussars harassed the enemy infantry and in turn were attacked by British cavalry. Pierre parried a lance thrust from an attacking lancer, his sabre deflecting the spear which passed between his body and his left arm, at the moment a tug at his jacket and a burning sensation. As the lancer drew away, reversing his weapon to pull it clear, Pierre swung his sabre, a vicious blow to the back of the neck killing his adversary instantly. Clamping his arm to his side he continued to hold the reins and carried on until, weakened by loss of blood, he began to sway in the saddle. His sergeant closed up on him and helped support him.

The battle raged on, stubborn contestants refusing to give in, the carnage unbelievable. Rivers of rain coloured by blood ran across the battlefield. The casualties were staggering, the men exhausted like zombies until both sides paused and drew back to catch their breath and prepare to meet a fresh assault. It never came. Soult withdrew back towards the start position on the Seville road and Beresford to the ridge positions. Each thought the other was beaten, but neither would give in. It was a terrible, never-to-be-forgotten day.

Back at the rear lines, Pierre, now in a state of collapse, was delivered to the regimental surgeon, who was swamped by the wounded, assisted by women camp followers who were quite skilled through experience in first aid. Eventually Pierre was seen by the surgeon, whose apron was drenched with blood. Pierre's chest was ripped open on the left side, a long slash exposing the ribs. The lance had then passed through the flesh of his arm, fortunately missing the bone. He was crudely stitched up and strapped with bandages, his arm also dressed and immobilised in a sling. He was then placed on the ground in a tent and given welcome coffee laced with cognac by one of the kind 'ladies'.

In the morning burial parties went to the battlefield to inter the thousands of dead. Both sides worked together, united in the common cause. The Hussar colonel visited the wounded, briefly chatting to those who were conscious, many obviously dying.

He came to Pierre and said, 'Ah, Flamand, I am glad to see you looking fairly well, You may not have been fully in your senses, but you led what was left of the Escadron away from the battleground. Benoit and most of his officers are dead. Your reconnaissance was not wasted. We did not lose, but the stubborn British would not give up. We are going back to Seville and then we shall see.'

The next day they left for Seville, leaving the bloody scene of such a terrible battle, the memory from which the survivors would never fully recover. Beresford also withdrew, back to continue the siege of Badajos. Wellington ordered that Albura was to be proclaimed a victory. Wellington himself undertook to reduce the fortress by all means, moving two divisions from the north. When Badajos was taken and one doorway into France secured, he would return to Ciudad Rodrigo. However, as the French were found to be strengthening their forces at Ciudad Rodrigo, he changed his plans and returned to the north. The fortress there fell after a stubborn battle and the way to Madrid was open.

After two days in the jolting, bouncing wagon, Pierre decided to get back on his horse, as the surgeon was agreeable.

'You must be feeling better, but take care, your wounds are far from healed.'

Pierre sent for his sergeant who brought his horse and helped him to mount. He could not use his left arm which was immobilised.

He first reported to the colonel, who said, 'Well done, now take over the Escadron and I will consider your promotion.'

Back at Seville the troop rested and re-equipped from the supplies available there. There was much talk among the men as to the next move: up north, most thought, but they were only about half strength and replacements were a long way off. The wounded were taken to Cartagena, to be shipped to France eventually. Pierre remained with the Hussars; he would recover just as well with the regiment. At Seville came the astounding news that they were going back to France along with other units. Napoleon was tired of the British stubbornly refusing to give up in Spain. Thwarted in his efforts to drive Wellington into the sea and in his plans to invade England, he decided impetuously to leave Spain to his marshals and turn his attention elsewhere, withdrawing some of the best battalions from the Peninsular.

Napoleon, unable to break out of Europe, thwarted in Spain and unable to cross the Channel due to the Royal Navy, or to the Orient by the refusal of the Czar to cooperate, in spite of his treaty with Russia in 1807 of non-aggression and mutual help, decided impetuously to raise a grand army against Russia. His act of folly lay in reducing the army of Spain, leaving affairs there to look after themselves.

The Hussars left with other units, first of all bound for Cartagena and the long march to the French border, along the coast to Perpignon some 800 miles. It was a hot summer, men and horses suffered from the heat and dust, slowed down by the baggage and commissariat wagons, thirsty always. Water sources were insufficient for such a large body. A soldier's lot. There was no threat from Spanish bandits or guerrillas, little chance of ambushes, but perhaps in the Pyrenees.

Before they left the colonel sent for Pierre and said, 'Flamand, I am glad you did not leave with the wounded. You appear to have recovered well. You will continue to lead the Escadron and you are as of now promoted to temporary captain.

Pierre was immensely pleased to have reached the 'exalted' rank so soon, a blessing of the war, when promotion came quickly for the survivors.

The coast road passed along very scenic Mediterranean country, the sea, the coastal plain with the foothills to modest rocky mountains. Blue skies, calm sea and the fragrance of pines and herbs. They passed through Alicante, Valencia, Castellon and to Barcelona. The Spaniards in the towns were sullen and unfriendly, looking askance at the hated enemy with an unsaid, 'Perhaps they are going home, good riddance.'

When they were near the border, much of the long march behind them, the infantrymen plodding along, placing one foot in front of the other, mechanically, seeing only the pack of the man in front, the road left the coast and entered into the high mountain pass. Without warning, in a narrow valley, shots rang out from the high slopes on the landward side, the crack of the muskets echoing and multiplying on the precipitous sides of the gorge. Men in the regiment in front of the Hussars fell dead or wounded and the colonel ordered the cavalry to move up, spurring his horse to a canter. The Hussars dismounted near the scene and took up positions where there was scant cover, and the colonel ordered Pierre and his squadron to advance towards the positions of the bandits or guerrillas above.

Pierre, somewhat handicapped by his wounded side and arm,

was aided by the big man, Jean, who was with him on the recce at Albura, and closely followed by his sergeant. Pierre ordered half of his men to halt and to cover the others climbing slowly through the rocks. As soon as shots were fired at them, an immediate volley of fire from the cavalry carbines was directed towards the snipers' position, the balls humming as they ricocheted off the rocks, some finding a target as men tumbled out of concealment. Some troopers were hit by return fire, and seeing their comrades fall angered the Hussars. The squadron pressed on, the rear leapfrogging those in front until they drove the ambushers out of cover into a valley. They followed the guerrillas to a small hamlet at the head of the valley, harassing them with some effective carbine fire. They found the place deserted and Pierre ordered his men to torch it, houses burning fiercely in the dry mountain air.

The march resumed without further hindrance and soon they found themselves in *La Belle France*, quickening the pace as they slipped out towards Perpignon. From there some units peeled off to their destinations, some to Bordeaux and the west coast, others to Marseilles and northwards, the Hussars onto Toulon, where they were to put things in order before taking the road to their depot at Lyons.

3

France

They arrived at the barracks at Toulon, where Pierre had stayed on the way to Spain, men and horses weary from the long journey. The colonel addressed the officers on the morning parade.

'We will rest here for a few days. Get yourselves smartened up and the men, remember we are now in France, no slackness! We will then ride to our own depôt in Lyons, where I hope to have further news for you.'

Pierre was aware that although he had only had a short experience in action on the battlefield, he both felt and looked different. Remembering how he was when he passed through Toulon, he would never be the same again. The first evening there, feeling that his reservoir needed to be emptied, he went to the brothel where he had enjoyed himself previously. The madam greeted him and sat him down with a glass of wine. She said she would bring some girls and he told her he would like to have the woman whom he had met before, describing her sufficiently for madam to understand who he was looking for. Shortly she arrived and without ado they went upstairs.

When they were in the room, she said, 'I believe you have been here before, a few months ago.'

He admitted that he had indeed and that she had pleased him very much. When he was undressed she saw the terrible wounds, healed and no longer bandaged, a grim reminder of the war.

'*Mon dieu, pauvre garçon, tu es blessé dans la guerre, terriblement.*' She insisted that he lie on his back. 'Lie still, I will do the work.' With professional competence she brought him to a very satisfying climax.

As they lay recovering from the exertions of the encounter, she suggested, 'Why do you not stay the whole night? It will be good for you and even I will enjoy having a young and handsome officer for a change.' Pierre thought so also and she said, 'I will go downstairs and tell madam and order supper to be sent up.'

They did not sleep at all that night. Pierre, young and vigorous, was easily able to undertake one sexual act after another. Even in the early morning, when he had to leave to go on the morning parade, she lay on her back, legs apart, inviting him to have a final go. In spite of her profession, she had genuinely enjoyed the night of love. The outcome was that Pierre came back to her for the few nights the regiment remained at Toulon, taking a fond farewell of her on the final evening and giving her an expensive piece of jewellery as a present. Love for a whore? He felt very much alive. The bout of sex had removed the stresses of the past weeks.

The regiment left Toulon on the secondary road through Provence to Grenoble and on to Lyons, the summer weather glorious, the Hussars splendidly smartened up, a gallant sight but the people in the villages were surly and uncommunicative, tired of the war, the soldiery and the shortages, going on endlessly it seemed. The Hussars were in good spirits; home, with no menace from a hostile population and with a good prospect of leave.

At Lyons the colonel held an order group for the officers. He told them that the emperor had declared his intention to open up a way to a world empire to the east, through Russia, and as the czar was unwilling to cooperate, he would be compelled to force Russia to submit by war. Napoleon had called up more conscripts, no Frenchman was exempt.

'However,' said the colonel, 'to bring us up to strength I would prefer to recruit volunteers and to do this, selected recruiting parties will be sent to districts where they have their roots and thus are locally known. The adjutant will advise those selected.'

The following day the adjutant sent for Pierre and said, 'Captain Flamand, yes, the colonel has confirmed your appointment. You are to cover recruiting in Normandy. You may make your own arrangements, but I suggest you take your sergeant, sergeant-major and five troopers. Take also two wagons with supplies and some basic uniform clothing. You should recruit sufficient men for your own squadron. There should be no difficulty, in view of the new conscription, to be selective and get the best recruits. If necessary you can send back batches of men with one or two of your troopers. I will also provide you with sufficient money, of which you must keep careful account. Good luck.'

Pierre took the adjutant's advice and in two days they were ready to leave. Pierre had, of course, included his orderly, Big Jean as he became known. They set off, a brave entourage, en route for Caen, where Pierre would make his headquarters and, of course, visit his home and beloved Collette.

The 300 mile journey via Tours and Le Mans passed very pleasantly and in a few days they arrived at the village outside Caen. Leaving the wagons in the village, he rode the troop to his parents' house. Alerted by the clatter of hooves, the household turned out, astonished to see the cavalry and then they recognised their son, returned from the war. Pierre sent the troop back to the village and entered the house with his mother clinging to his arm. They were overjoyed to see him and proud of his rank, so soon earned. They told him that Collette was at the small house across the meadow which she had furnished and added extra rooms to, their first home. Without delay he crossed to the house and called for Collette, who came running from the kitchen.

'Pierre, my darling, how marvellous to see you again. We had no word from you since you came back from Spain, and here you are.'

Inevitably, they went upstairs and feverishly undressed. He noticed that she was not showing any noticeable change in her abdomen.

She noticed his glance and said, 'No, Pierre, I am not pregnant yet but come, we will try hard to change that.' It might have occurred then that the earth moved as they climaxed together. Afterwards, as they dressed, she saw the still vivid scars of the terrible wounds and woman-like she burst into tears.

'My poor darling, how terrible for you, you might have been killed. Those awful English!' She traced the scars with a gentle finger fearing to cause pain, then said, 'Oh well, it is nothing now, all over, nothing to weep over. Let us go over to the house, we can all talk together.'

At the house after renewed greetings, hugged by his mother and hands warmly clasped by his father, Pierre told them of his adventures in Spain. Collette interrupted to tell of the wound and all were alarmed and sympathetic until he assured them that all was now well. He explained that his squadron was reduced to half-strength from the fighting at Albura and that he was here to recruit young men from Normandy and that after looking around the village would make a small tour of the province. He stayed for a few days, enjoying an extended honeymoon and planning his operation with the help of his father who knew the country well. They decided that he would go to Evreux first and then on to Argentan, Vire, St-Lô and Mortaine, the heart of the Maquis, a countryside of high hedges and sunken roads, perfect for ambushes. Finally, to Domfront and Coutance and then back home, purposely avoiding the cities of Cherbourg and Le Havre.

The entourage set out after a few days, Pierre promising that he would be back when he had sufficient recruits. Ten likely fellows he had found locally he sent back to Lyons with a trooper. Most of the men had their own mounts, for the rest he requisitioned horses through the mayor's office. Hopefully, they would be paid for in due time. At Evreaux he found accommodation at an inn on the town square and in the morning set up a table and chairs in front of the inn, the tricolour and the regimental pennant planted either side. The sergeant importuned likely young men passing by and if they were acceptable and willing sent them into the inn with a trooper to refresh themselves before being enlisted.

During the morning a smart carriage stopped in front of Pierre and a well-dressed lady, whom Pierre judged to be in her mid-thirties, got out accompanied by a youth.

'I am Madeleine Oudinot,' she introduced herself, 'nothing to do with the emperor's favourite marshal, only the name. My husband, a major of cavalry, was killed at Torres Vedras too, two years ago. This is my son, Jacques, who wishes to join the army and would like to ride with you to your regiment.'

Pierre invited them into the inn, where in a private room he entertained them. He said that Jacques could go to Lyons with the recruits from Evreaux in two days. He would give him a letter to the colonel. Madeleine invited him to dine that evening. She would send the carriage for him.

Several of the local gentry were invited to dinner and were interested to listen to Pierre's story of his experiences in Spain.

'How was the war going there? Was Wellington going to be driven back into the sea? It had already been a long drawn out campaign in the Peninsular, when would it end?'

Pierre could only tell them that the emperor had other plans, which might end the war and force England, the stumbling block to the empire to the west, to capitulate. The widow, who had been eyeing Pierre during the evening, with that certain look, said a warm goodnight to him and said she would drive by in the morning.

In the morning Madeleine duly turned up, looking especially attractive. Pierre appreciated that it was a show put on for his admiration. Over a glass of wine Pierre said that he would be ready to leave the day after tomorrow. He outlined to her his programme and was surprised when she offered to go with him.

'I know the country well and, in any case, I can make the journey more pleasant for you.'

Pierre was quite willing, suspecting her motive. He thought of Collette, his conscience pricking a little, but put it behind him. The temptation was here and Collette was far away. Madeleine said she would be ready to leave and would bring Jacques with a spare horse to carry his baggage. Pierre arranged that he would provide the coachman, which she agreed to. No tales to carry back to Evreaux, she thought.

The carriage arrived at the agreed time and Pierre appointed Big Jean to sit on the box. The coachman was sent back to Evreaux. Soon after they were on the road to Argentan, they halted to take refreshments and rest the horses. The wagons were well stocked and the widow had brought a large hamper of delicacies and wine.

When they were ready to carry on, Madeleine suggested, 'Pierre, why don't you ride with me in the coach? It will be a rest for you.'

She was looking quite ravishing and Pierre thought to himself, Why not, who knows what might happen? A soldier's luck, maybe. So they went comfortably ensconced in the cosy interior.

Whatever happened, on a bumpy stretch of road, she was thrown against him, or did she contrive it? Pierre clasped her to prevent her falling and inevitably they embraced. She made no move to free herself and it developed into a frantic exchange of kisses and fumblings.

She said, 'I have been so long without a man, faithful to the memory of my dead husband. Please take me.'

She reclined back on the seat, one knee resting against the back cushion and the other leg with her foot resting on the floor, clothing pulled up round her waist, drawerless as was the custom.

Pierre thought, 'Well, how expertly contrived, she has done this before.'

Nothing loath, he lowered his breeches and, well and truly aroused, entered her. Their coupling was very satisfying and Madeleine was very affectionate towards him. 'We can stay together when we reach Argentan. We are not known there and your wife will not find out.'

Pierre had told her he was married.

Having successfully recruited some fine young men at Argentan and sent them off to Lyons, they carried on to Vire, St Lô and other places, ending up at Coutance.

Pierre had very much enjoyed his liaison with the amorous widow and when they parted, she to return to Evreux, she said after their last night of love. 'It has been wonderful, I feel rejuvenated, a new woman. We may never meet again, but I shall never forget you.'

Big Jean was to drive her home and then make his way back with the carriage and pair, which Madeleine had made a present of to Pierre. It would call for an explanation, but he would conjure up a likely story.

Pierre arrived home alone, having then sent all his party back to the depot. He would take a few days' leave with Collette and the family. When the coach arrived, he suggested that Collette should come with him to Lyons and afterwards possibly go with him when the regiment moved on, as it inevitably would.

Saying goodbye to their families, they set off for Lyons, Big Jean on the box and Pierre taking turns to ride or join Collette in the coach. At Lyons they first of all found suitable accommodation near the depot and then Pierre reported to the Adjutant. 'Your squadron is now up to strength and for the time being you are to concentrate on general military training for the new recruits, in mounted and dismounted drill, swordsmanship, pistol and carbine, gradually infiltrating them with the trained soldiers. In about a month you should be ready for exercising as a squadron out in the country. Avoid damage to property. The people, as you will have doubtless noticed, are not favourably disposed towards the military, being tired of war.'

They settled down very well, the squadron shaping up to Pierre's satisfaction, his troop officers quite happy with him as their squadron leader. After all, they were mostly new boys. There was a great deal of sport, hunting, horse races and regimental balls. The cavalry excelled in having a good time and wining and dining with the local gentry. Collette mixed very well with the other wives and their cup of happiness overflowed when Collette told Pierre that she was pregnant. Pierre fussed over her and she assured him all would be well, she would be careful and in due course would return to Normandy to deliver her baby with the family. Pierre had promoted his sergeant to squadron sergeant major and altogether the squadron was in fine fettle, ready to go to war.

The squadron manoeuvres out in the countryside were enjoyed by all, lasting several days: bivouacking at night in the late autumn weather, tolerable out in the open, conditioning men and horses. They had a troop of artillery with them, detached from the battery, which was part of the brigade group. It was soon time to integrate the squadrons and carry out regimental exercises.

At the onset of winter the whole regiment, with the gunners and baggage wagons, set out for a two-week exercise from Lyons, along the road which eventually led to Geneva across the Haut Savoie. The colonel had given strict instructions that none must cross over the Swiss border, explaining why to the officers at the briefing before the exercise. He told them that France had occupied Switzerland in 1798; its sovereignty was restored in 1883 by Napoleon at the Treaty in Paris, guaranteeing the Swiss perpetual neutrality. The Haut Savoie was not good cavalry country, scrub and rock and already cold with quite severe frosts at night, although they were unaware of this, a small foretaste of things to come.

The exercises concentrated on a sufficiently barren area where cavalry could move as they were intended to, practising charges supported by the artillery against enemy positions; Pierre found himself thinking about the real thing at Albura. He appreciated the especial comfort of the cavalry all together in an exhilarating gallop, all together men and horses, the horses apparently, equally enjoying the excitement.

One morning the guns were firing not far from the road when a passing carriage was obviously in trouble. The horses shied and then bolted. Pierre was near the road and, realising the predicament, spurred his horse to a gallop after the swaying, jolting coach. He overtook them with some risk and closed with the lead horses, easing them to a halt. He dismounted and approached the carriage where the occupants, a lady and gentleman and a young girl, were recovering from their fright. Pierre helped them down and they thanked him effusively.

'We might all have been killed. Our coachman is too old to cope with such incidents.'

Pierre said it was a mistake that the guns were firing too close to the road. He was sorry that they had to suffer such an ordeal.

They introduced themselves as German Swiss, going to visit friends in Lyons with their daughter, Heide. Daughter Heide, Pierre saw, was a very beautiful, golden-haired, blue-eyed, young lady.

Well, well, he thought, what have we here?

The father reached into the coach and brought out a small hamper fitted with drinks and glasses.

'Shall we take a glass of wine or brandy?'

Pierre assented. 'A brandy would be most acceptable. I must hurry back, we are on exercise.'

He told them he was stationed in Lyons.

'My wife is there. I will give you a note to her, you may like to call sometime.' He drank his brandy and said, 'I think your man is too disturbed to drive the coach. I will send one of my men to take you on to Lyons.'

They parted with a show of grateful cordiality on the part of the Swiss family, the girl shyly shaking hands. Pierre, kissing hers and her mother's hands, went back to the squadron to send Big Jean to drive the coach.

The exercise carried on for a further week, the regiment becoming a composite fighting unit, ably commanded by the colonel, the epitome of a dashing cavalry commander in whom his officers and men had every confidence and would follow unhesitatingly, a very happy state to be in for a cavalry regiment. Back at the barracks, they settled down to a peaceful routine, pondering on things to come. It was too good to last. The news from Spain was not good. Wellington was on the offensive. Ciudad Rodrigo had fallen and the enemy's attention focused on taking Badajos; the roads then would be open for an advance to the French frontier and then what?

As they returned to Lyons, Pierre was joyful at the prospect of meeting Collette, but also his thoughts, unbidden, strayed towards Heide Strauss. Had the Strausses been to see Collette? He hoped so. He found Collette very depressed, maybe because of her pregnancy. She had not made friends with anyone in Lyons and was missing her family and friends in Normandy.

'Yes, the Strauss family called quite often. They are hoping to see you, to express their thanks for your help.'

Pierre said that he understood and as the regiment could be on the move anytime, she would be better off at home. He would ask for leave of absence and they could go together.

Pierre was granted two weeks' leave and they prepared for the trip back to Normandy. Big Jean would drive the carriage and Pierre would obtain another charger and both ride back to Lyons, leaving the coach with Collette. Before they left the Strauss family called and Pierre was very pleased with their warm welcome, but after all, he thought, I probably saved their lives. Heide was a bit shy, but underneath he felt he could detect a certain warmth of feeling, who knows? He would work on it when he came back from Normandy.

With Collette happily back with her family, Pierre took a fond leave of her,

'I will try to come again, but the future is so uncertain, heaven knows where the regiment will end up.'

On the way back he decided to go via Evreux and to call on the widow; a social call he persuaded himself. He found Madeleine at home and she was delighted to see him. He said he was passing through and must hurry back, his leave was nearly expired. However, she persuaded him to at least stay for the night, 'for old times' sake'. Well, of course, he did and they renewed their rather energetic sexual activities of the past, a very enjoyable encounter. Pierre rose in a good mood, sad at leaving his wife, but comforted by the widow's warm welcome and thoughts about the future, the coming new adventure into war and, also, a little about Heide. Well it was expected of a dashing cavalry officer.

Pierre kept the house at Lyons and the maid. Who knows, he might be entertaining! He visited the Strauss family and in the course of conversation Heide remarked that she missed riding. Pierre said that he had brought a spare horse from Normandy and she could borrow one occasionally. 'But cavalry horses are rather high spirited and it would be best if we ride together.'

(Foot in the door, he thought.)

They went over s stretch of moor outside the town. Heide looked ravishing, her cheeks glowing after a gallop. She managed her horse very competently, was not just a pretty face. Pierre suggested that they went back to his house for coffee and she accepted with what he thought was a twinkle in her eyes. Back at the house the maid brought coffee and they sat chatting until he got up and went over to take her cup. Pausing, he bent down gently, raised her face and kissed her. She responded eagerly. Putting down the cup, he felt down her body, over her breasts and down to the great divide. She made no effort to resist and even parted her thighs, whereupon he explored under her skirts and found the moist place, warm and wet from the excitement of the ride and the motion of the great body underneath her bottom.

Pierre said, 'I will send the maid out on a lengthy errand and we can go upstairs.'

His probing finger had found that in fact she was not a virgin and a slice off a cut loaf would not come amiss.

Heide proved to be a perfect match for his ardour: very enthusiastic, arching her body under him with considerable strength to get more of him into her. Skilfully delaying the climax, they finally came after a vigorous burst of movement. Both were well-satisfied and realised that their future would be rosy. They thought it would be wise to meet perhaps once a week.

She told him, 'I hope nothing happens, but in any case if it does, I am expected to marry a neighbour's son at home in Switzerland, so *n'importe de quel!*'

He obtained leave for Christmas and the New Year, good to be off to Normandy, away from barrack life and the endless training. Collette was overcome with emotion when she greeted him.

'Pierre, my love, I have missed you so much. Why cannot we be together always? This terrible war, when will it end?'

However, Collette was mollycoddled by the families and now, although showing her pregnancy a little, was very well and insisted they make love.

'If we are careful and not too rough, he will enjoy your attention.'

Pierre enjoyed himself. Although he had been a bit of a naughty boy, it was to be expected of a young, high-spirited cavalry officer and his conscience did not trouble him.

In 1812 they welcomed the new year in with a party for the families and intimate friends.

Pierre told Collette, 'This time next year it will be all over and our son will be born.'

He was not to know when they said a fond farewell, she tearful, that it was the last time they would see each other. Forbearing to call on the widow at Evreaux, he rode straight back to Lyons and the regiment.

He was disappointed to find the Strauss family were leaving for Switzerland almost at once, having, fortunately for the lovers, waited to say goodbye to Pierre. They managed a last afternoon together. Whatever the future, they had enjoyed each other. She was so beautiful that he would certainly never forget her.

As they parted Heide said, kissing him fervently, *'Pierre, cherie, mon amour, je ne regrette pas, jamais.'*

Another parting for ever, although they hoped to meet again, whatever the circumstances.

Pierre gave up the house and moved into the barracks. There was a feeling in the air that things were about to happen and it was a relief then the colonel announced in the early spring that the regiment was to move eastwards. All were filled with excitement, bored with peacetime soldiering and endless training.

'Away and let's at 'em, come what may.'

4

Prussia

Spring of 1812 saw the roads of Europe choked with marching men, infantry, cavalry, guns and wagons, bound, at the emperor's will, for the concentration area in Prussia. Over half a million soldiers were gathering in the east. Napoleon's *Grande Armée*, the greatest ever seen, surpassed even the armies of Alexander, Genghis Khan, Tammerlane and Caesar. In the past 14 years the army of the revolution, driven on by the genius of Napoleon, had conquered all of Europe, except for Portugal, part of Spain and the real enemy, England, who commanded the seas, stubbornly refused to surrender, leaving Bonaparte no choice but to move eastwards.

The treaty of 1807 that Napoleon signed with the Czar Alexander guaranteed peace between France and Russia, agreed also that together they would advance across Asia, giving them the whole of mankind. Czar Alexander was cautious. He wanted only Poland and Constantinople, an outlet to the sea through Turkey. So already there was a crack in their agreement and treaties can be ignored or torn up. Napoleon began calling up more conscripts and demanded his subject countries of Europe, Poland, Germany, Holland, Spain, Italy, Denmark and others, to arm against Russia and to swell the ranks of the *Grande Armée*. The dice were cast when in May 1812 the czar refused to come to a settlement and increased the size of the Russian army and built fortifications on the roads into Russia. Napoleon set out to join his army and made Königsberg in Prussia his headquarters. With his skill in planning he must have known of the impossibility of supplying half a million men in the waste lands of

Russia but, falsely buoyed up by his pretensions of invincibility, he entered into an enormous military folly.

The Hussars left Lyons on a bright spring morning. Many of the town turned out to see them go. The regiment was quite popular and furnished a brave sight: splendid horses and uniforms, the guns and finally the wagons. On the colonel's order camp followers were cut to a minimum, only those 'ladies' who could be used as nurses and laundry women. The men would doubtless pick up other willing young women along the road. To move the regiment across a crowded Europe, out of France, over Germany and Prussian Poland, some 1,500 miles was no mean task, but Napoleon's soldiers were well acquainted with such seemingly impossible feats. The colonel sent for Pierre.

'You will be in charge of movements, planning each day's journey and night stop. It is a very responsible job, we must not get lost on the way. We should be in Poland in the region of Königsberg in just over a month.'

A very worried Pierre went off to study the maps. In France it was not very difficult and once over the first day, having successfully ended up the march at a place sufficiently big enough to park a whole regiment, he felt better. The colonel arrived at the chosen area ahead of the main body.

'Well done, Pierre,' he said, 'this will do fine. We have made good time, keep it up.'

The colonel had ordered a complete day off each week to rest the horses and make and mend and not to stop near large towns where men might be tempted to desert.

The journey along the Vosges mountain range was very pleasant and they crossed into Germany at Karlsruhe. In spite of orders regarding camp followers, the number of women joining the march grew each day. Love of adventure, free food, such as it was, and a man to look after, drew all kinds to follow the colours. Even in Germany and Poland other women joined in until there were almost enough to go round.

Their route took them to Dresden. The way was easy to find now, so many other units going the same way, so it was hardly a problem for Pierre to find a place to stop overnight. They just halted when the troops in front stopped. At Dresden the colonel ordered a few days' rest. They were well on the way and soon would be crossing into Prussia-dominated Poland, on to Prague, to Poznan and their destination, Königsberg. A few officers' wives had accompanied their husbands but mainly they were travelling alone. Pierre very much felt the need to relax, the responsibility of being transport officer was very nerve-racking. He had to know exactly when and where to stop. Have I taken the wrong road? It could be disastrous, and with no turning around, a very worrying affair.

In fact, all went well and the colonel was pleased and said to Pierre at Dresden, 'You have done well, go into the town and have a good night.'

On the road in, Pierre had noticed a pleasant, inviting *Bierstube* and so he took his squadron officers there. Although the French were not very popular, they were made welcome. Officers were quite something whatever their army. Tables were put together and without asking what they wanted, two young women in traditional dress appeared with handfuls of great biersteins, foaming with good, strong German beer, following this with plates of sausages, bread and gherkins. The girls were almost twins, blonde, blue-eyed and buxom. Pierre absently fondled a plump backside as one of them leaned past him to the table. She looked back unsurprised and he thought, well, well, what have we here? During the evening he spoke to her in his schoolboy German and she replied in excellent French. As the evening wore on some of the officers were well away and Pierre thought it was time to go.

Gretchen, that was the girl's name, said to him, 'We shall be closing now, wait for me in the porch.'

Gretchen, when she appeared, took his arm warmly, saying, 'Come, I have a small house nearby. We can be cosy and have a chat.'

A gentleman and an officer, he responded by halting and turning her towards him, embracing her very comfortable body which at once fitted into his own, made for the job.

They kissed and she murmured, 'The first time I have been kissed by a real live *Hauptmann,* such a gallant captain of Hussars.'

At the house, very small but comfortably appointed, she suggested, 'Coffee and brandy. You have had enough beer. If you want to relieve yourself, go out there into the back yard, through that door.'

Pierre went out and pissed on the ground, emptying his bladder and looking up into the velvety, starlit sky with a brilliant quarter moon. How lucky I am, he thought, the gods must favour me. Wine and women, a soldier's luck follows me around.

They sat comfortably on the small settee and she told him her story. She was born in Berlin, her father was a teacher at a *Hochschule* and he himself had taught her beyond elementary school, French and history so that she was able to get a job as a *Hauslehrerin*, a governess for children. Gretchen had been employed by an aristocratic family to teach their two youngest children. Their elder son had seduced her and she became pregnant; the family looked after her and when the child was born, gave it over to a foster mother. Gretchen told him that they paid her off handsomely and she came to live in Dresden; she was unattached and did not bother much with men . . . however! Pierre in turn told his story, including his experiences in Spain.

Gretchen said, 'Your wife is far away, enough of this talk, there is a fine bed upstairs.'

Indeed, there was a splendid bed, a soldier's featherbed on a German *Federbett*, just the job. Without delay they shed their clothes.

Gretchen fingered his scars and he said, 'Spain.'

Gretchen was indeed beautifully formed, plump in the right places, and for Pierre their coupling was very enjoyable and, judging by her ferocious clawing and exclamations, she also was transported into a sexual heaven.

Pierre came straight into Gretchen's house as soon as he was off duty. She had stopped away from the *Bierstube* and after they had frolicked on the *Federbett*, fed and wined, Gretchen said, 'Pierre, my dear, we get on well together, don't be shocked at what I am going to say. I am going with you. It is not secret that your beloved emperor is going against the Russian czar. Lotte, my friend at work, is coming with me. She met and became involved with one of your officers. We will have our own transport and can leave with you from Dresden.'

Pierre was dumbfounded. It would, of course, make life much more enjoyable. It was rare for an officer to have a lady with the camp followers and few officers' wives went along on campaigns. However, he quickly made up his mind.

'All right, Gretchen, you will be very welcome. It is a hard but exciting life, but I can promise you some fun. My orderly, Big Jean, has his wife with us and he can be our go-between and she can help you.'

He thought privately that Gretchen and Lotte might well live to regret their spontaneous action.

They left Dresden and crossed into Poland through Poznan and in a week or so arrived near Königsberg and their marshalling area. The regiment was to join a division in Marshal Oudinot's Cavalry Corps, the elite of Napoleon's cavalry. Marshal Oudinot, a young man for such an exalted rank, who was also the emperor's favourite marshal, was to survive the wars and later was Duc de Reggio and commander-in-chief of the National Guard. On the march Pierre had managed to spend some nights with Gretchen and no matter what, they truly enjoyed each other, having a very successful sexual rapport between the blankets.

When the colonel told them they were joining Marshal Oudinot, Pierre, of course, thought of the widow, Madeleine Oudinot at Evreux, a long way away, but what good times we had: since I put on a uniform it has been one woman after another.

Early in June the *Grande Armée* marched towards the Polish frontier with Russia. Napoleon chose the time-honoured season for the invasion of an enemy: just around harvest time, when the gathering of the crops would be interrupted by being in a war zone or by a shortage of manpower, due to conscription. Before they left Pierre received news that Collette had borne him a son, whom they had agreed was to be christened François. He celebrated the news by getting drunk and spending a riotous night in bed with his lovely Gretchen.

The *Grande Armée* now numbered some 600,000 men and the movement of such a stupendous body across some 200 miles of the Polish countryside was a daunting task, problems however overcome by Napoleon's genius in planning such operations. The first troops arrived at Kovno and crossed into the Russian plain, part of the all-important granary of Russia. Marshal Oudinot's corps were the first to deploy, the advance guard, which was prepared to meet with resistance from the czar's troops. Nothing happened. The two cavalry divisions were strung out all prepared but encountered only the stillness of an apparently empty countryside.

5

Into Russia

The czar had ordered Kutusov, his commander-in-chief, to withdraw before Napoleon, reluctant to face the superior French forces, and also to lay waste the countryside before them, following a scorched earth policy. The plain stretched interminably, a vast, seemingly empty space. Oudinot's cavalry, the advance guard, were ordered to probe forward as soon as the main body of the *Grande Armée* had crossed over the River Niemen at Kovno. At the river they had replenished their canteens and the numerous water carts. As always on the march with so many men and horses, thirst was a problem.

The Hussars on the right flank were ordered to take a look at a hamlet which was discernible on the horizon. They crossed wheat fields which, if not already harvested, were burnt. The hamlet was deserted, not even a dog nor cat was to be seen. The small stream adjacent was fouled by the rotting bloated carcasses of dead farm animals, the stench awful, a foretaste of things to come, bringing death-dealing cholera and dysentery. Away from the houses across a mile of stubble was a copse, its trees not destroyed by fire. They had a feeling that they were being watched all the time, certainly there were Russian Cossacks somewhere out there, following the movements of the French, but this was from not far away.

The colonel ordered Pierre to take his squadron over to the copse and see if anyone was there, maybe some peasants who remained behind. As they approached the wood, shots rang out and two troopers fell, dead or wounded: the very first casualties of the war, a doubtful honour. Pierre wheeled the squadron out of musket range and sent word back to the colonel that there were armed irregulars or guerrillas in the copse and he would smoke them out. Pierre sent half a dozen troopers on foot to approach the trees from the cover of a small valley to the rear with enough gunpowder to start a blaze. The party was successful and the timber, dry from the summer heat, blazed and swept towards them. The troops were spread out to intercept the Russians, who inevitably would run out.

As the fire spread, men could be seen emerging from the smoke. Some shots rang out, aimed at the Hussars, and Pierre said, 'Right, kill them all, no surrender,' and spurred forward. Any others remaining in the wood were overcome by the fire and dead in any case. He decided to take one prisoner for interrogation and told Big Jean to weed one out. It was quickly over and they counted some 50 bodies, cut down or pistoled, a good haul. The colonel was well pleased and sent the prisoner, a burly, black-bearded peasant, back to brigade.

He remarked to Pierre, 'This is what we must expect until we catch up with them.'

The advance was ponderously slow. Napoleon, of necessity, had to keep his enormous force closely knit, no staying behind, the distances covered day by day governed by the slowest, the vital supply wagons. They must not become isolated and targets for any wandering Russian-shadowing Cossacks.

The colonel of the Hussars was called away to headquarters and was told that his regiment were to be the eyes of the grand army, to keep in close touch with the ever retreating Kutusov and to report back. The colonel was told not to get involved in any fighting, but nevertheless might profitably intercept Russian patrols on like missions: see and not be seen. The colonel briefed the squadron leaders, emphasising the role of close reconnaissance as instructed by headquarters. He pointed out that above all they must be self-sufficient, could not live on the land which was laid bare and could only be supplied at weekly runs by the regimental quartermaster.

The regiment pressed on across the endless plain, through villages, with eternal smoke on the horizon until they were close enough to be able to observe the rearguard of the Russians. Pierre was able to get back to the wagons and Gretchen for a night's 'blanket drill' and be back before daylight as the army was closed up for security reasons: no tail-end stragglers. He found Gretchen and Lotte remarkably cheerful and enjoying the excitement of being part of something big and the comradeship of their fellow travellers. Pierre warned them to conserve all supplies and to be particularly careful with water.

Pierre was on the forward patrol when he saw a patrol of some 50 Cossacks ride away from the main Russian body to outflank the French, bound on the same mission as their own. He sent word to the regiment to intercept them and when the enemy patrol were out of sight moved to place his squadron to cut them off. Inevitably, faced at their front by a considerable force, the Cossacks turned back towards the safety of their own lines. Pierre was in a position to attack them when he chose and at the right time ordered the squadron to advance in two extended lines abreast, walk, trot, canter and into a galloping charge, hitting the surprised Cossack like a thunderbolt. Pierre, up front, picked out an officer who appeared to be their leader and ran him through under his chin, straight through the neck, withdrawing his sword as the officer fell dead and selecting his next opponent. It was soon over. The Cossacks refused to surrender and were cut down to a man. The troopers went round finishing off those wounded and obviously dying. A few who were lightly injured were taken prisoner for questioning. The Hussars got off lightly with two troopers killed and six wounded.

Division decided they wanted more prisoners. The czar's movements, even backwards, must end and it was vital for the French to discover his intentions. They were now some 200 miles inside Russia and had met no resistance. The Hussars were ordered to carry out a night raid and the colonel, recalling Pierre's success at Albura, ordered him to perform the operation, using his whole squadron dismounted.

Before dusk the squadron approached the Russians without being observed and Pierre went forward on foot to have a look-see. He discovered that there was a patrol of Cossacks covering the rear and could identify two officers, one by his dress a Cossack, the other could be a staff officer. There is our target, he thought and observed them until he was sure they had halted for the night. Back with the squadron, he decided against an attack by force of arms and told a troop officer, who happened to be Lotte's friend, to select six of his men armed with knives and pistols only. He would lead the party with Big Jean and another trooper equally reliable. He explained that he and his two men would take the officers and the others act as a screen for the getaway.

Silently they crept forward. It was now dusk and the Russians could be clearly seen by the light of their cooking fires and, to one side, the two officers. Pierre and his men covered the rest of the ground at a run and fell upon their object, completely silencing the pair by heavy blows to their heads. The following troopers placed themselves in between. Pierre hurried his men away as fast as they could go, carrying the prisoners. Safely away towards the squadron shots rang out behind them. Their screen had been detected. It was too late. They all got back to the horses and only then did Pierre learn that the officer had been shot in the head and was dead, also that one trooper was probably fatally wounded. Nevertheless, Pierre was elated, a most successful mission, and the colonel thought so also.

'These two must be a mine of information. Division will be pleased.'

The following night Pierre went down to the wagon lines. Apart from seeing his beloved Gretchen, he had the unpleasantness of telling Lotte that her lover was dead. Lotte was, of course, terribly upset. After all, she had lost her protector on this journey into the unknown. There would be others, of course. That was life.

Gretchen produced some preciously hoarded schnapps and they sat quietly getting a little bit tipsy.

Lotte was maudlin and Gretchen, seeing she needed to be comforted said, 'Pierre, let's put her to bed, we can get in with her.'

So they undressed and went to the large mattress on the floor behind a curtain, which served as the bed. Pierre was in the middle and found it a very exciting situation and he did not know which way to turn until Gretchen said, 'Comfort Lotte, she needs it to help her forget.'

Lotte was most willing, strangely sobbing for her lost lover but responding to his thrusts with vigour.

Gretchen inserted her hand between them and screamed, *'Mein Gott,* I can feel it, *ich bin bestimt verück.* Hurry up, Pierre, I am on fire inside.'

It was an unforgettable experience and although Pierre was exhausted, it put him in a very happy mood.

In a few days they reached Vitebsk on the River Dvinar, some 250 miles from the border. Would the Russians make a stand here? The Hussars reported back that the enemy was crossing the river over the bridges and by ferry and they could see elements passing out of the town beyond. The colonel suggested that they would cut off the tail-end of those waiting at the bridgehead and the ferry and he asked for an infantry brigade to carry out a combined attack. Very soon the cavalry were joined by units of the prestigious Imperial Guard, Napoleon's best, coming up at the double. Without delay the infantry advanced with the Hussars on either flank and reached the river without much fire from the Russian rearguard who were too anxious to escape, except for a battery of artillery enfilading the French from a flank position.

The phalanx of Imperial Guards advancing at the double was a brave sight, steadily closing ranks when cannonballs from the Russian guns cut swaths in their ranks. The colonel indicated that two squadrons were to follow him standing on his stirrups and pointing his sword at the guns. Coming on the Russian gunners from the right rear, the Hussars tore into them, scattering the company of infantry who were their protection guard. Second-class troops, it was quickly over, prisoners corralled and the guns turned round. Pierre had arrived at the scene right behind the colonel and, singling out a crew about to fire, despatched the three with savage blows to right and left.

As the squadrons wheeled and emerged from the battery, leaving a troop with the prisoners, the colonel indicated a formation of Russian cavalry which was moving cautiously towards the guards, as if undecided whether to attack. The Hussars without hesitation charged the Russians. It was true cavalry work, men and horses all in the spirit of the game. They hit the Russians, who were heavy boys, breastplated cuirassiers, no match for the Hussars. It was soon over and those who survived the charge surrendered forlornly. If this was the spirit the French were to encounter, then it would be a walkover when they came to grips with the main formations, if they ever decided to stop and face the invader.

Meanwhile, the Guards had reached the Dvinar, capturing whatever remained of the rearguard: quite a few welcome laden wagons, camp followers, who would be shared out as comforts for the troops, and some Russian infantry who gave up readily. The Guards advanced across the bridges and set up a bridgehead on the other side. They met with no resistance and the Russians had got away. Pierre's squadron had suffered relatively few casualties. He had been slashed across his left forearm by one of the 'lumpers', as the heavy cavalry were known, nothing incapacitating but a lot of blood. Pierre thought, my poor left arm again, more scars to cause interesting comments by the ladies if he was lucky enough. He sometimes thought of his wife, Collette, and his son, François, but they were so far away. Gretchen, and perhaps even Lotte, was on the spot.

The *Grande Armée* crossed the Dvinar. The Russians were gone, retreating with all speed, a cloud of dust on the horizon and columns of smoke, nothing left behind. The French were beginning to conserve their supplies. The nearest source of replenishments hundreds of miles behind them, even the small amount captured at Vitebsk was more than welcome. The end of July weather was very good, long hot, sunny days, water not so much a problem as envisaged. On to Smolensk. Would the czar make a stand there?

6

Smolensk

The Hussars were once more out front keeping a close watch on the retreating Russians. Occasionally there were opportunities to harass the rearguard, the colonel ever alert to send in a squadron when detachments became isolated from the main body. Wagons broken down were invariably captured. By mid-August 1812 the Hussars came in sight of Smolensk, an important trade centre, sprawled across the great Dnieper River, and reported back that the Russians had halted at the approaches to the city and were digging in and throwing up fortifications. Napoleon thought that at last he had them. Moscow was waiting out there and Czar Alexander would be forced to submit.

When Napoleon had assembled a force of some 50,000 men he decided to attack frontally and to cross the Dnieper either on the bridges or by the pontoons which had been lugged up from the rear. The Hussars were ordered to cross the river by whatever means they could find and report back on the Russian positions, a daunting task, but the cavalry were well versed in the role of reconnaissance in and behind the enemy.

The colonel decided that the best way across the Dnieper was upstream at a village almost certainly deserted and where there would be a crossing by bridge, ferry or ford. The regiment set off at first light, keeping out of sight of the Russians, and away from the river for several miles until the leading squadron reported a likely village which appeared to be deserted. There was no bridge across but they located a ford which took them without difficulty to the other side, where the houses were also empty and bare, all inhabitants gone. They continued away from the river making for the Smolensk–Moscow highway. By mid-morning they reached the highway where it ran through a wooded area which covered a few miles and could easily conceal the regiment.

The colonel placed Pierre's squadron on the Moscow side and another some distance away towards Smolensk, concealed to prevent any escapees and where Pierre could stop travellers likely to be of interest. He ordered that whatever occurred, none were to get away.

'Kill them all, we must not be discovered or our missions will be in vain.'

The other squadrons were in the wood behind with the packhorses. There were several riders and some carts going to Smolensk, which were allowed to carry on, then came a carriage with a mounted escort of an officer and six troopers.

The colonel who was with Pierre said, 'Right, this is yours, Pierre, stop the carriage, shoot the coachmen and cut down the escort. Use two troops, one in front and one behind and clear the road at once.'

As the carriage approached at a canter Pierre rode out with his troop and blocked the road. Two troopers seized the carriage horses, another shot the coachmen. Both troops, front and rear, closed with the escort and in a trice the poor fellows were no longer with the living. With great urgency, the horses were rounded up, bodies dragged into the undergrowth and the carriage brought to a clearing away from the road.

Pierre opened the carriage door and ordered the occupants, 'Out, out, quickly.'

Out came an elderly staff colonel, falling over his sword, very agitated, astonished to see French cavalry, followed by a lady, who might have been his wife or mistress. Pierre found two despatch boxes, which he brought to the colonel, who had with him a Russian-speaking officer borrowed from Division. The officer examined the boxes and said that one was for General Barclay de Tolly and the other for General the Prince Bagration.

The colonel was very pleased, and said, 'This is very important. We are in luck. Ask the colonel who the generals are and what they are ordered to carry out. Tell him that if he does

not immediately answer, we will kill the lady first and then him.'
He turned to a sergeant and said, 'Shoot the woman.'

The sergeant placed his pistol on the back of the woman's head and the Russian colonel fell to his knees imploring, 'No, no, my poor wife, don't kill her. I will tell you anything you wish to know.'

In reply to questioning he told the colonel that de Tolly commanded an army which was to defend Smolensk at all costs and Prince Bagration another army positioned to hold any breakthrough the French might achieve. The colonel ordered Pierre to send the colonel and his wife back to the rear squadrons for them to be escorted by a troop back to Division, with the despatch boxes. He wrote a note to be given to the troop officer for Division, requesting an urgent reply. The carriage was to be hidden and the prisoners were to go on horseback, like it or not.

The regiment continued to raid the road successfully, taking anything of military significance that could be carried out swiftly without distraction, also likely carts which were carrying produce. Regrettably, no prisoners were taken and, apart from some Russian officers who were escorted back, all others were slain out of hand. The colonel reiterated, it is them or us and the success of our mission. On the third morning, at daybreak they heard the rumble of artillery and could see the flashes in the sky. De Tolly had held and the battle was on. The troop officer who had escorted the Russian colonel returned with an order for the regiment to remain behind the Russians and contrive to harass them.

'We shall be with you soon.'

At dark that day they observed a supply column with a few wagons but more important, a dozen pieces of artillery, a great prize, captured guns regarded as confirmed victory.

The column left the highway and prepared to bivouac for the night and the colonel said, 'We will have them, the guns are for us.'

He ordered two squadrons to place themselves round the target, dismounted, and said that they had two hours to get in position, by which time the Russians would be settled down for the night.

'The trumpeter will sound a single note and then get in, kill them all. Before daybreak all must be cleared away as though nothing had happened. Our woods are filling up, but our friends will be here soon.'

All were in position when the trumpet call came. Pierre, in the centre of his squadron, ran forward closely followed by Big Jean. An unsuspecting sentry (who would expect trouble out here?) was silently despatched and all along the line the Hussars moved in. The column escort and drivers were not front-line soldiers and apart from a few pistol shots, there was no resistance. Then came the hard part, to clear all away before dawn, but it was done and it was as though nothing had happened. The regiment had a few casualties, men injured falling in the dark.

So it went on, 'fishing' the highway.

The colonel was very pleased, but he said, 'I hope the Russians break soon or we must inevitably be discovered and have to make a run for it. The sound of gunfire continued all day – the Russians must be holding at Smolensk.'

At dawn they could see that the whole Russian force was withdrawing. So it turned out. As they discovered later, de Tolly feared that the French would bypass him and press on to Moscow. Bagration was obliged to conform. Both sides had suffered several thousand casualties, but Napoleon was elated. The way to Moscow was open and the humbling of the Czar.

Two days later the vanguard of the French appeared and the Hussars lined the road with their prize guns displayed.

Pierre managed that night to get back to the wagons where he found Gretchen in good spirits. Lotte had gone.

'I am glad, I do not want to share you again with anyone,' she told him.

Gretchen told Pierre that supplies were getting short and some things were rationed. She had seen that many wagons had remained behind in Smolensk, supposedly to make a supply depot. She also said that there was nothing to be had in the town, all had been taken by the Russians.

'Never mind, we shall be all right when we get to Moscow.'

7

Borodino and Moscow

The colonel of the Hussars, at a situation report, told the officers, 'Marshal Oudinot has expressed his gratitude for our successful performance at Smolensk. The Russian staff colonel was of great help regarding the czar's plans. We now know that Alexander has instructed his commander-in-chief, Kutusov, to block our advance on Moscow at Borodino.'

The colonel went on to say that the regiment would resume the role of forward reconnaissance, keeping the army informed of the enemy's movements.

The *Grande Armée* was now some 300 miles inside Russia and Moscow another 200 miles further on. The going was good, the weather warm and sunny but the nights colder, with a hint of the coming winter frosts. The regiment soon caught up with the tail-end of the retreating Russians. The wagons, inevitably the end of the line, were escorted by a squadron of Cossacks.

The colonel said, 'Right, we will take out the Cossacks. And capture some wagons, but we must not become involved in a battle. Our role is to watch and report. However, a little harassment is quite in order and we might be lucky with the wagons. Two squadrons, you and you, ride on the Cossacks from each flank.'

Pierre led his squadron at a smart pace towards the Cossacks who immediately formed up in battle line to meet the Hussars. The three elements met at the charge, a furious tangle of horses and slashing swords. The Cossacks stood little chance and it was over as soon as the Hussars met in the centre. The remnant broke away back to their lines where infantry were halted to prepare to receive the French. Pierre signalled to the other squadron leader to keep the Russians busy, whilst he turned some wagons. It was very quickly over and the Hussars were galloping back with their booty, followed by a few musket balls. There had been a few casualties, but the Russians had left more of their dead behind than the French. The wagons contained flour and sugar, some other useful groceries, such as tea and, above all, vodka and women, the usual camp followers.

The colonel said, 'The supplies are ours but regretfully the women must go back to Division. They can have the pleasure and the trouble.'

The Hussars resumed their proper role of shadowing the enemy who, as previously, left nothing behind, only empty villages and scorched earth. Napoleon urged the *Grande Armée* on, hoping to catch Kutusov unprepared at Borodino. Realising that this was The Battle of Moscow, the Russians would be unable to prevent the French from reaching Moscow, which was only 50 miles away. Supplies were getting short and it was essential to reach a conclusion to the war, when the czar would come to terms. The Hussars reported that the Russians had halted at Borodino and had drawn up battle lines. They estimated that Kutusov had some eight divisions. The army that was following close behind the Hussars comprised of some ten divisions of the *Grande Armée*'s best, led by the staunch troops of the Imperial Guard, Napoleon's favourites.

On 7 September 1812 the battle for Moscow commenced with barrages of artillery from both sides followed by an advance against the Russians by massed regiments. Oudinot's cavalry divisions were on either flank to protect the infantry from Russian cavalry attacks and to exploit any movement by Kutusov back towards Moscow. To Napoleon's surprise, the Russians held firm, even when hand-to-hand fighting occurred. On the first day casualties were very high on both sides. The Hussars were stationed in the front of their division when their leading squadron observed a mass of Russian cavalry approaching towards the French flank, the ideal cavalry role, seldom happening, of cavalry against cavalry.

The division formed up in battle array, two brigades up and one in reserve, each brigade in three regimental columns, each regiment with three squadrons in line ahead, a formidable sight. Brigade commanding generals and regimental colonels in front of their formations, accompanied by their Staff Officers, orderlies and trumpeters. The division commander-in-chief, a splendid figure in his general's uniform, was at the front, alone, a staff colonel, trumpeter and orderlies some way behind him.

The French infantry were moving forward at a steady pace, perfectly aligned. The French and Russian artillery were banging away, the Russian guns cutting swaths in the ranks of the infantry, the lines closing up to maintain a solid front.

The French guns were hammering away at the Russians in the fortifications hastily constructed by Kutusov. The Russian cavalry some way off were milling around, raising clouds of dust, as they assumed battle order.

The colonel sent for the squadron leaders and said, 'We will go in as a solid wedge to split the enemy apart.' He ordered, 'You must keep together, so that we emerge from the Russians as a unit, ready for a counter charge. Remember, keep together, dress ranks, *bon chance mes braves.*' Pierre went back to his squadron and passed on his message to the troop officers. The troops were aligned two up with his headquarters troop in the centre and the other three troops behind. The squadron was the first in line behind the colonel. A trumpet call from the general's trumpeter out front signalled the order to advance and the formations moved off in perfect drill order, the commander leading. Intense musketry fire told them that the infantry were engaged.

As they moved forward they came under fire from Russian artillery on their flank. Four guns had been hurriedly positioned and the cavalry were within range. The first casualties occurred, horses and riders down. The nearest brigade ordered a regiment to silence the guns, even if it were necessary to charge them, which would be very costly. The regiment advanced towards the guns, one squadron frontally and the remainder to execute a flanking attack. The squadron charging the guns was cut to pieces but the rest of the regiment rode at the guns and within minutes it was over. The precious guns, victory trophies, were limbered up and sent away from the front. The much depleted regiment resumed its position in the formation, which was approaching the enemy cavalry who were also on the move.

The order came to charge and they came together in a thunderous fracas: the clash of swords, clouds of dust and whinnying, plunging horses. In the confusion of the hand-to-hand mêlée, miraculously the Hussars emerged behind the Russians somewhat depleted, but ready to countercharge, back into the cauldron. So it went on all day, continual charges and countercharges, a cavalry fight as such had probably never been seen before in the history of warfare. At the end of the day both sides had had enough, fought to a standstill and, as though by mutual consent, withdrew. The various units sorted themselves out. Miraculously, the general had emerged unhurt and quite unperturbed; the Hussars' colonel was sorely wounded, his uniform a bloody mess, his right arm dangling, the sword held on by the knot. Blood was pouring from one leg. His orderlies got him down from the saddle and set about binding his wounds. At a rough count half the regiment was missing, either killed or wounded. The wounded would be picked up later, when it could be organised. The Russians would also collect their wounded, both enemies meeting in a common cause.

The infantry had also fought to a standstill and were withdrawing. The Russians had made a heroic stand and casualties were unusually high. Some 80,000 perished, 30 per cent of the forces involved. Kutusov withdrew swiftly along the highway to Moscow 100 miles further on. The French reorganised, the wounded being sent back, including Pierre's colonel.

Before he left he told Pierre, 'I am done for, you will take over the regiment, promoted to Major. The Brigadier will be informed.'

Pierre was unharmed, not even a scratch. His squadron had kept together throughout the fight and had fewer casualties.

The brigadier sent for Pierre and confirmed his appointment.

'Major Flamand, you will organise the Hussars. I leave the details to you. It must be carried out quickly as you are to resume your previous role of being the eyes of the army. You are to avoid any action against the Russians. It is more important that you keep us informed of Kutusov's retreat. The Russians are "going home" and we are getting further away.' He added, 'If you see your colonel before the wagons leave, please give him my best wishes. He is unlikely to survive the awful journey in a jolting wagon.'

Pierre had, of course, been considering reorganising the regiment and straight away put his conclusions in hand. There were sufficient men to make up two fighting squadrons; officers were insufficient in number after he promoted the two most promising troop officers to squadron commanders as captains. To make up the necessary ten troop officers, on the advice of the regimental maréchal, regimental sergeant major, he selected four sergeants to command troops. He would dispense with a second-in-command and use the RSM, a very experienced old soldier in that role. Very quickly they were ready to move out.

Before leaving, Pierre went back to the wagon lines and among the hundreds of wagons going back for supplies from Smolensk and carrying the sick and wounded; the dreaded typhus and dysentery were rampant, with little chance of survival for those affected. With much difficulty he found the colonel in a wagon with another senior officer. The colonel was far from well and could barely interest himself in Pierre's details of the regiment's reorganisation. Pierre judged that he would not reach Smolensk alive. The wagon columns required a considerable escort as the half-starved marauding bands of Russian brigands, or partisans, seized any opportunity to raid them. Even if going back empty, the horses made welcome eating and the wagons the firewood for cooking and warmth. It was getting cold at night. Such was the problem of supplies that out of the remaining force of the original 600,000, Napoleon could only manage to provide a front-line army of barely 100,000 strong.

Pierre went on to find Gretchen, who was expecting him as they were halted and the sounds of battle had died down. They made love and Pierre was a new man. Relieved from the stresses of the past days, his troubles poured out. They lay talking and drinking a bottle of schnapps Gretchen had saved up. He told her about Borodino, the horrors of the battle, the great cavalry fight, probably the biggest ever such engagement. He spoke of his colonel, whom he had just left in the wounded wagons, a very gallant gentleman, sorely wounded and unlikely to ever see France again. Half the regiment were slain, horses slaughtered, fit only for horsemeat, good to augment the now insufficient supplies, but so sad.

'Gretchen, my love,' he told her, 'we are going to Moscow for certain and the Russians will not stop us. They will probably keep going back into their own vast country, whilst we get further away from our only source of food and sustenance. The days and nights are getting cold even in September. What will it be like when the Russian winter comes, how shall we survive?' He went on, 'Perhaps you should return now with the column forming up outside. You can reach Smolensk and then without difficulty your home in Prussia.'

Gretchen said, 'No, Pierre, I will stay and offer you always the comfort of my love and my body. Also I have grown to enjoy this *Zigeuner* life, it grows on one in spite of the problems of just surviving. I will carry on, whatever comes. There are many of us followers of the soldier who feel the same.'

When Pierre returned the next morning the regiment was ready to move out. He reported to the brigadier and was told, 'Right, off you go, Moscow here we come. Keep me fully informed. You are our eyes, remember.'

The Hussars moved on up the Moscow highway, well strewn with useless rubbish discarded by the Russians. The turnout of the regiment was good, replenished from their dead comrades, knapsacks and saddlebags full, weapons and saddlery in good order. After some days they caught up with the Russian tail-end and came across a few broken-down wagons and stragglers, but made no attempt to attack the rearguard. Their continuing situation reports were more important.

Kutusov hurried on back to the haven of the homeland, nevertheless destroying all behind him, leaving nothing of use to Napoleon, neither food nor fodder. Pierre kept in close touch and sent back regular messengers to report the situation. In a few days they came to the Moskva River, with its many bridges still undamaged. The Czar had reasoned that the French would not be here for long. Let them have Moscow, they will find nothing and will have to go away, over the barren wastes they came by.

Pierre decided to wait for orders to enter the city. He could see that Kutusov was not halting, the streets sucking in the last of his army like water down the gutters, leaving all still and deserted. Word came to press on and to continue to monitor the position of the Russians. He led the regiment across the nearest bridge and over the island to midstream from where could be seen the onion domes and spheres of St Basil's Cathedral. He pressed on towards the cathedral, a truly breathtaking cluster of variegated domes decorated with splendid colours and intricate masonry, a part of the lands east of Europe they had not ever imagined in its strange splendour.

The emerged up a steep slope into the vast Kremlin Square, on one side the vast red-brick walls surrounding the Kremlin complex of palaces, cathedrals and government offices and all round magnificent palaces, galleries and museums, where the czar's great collections of art, paintings, statuary and many forms of the arts of jewellery, tapestry, collected from all over the world were stored.

Pierre sent patrols to explore to the south and east and himself took a squadron into the Kremlin through the massive gateway into the labyrinth of streets. All was eerily still and deserted, not even a cat to be seen, probably eaten anyway; only the clatter of hooves and jingle of harnesses disturbed the stillness. All signs of life were gone. Dismounting and entering some of the palaces, they found them stripped of most of the moveables as though by a host of furniture removers. The population had been obliged to carry all with them as they were driven to the east of the city by Kutusov's soldiers. Much however remained, loot for Napoleon's men, which would probably never reach France.

The patrols all reported the same situation; all deserted, no mean feat to empty a great city with such speed, leaving nothing of any substance for the hated Napoleon. The Russians, downtrodden and oppressed, just obeyed their lords and masters, like dumb animals, in spite of the additional hardships to themselves in leaving their albeit miserable homes behind. All gone as if by magic! The Hussars spent the night in the square with plenty of wood for welcome fires, sentries alert, but all was still; a quiet night in a deserted metropolis, quite unrealistic. In the morning the regiment set out to find the Russians. Pierre left one troop behind to meet the advance guard of the *Grande Armée* and proceeded eastwards on the main road to Vladimir, passing through miles of empty streets with nothing to stop their reconnaissance. They arrived at a clearing beyond which was a great forest of pines: Babushkin, the place where the rich élite had their country houses and dachas. Smoke from fires could be seen rising above the pines, so they decided that Kutusov had halted there. Pierre ordered the regiment to stay out of sight. At nightfall he would send in a small group to find out what was in the woods and try to capture any Russians they could without raising the alarm. Although he was by now experienced in such operations, he decided not to go in himself.

After darkness fell, one squadron commander, a troop officer and six troopers went out dismounted and lightly armed to reach the woods. Big Jean went with them. He was most likely to bring back a prisoner. Within a few hours they were back, bringing with them a junior infantry officer who was picked up with his trousers down behind a bush!

'Yes,' reported the squadron leader, 'we are fairly sure Kutusov has stopped there. There was quite a lot of noise, chatter going on, and fires to be seen. This chap is quite nervous and humiliated at being caught in such an embarrassing situation. He will probably tell us all.'

Pierre left one troop behind to keep watch and returned to the Kremlin Square, where he found part of the army had arrived. He sent the news back to the brigadier and waited for orders. A troop officer told him that some of the men had found a great store of vodka and brandy in a warehouse, concealed in a vault by a hidden entrance.

The finders were considerably drunk, but he had closed the vault up until the spirits could be distributed properly by the commissariat, and he said, 'Sir, I have sequestered some for the use of the regiment.'

Jolly good show.

Napoleon brought his army, the sick and the camp followers, including Gretchen, into Moscow. Out of the 600,000 of the *Grande Armée* which entered Russia, less than four months beforehand, there remained in Moscow 120,000 fighting troops, 20,000 sick and 40,000 camp followers. Some were at Smolensk with the supply depot and others on the wagon columns operating through some 300 miles of hostile, barren countryside.

September was drawing to a close and the tentacles of chill winter were in the air. Napoleon realised that he could not continue chasing Alexander into the vastness of Russia and that if it came to a fight, the French, splendid soldiers though they were, had shown signs of weariness. Tired and undernourished, they might be defeated. At Borodino, a draw, it had been touch and go. It could not go on. The Czar must be persuaded to show reason. After all, together, France and Russia could conquer the far-off lands of Asia. Secretly, he considered that Alexander would not come to terms, but an attempt must be made.

The Brigadier sent for Pierre and told him that as he had already been to the area where Kutusov was encamped, he was to deliver a message from the emperor to the czar of greatest importance.

'You will go under a flag of truce and I suggest your orderly and the RSM. You will, of course, be properly turned out to impress the Russians. Make it a ceremonial occasion. Be as quick as you can. You will not reach the czar but so long as you hand over the missive at Kutusov's headquarters, it should suffice. Wait for the answer.'

The trio rode off on the errand which Pierre understood was of the greatest import. Much would depend on the reply. He planned to arrive near enough to the Russian positions in broad daylight. As they drew close enough to be observed, Big Jean waved the large white flag of truce. They waited for almost an hour and finally an officer, unaccompanied, rode out to them. Pierre told him that he had a message from the emperor to the czar which he was instructed to hand over to General Kutusov to be conveyed to Alexander. The Russian colonel told him to follow and passing along seemingly endless forest tracks, they arrived at Kutusov's base. Pierre insisted that he would only deliver his message to the general personally, and eventually reached him. Kutusov told him he would have to stay for at least two days for an answer and sent him away to be kept under guard. From what Pierre could tell, the Russians were no better off than the French. However, he and his escort were well looked after and fed.

In due course, Kutusov sent for Pierre and told him, 'Here is the reply. Just tell your master that our czar refuses to negotiate. There will be no treaty.'

Pierre returned and informed the brigadier, who said, 'We will go to see the emperor together and you can tell him what happened at first hand.'

Napoleon was using the czar's great palace in the Kremlin, the entrance guarded by his ever faithful Imperial Guard. They climbed the great staircase up to the reception rooms, where they were taken to a room cluttered with work desks, strewn with maps and papers and endless reports. Napoleon was a demon for work and kept in touch with all and sundry concerning the enemy, the supply situation, etc. Outside were several high-ranking officers and a host of orderlies.

Napoleon was deep in thought, as always, planning and scheming. Pierre could at once sense the power and genius of the great man, bogeyman to his enemies, but what a powerful presence.

The brigadier said, 'Your majesty, Major Flamand has been to Kutusov's headquarters and I have brought him to tell you the outcome in his own words.'

Napoleon listened in silence and without emotion until Pierre had told all: no parley. Then the Emperor was suffused with fury.

'All that we have achieved will come to naught. I have lost France the world!'

Pierre went back to the regiment, collected some flasks from their store of vodka and went off to find his piece of comfort, Gretchen. She was rested after the arduous journey in the jolting wagon, over the awful roads, unimproving with the passage of so many hooves and wheels. What would they be like when the snows came? Pierre immersed himself in her warm body, which was still comfortable in spite of the meagre rations. They made love very enjoyably, by now very accustomed to each other's peccadilloes. He rarely thought of Collette, his wife, or of his son, François. These German girls are the best, he mused, better than the others, or perhaps it is because she is here and the others far away. Widow Oudinot was exciting. Perhaps I will have the pleasure again some day.

The troops found many valuables, mostly cumbersome, which the Russians could not easily remove and hundreds of wagons were loaded with many treasures destined for France. Almost before the French had settled down, a fire broke out, probably started by looters. The entire city was burned down except for a few stone buildings, the flames burning brightly in the cold crisp atmosphere. This unfortunate occurrence was the final straw. There was nowhere to go and the French were forced to begin their disastrous retreat. It was mid-October and the first frosts of winter occurred, the temperature falling at night to hitherto unexperienced levels. The soldiers had extra blankets and clothing obtained from their fallen comrades, but these were insufficient to combat the dreadful cold.

8

The Retreat

Napoleon decided that he would go south to the warmer lands of the Ukraine. After a week on the road to the south and only a few miles from Moscow they reached Maloyaroslavets, where they found the way blocked by Kutusov with a considerable force. The ensuing battle was bitter, both sides determined to outdo the other. Napoleon ordered Oudinot with his cavalry to clear the way, a fatal move, cavalry against prepared positions. Oudinot could only manage to field a division out of the former cavalry corps. Knowing the importance of breaking out to the south, the cavalry made an all-out effort. The brigades charged the outposts, who were quickly swept aside.

Pierre with the Hussars penetrated into the town and gained the main square. They were met by a hail of musketry and, without infantry support, were forced to withdraw, leaving many dead and wounded, horses sorely injured and screaming in their agony. Napoleon ordered his infantry to attack and forward they marched in close order rank upon rank, not even breaking when met by a withering fire from cannon and musket. The Russians had regrouped outside the town. Hand-to-hand fighting ensued, bayonets clashing, men falling dead or dying. The French were desperate to win, knowing the consequences of having to go back. The cavalry regrouped and were sent on a wide sweep to encompass the town, no longer a full division, only three brigades at half-strength. They were met by a swarm of charging Cossacks and the two met with a great clash of arms. Formations split up and individual combat, man to man, went on with demon-like fury. Pierre survived, he and Big Jean fighting together, a well-tried team, the one guarding the other. At the end of the day the French withdrew, beaten, no longer able to go on. The only way was to retreat to the pestilential road to Smolensk, leaving more then 6,000 dead on the field of battle.

The road back was unbelievably chilly. There was nothing for the *Grande Armée* to eat apart from what it carried in pockets and knapsacks, nothing to sustain themselves until they reached the supply depot at Smolensk. In addition, they were harassed by the savage partisans, who seized any opportunity to cut off stragglers and rob the wagons. The way was littered with abandoned wagons, loot-laden with the treasures of Moscow, and horses dead at the shafts.

The starving army retraced its invasion route through charred hamlets. There was no cheer in their surroundings. Typhus was rampant and when they reached Borodino, scene of the old battlefield, the charnel house was strewn with thousands of unburied corpses. Sick and wounded left behind there were frantically trying to find places on the remaining wagons, already overloaded.

Then it snowed, not as gentle white doves descending from heaven, but accompanied by an overwhelming fog and, finally, a terrible blizzard blew from the frozen north across endless miles of steppe. The path of the invaders was blocked by drifts of snow. Staggering blindly on, they were exhausted. The once vast army began its final disintegration, an unparalleled disaster. The snow continued endlessly, it was a matter of *suave qui peut*. Napoleon was forced to abandon any attempt to make a stand and to crush the Russians.

By mid-November they had reached Smolensk, where they found the supplies inadequate, even though Napoleon had some 50,000 fewer mouths to feed, 50,000 being lost since leaving Moscow. The discipline of the Imperial Guard kept a semblance of order. Those that remained of the Hussars, once proud cavalry, struggled along on foot, horses all starved to death. Pierre kept together as many as possible. They must be able to fight as a unit, if called upon to do so. He had abandoned any hope of finding Gretchen and at Smolensk decided she had perished.

The Russians, almost as badly off as the French, staged an offensive at Knasnoi and in spite of the appalling state of the combatants, they slogged away at each other for three days. Hundreds more were lost in the battle and only 30,000 French remained with the colours.

By the end of the month the French reached the Berezina River where the Russians barred the way to the pontoon bridge which the engineers had strung over the wide river. The emperor broke through by sheer willpower. Many drowned in the current or were captured by the Russians.

Pierre, struggling over on a pontoon, was killed outright by a shell which struck in front of him. Big Jean, with him to the bitter end, went with him into the icy waters

The emperor, succoured by his faithful Imperial Guard, abandoned the survivors and departed for Warsaw in a sleigh, reaching Paris a week later.

He brushed aside the calamitous campaign by explaining, 'It is nothing, only the effects of the climate. In six months I shall be again on the Niemen.'

So for the second time, the first being his attempt through Egypt in 1798, where he was defeated by the British, in particular by the Royal Navy, Napoleon returned to France without the troops he had set out with to conquer the east.

The tragic remains of the 600,000 *Grande Armée*, which had set out a short six months earlier, a mere 10,000 men crippled by typhus, crossed back over the Niemen into Prussia, all who remained of the army, the rest destroyed by the freezing snows, or in battle.

If there had been no Russian campaign and no retreat from Moscow, then we would not have had Tchaikovski's glorious *1812 Overture*, or Beethoven's *Fifth Symphony* or *Emperor Concerto*: some consolation.

9

Paris

Collette, in Normandy bringing up her son, François, now in his second year, had not received any news from Pierre since a letter from Prussia, before the ill-fated Russian adventure. Gradually news spread of the disaster that had overtaken Napoleon's army, most of it buried in the snowy wastelands. She guessed he might be dead, but with so few survivors there was no means of finding out. The Hussars' depot at Lyons could only tell her that he was missing, believed dead.

One day she was visited by a lady riding in a grand carriage, who introduced herself as Madeleine Oudinot, a widow living at nearby Evreux. Madame Oudinot told her that she had met Pierre when he was recruiting for the regiment.

'Pierre helped my son, who went to Lyons and is even now serving there with the Hussars.' She went on to say that Lucien had recently returned from Spain. Wellington had finally driven the French out of the Peninsular. Lucien, remembering Pierre, had closely questioned the few survivors who had returned to Lyons. He ascertained that Pierre had eventually commanded the regiment and had finally perished, during the retreat whilst crossing over the Berezina. 'So you are now a war widow, like myself. My husband was killed at Torres Vedras.'

Madeleine mentioned that she had 'helped' Pierre when he was recruiting in Normandy and Collette thought to herself, I wonder how?

They became good friends, war widows together, and Collette spent half of her time at the grand house at Evreux. Like most people tired of the endless war still continuing after twenty years, and Napoleon's erstwhile occupations of Europe shrinking, the ladies devoted themselves to fashion, anything to take their lives away from the misery brought on by the privations of the conflict. Madeleine was rich, they had much in common and were able to indulge themselves, even in the drab surroundings. They made a trip to Lyons to see Lucien, and Collette was welcomed warmly by the colonel commandant as the widow of a respected officer of the regiment.

It was spring of 1814. Napoleon had been defeated at Leipzig by a coalition of Russia, Prussia, England, Sweden and Austria. Pursuing him into France, they obliged him to abdicate. He was exiled to Elba, a small island in the Mediterranean between his beloved birthplace, Corsica, and the Italian mainland, too near to home as time would show.

Madeleine pointed out to Collette one day soon after Napoleon had gone, 'Things have changed. I am tired of Normandy. We are both still young and free, let us go to Paris. We have a common interest in fashion and French women are in the mood to shake off the miseries of wartime. We can start a business. Let's go!'

Collette was very agreeable and without delay they set off for a new life. François remained behind with his grandparents for the time being.

Madeleine knew her way around Paris and exactly where she wanted to establish the *maison de haute couture* and straightaway found premises for rent on the *Champs Elysées* near the *Quai d'Orsay* and the *Arc de Triomphe de l'Etoile*. The arc had been under construction since 1806, to commemorate Napoleon's victories. It was still unfinished and would be many more years in the building. The building was well-chosen and had apartments above for each of them. The Oudinot, (they chose to use Madeleine's name because of the association with the popular marshal, who had survived the Russian campaign), *Maison de Haute Couture* prospered as Madeleine had predicted and within a year they had purchased the building.

Early the following year, 1815, Napoleon left Elba and landed in France. The French, as always mesmerised by his magnetism, rallied to him and in no time he had raised an army. His rule lasted only a hundred days, culminating in a disastrous defeat at Waterloo by his old adversary, the Iron Duke of Wellington, and his Prussian ally, Blücher. This time the allies made no mistake. He was exiled to the tiny island of St Helena in the South Atlantic. End of Napoleon, after all an exceptional genius with a tremendous impact on history, a dictator with the power to sway a nation of millions of people. His son, Napoleon II, succeeded the emperor, but he never ruled France, spending his life in Vienna as a 'guest' of the Austrians. He was known as 'The Eaglet', *L'Aiglon*, and died of tuberculosis at the age of 21, not carrying on the greatness of his father.

Freed from the tyrannies of war, France flourished and Paris became the most popular capital city of Europe. The French way of life was exciting to the cold northerners who flocked to sample the fleshpots. Maison Oudinot became very popular in the world of fashion and the owners had made themselves very prominent in the business. Collette brought François to Paris where, at four years of age, he attended a good *école pour les enfants* on the Quai d'Orsay. Both widows had admirers and, very discreetly, carefully chosen gentlemen inserted themselves between the sheets. Until . . .

One morning a group of three ladies and a man came to the salon. The man, well-dressed, tall, blond-haired and blue-eyed, had a soldier-like bearing.

He introduced himself. 'Kurt von Winterstein, this is my mother Gräfin von Winterstein and my two sisters who wish to be shown suitable dresses and accessories.'

Whilst Madeleine and her assistants were attending to the ladies Kurt chatted to Collette.

'We live temporarily on the Quai d'Orsay and I have sometimes seen you passing with a small boy.'

'He is my son. I am a widow and my husband was a Hussar. He perished during the ill-fated Russian campaign. I had not heard from him since he left Königsberg with Napoleon's army and he never saw François, our son.'

Collette invited him to sit and have a glass of wine whilst the ladies were occupied. She looked enquiringly at his gloved left hand.

'Waterloo,' he said, rapping wood against wood on the table. 'A

French musket ball. We were on the same side as the French in Russia. My home is at Tilsit but luckily I did not go to Russia. I may well have met your husband. We entertained a great deal.' He told her of the great family estate. 'My father is Gräf Otto von Winterstein and I am the only son. The land at Tilsit is mainly sand and rock, but we have enormous forests.'

He told of the Baltic Sea, good fishing and sailing in the summer, frozen over in the winter; one could skate across to Switzerland.

When the party was ready to leave, the purchases would be delivered by the maison, the Gräfin said, 'I am giving a soirée this week. I will send you both invitations.'

The Gräfin understood that although Collette and Madeleine were in 'trade', at least they were 'officer class', an all-important distinction for Prussians. Her son, Kurt, a major of cavalry, was now military attaché to the German minister to Paris. Kurt said a warm farewell to Collette, kissing her hand, his eyes revealing that he was interested to say the least.

'Until our next meeting,' he murmured..

The party was a grand affair, the guests mostly from the diplomatic corps, with a sprinkling of splendid uniforms. Collette realised what a fine figure Kurt was in cavalry officer dress and perhaps began to have thoughts. The ladies of *Maison Oudinot* were delighted with the scene. Both elegantly turned out, they were much admired and sought after by young and old admirers. When it was time to go, Madeleine was not to be found, obviously off somewhere with a beau. (Collette knew she was a lady with warm feelings and sometimes wondered what the relationship had been with her and Pierre). So Kurt took Collette home, suggesting that as it was a fine night they could walk the short distance to the Champs Elysées.

At the house, Collette invited him to the apartment. François was almost certainly sound asleep in a room at the back. It was a calculated move. Kurt was an attractive man and she a widow, no shy young girl. In the salon, Kurt helped her off with her cloak, contrived in doing so to touch her breasts more lingeringly than was necessary. Collette suggested he sample some calvados brandy from her native Normandy and they sat close together on the small settee, talking about themselves, their homes and upbringings widely different. Inevitably, they came together, as though deciding enough playing games, we both know what we want. Let's get on with it!

Collette said, 'Not here, let us go to my bedroom,' practically dragging him to the door.

Kurt, accustomed only to ladies of easy virtue to be had in the villages at home, was overcome with the experience of a beautiful woman giving him freely the most intimate parts of her still young and lovely body. They made love until dawn, when Kurt felt it prudent to leave, vowing that he must see her again very soon.

The relationship developed to the point where Kurt began to have serious intentions, reaching a stage when he felt obliged to have a talk with his mother.

He told her of his involvement with Collette and went on, 'You know that I may not have children, due to my riding accident.' (Although his sexual performance was undiminished). 'Collette is a suitable person and, more importantly, has a prize son. There should be no objection to having a French wife. After all, Father's grandmother was a French countess. The boy François would have his name changed to Friedrich and would be brought up as a Prussian. He is too young to appreciate the change.'

The Gräfin agreed that this could be a happy solution to the problem of inheritance.

"Kurt, I am sure your father will agree, but I will write to him, so wait until we know his reaction.'

The Gräf came to Paris when he received the letter to see the situation himself and, having met Collette and the boy, approved of the choice.

He told Kurt, 'Go ahead, she is a fine woman. I could fancy her myself,' fathers usually being attracted to their sons' young ladies, whereas mothers instinctively dislike them. In this case, the Gräfin approved.

So Kurt proposed marriage to Collette, who, privately, was not surprised and accepted with evident pleasure. Kurt explained to her what was proposed: eventually they would live at Tilsit and he would inherit the estate.

'In due course, François will carry on and to this end I propose that we change his name to Otto and, of course, when we marry, he

will be a von Winterstein.'
Collette was horrified.
'He is my late husband's son and French also. My parents and Pierre's would never agree.'
Kurt said, 'Well, it is a pity, but we shall marry nevertheless, then we shall see.'
Madeleine, when told the news said, 'I am not surprised. Your Kurt is a fine man, quite a catch. I shall miss you. Oudinot is well-established now, so there is no problem there.'
Then Collette went off to Normandy to tell the families, leaving François in the care of the gräfin, a good move since they were likely to know each other in the not so distant future. Collette told her mother and father of the proposed marriage and the suggestion of changing François's name. They were happy for Collette.
'You are young and unfortunately widowed. Go ahead. We give you our blessing. Regarding François, his paternal grandparents will never agree to a change of name. His new family name perhaps, but he must never be induced to believe he is other than French.'
Following a talk with Pierre's parents they decided to go to Paris to see for themselves.
Eventually, the interested parties met and, contrary to Collette's fears, they got on very well and, surprisingly, agreed that eventually the couple would live in Germany and François would be brought up as a Prussian. There would be no change of name. He would no longer be François Flamand but François von Winterstein and never be persuaded to forget his French origin. This was agreed and they decided to remain in Paris for the wedding, which could be arranged very quickly by means of a civil ceremony by the German minister.
The newly-weds went off to Deauville for the honeymoon, ironically to the hotel where Collette had spent her first, with Pierre, although she did not enlighten Kurt.
At first she thought the proprietress remembered her and quickly said, 'What a nice place Deauville is. Although I live in Normandy, I have never been here before.'
Kurt might have felt a little upset. When they returned to Paris, the von Wintersteins left and the couple, with François moved into the grand apartment. François was enrolled in a school which

catered for both French and German pupils and taught in both languages. Kurt had another year to serve in Paris and then they would go to Tilsit.

The year passed very quickly and happily. The diplomatic service was tied up in an endless round of entertaining, mostly confined to those representing other foreign countries.

Before leaving for Germany, (now so known, being the confederation of the several former sovereign states by Napoleon and, latterly, by Bismarck), they went for a holiday to Normandy, when Collette's parents remarked, 'François is becoming a proper little Prussian.'

10

Germany

Firstly they went to the von Winterstein estates in Tilsit. Collette was astonished by the extent of the property, requiring several days of riding to cover it all: great forests and farms with scattered hamlets, one day to be François's domain. Kurt reported to the war office in Berlin and, having decided to soldier on, was promoted to major and given a squadron of the prestigious *Ulhanen*, cream of the cavalry, the regiment being stationed at Spandau, outside Berlin. The officer he was replacing rented a splendid villa on the shore of the nearby Havel Wasser which he handed over to Kurt with the owner's consent. There was a small sailing boat moored at the jetty, which went with the villa, and there were wildfowl in abundance and the lake was good for freshwater fish.

Collette was delighted with the villa and its surroundings and the prospects of a good new life. Adjacent dwellings were mostly occupied by military officers' families and she should make many new friends. François was enrolled in a school at Spandau which specialised in teaching officers' children. The Spandau area was home to many regiments, so there was no shortage of pupils. Collette explained the seeming oddity of François's name.

'His father is French, as I am. He was killed during Napoleon's campaign in Russia, where he was commanding a Hussar regiment. I hope other boys will not trouble him because of this.'

Of course he was teased and bullied, but very quickly he was accepted.

Some very enjoyable years were spent at Spandau. They went

several times back to Tilsit. There were no children and they were so glad to have François, whom Kurt now thought of as his own son and he, not having seen his real father, was very happy with the only one he had known. On their last visit to Tilsit, they found Otto, Kurt's father, very frail and beginning to neglect the estate, although there were competent foremen. The Gräf was not just a nominal head, he was also called on to make all decisions regarding management, even in day-to-day affairs. So Kurt decided to leave the army and go back to take over the reins from his ailing father.

They settled quite happily into the von Wintersteins' schloss, the family castle, and François who was now old enough, was enrolled as a cadet in the Prussian military academy in Königsberg, destined for the army, like his 'fathers'. He came on long leave and on arrival at the schloss, one of the housemaids was told to take him to his new quarters. Carrying his hand luggage, she opened the door and turned to let him pass. He brushed past her and involuntarily his body touched hers. He could feel the firm, soft cushions of her buttocks and a shock went through him. She could see he was aroused, the bulge in his tight uniform trousers bursting to get out.

'Come,' she said, 'we must do something about that, it is suffering,' putting her hand on the lump and closing the door. Deftly she removed his trousers and was astonished by the monster that was revealed. 'God in heaven, so young and so big,' she said. 'Come.'

François, although a virgin, was not backward and with her help guided his extra large member into her. Even though she was well used he only penetrated a few inches when he discharged copiously. She clung to him desperately.

'Don't leave me, you will soon be ready again.'

And he was. She cried out with pleasure and so François lost his virginity.

The maid made the mistake to tell the others and François was besieged by imploring females and whenever he chose bedded them. So his reputation grew. Finally, he took one very young kitchen maid who although a virgin begged him to break her in. It was quite a disaster. Forcing entry, she screamed and fainted and as he withdrew she bled profusely. Something was ruptured. He opened the door and as bad luck would have it there was his mother, coming to see what the screaming was.

She exclaimed, 'What on earth have you done? You are too big I see for such young women. I will deal with her. Wait in my room until I come. We must have a talk, you must be more careful. I am astonished to find you behaving like a grown man.'

When his mother came, she told François, 'It is all right now. The girl is attended to and will be sent away.' She continued, 'You have been a very naughty boy, François. I will ask your father to speak to you. You must be careful.'

Although his son was a little young, Kurt realised that François was advanced for his age and could go to the university, the oldest in Germany, founded in the fourteenth century. Heidelberg, a must for the privileged ones. He was admitted to the university as a student of military history and in view of his future career enlisted in the associated *Officer Korps* as an extension of his cadet school experience. In view of the dreadful experience with the young virgin, he decided to avoid seeking casual intercourse and that it would be less troublesome to use one of the *bordels* catering for the upper classes.

The first girl he chose took one look at his large plaything and said, 'Oh no, such a monster would ruin me but I will introduce you to my friend. She can take it, I hope.'

It proved to be very satisfactory; one problem solved and now he could concentrate on his studies. The association went on for several years, trouble-free sex with no complications.

The whore grew very fond of him and told him, 'There is no sensation for a woman to equal big men and I have never in all my very many encounters met anything like you.'

However, his peaceful sojourn at Heidelberg was to be rudely interrupted. There was an inn that was very popular with the students and the innkeeper's daughter, a buxom blonde named Gerda, was even more a favourite with those who were permitted to share her favours. When inclined, the lucky ones were invited to a makeshift bed she had contrived in the stables. One of her favourites was a swaggering, loud bully, an older student who tended to regard her as his property. She had made sheep's eyes at François, who had not responded until, very drunk, he allowed himself to be led to her lovenest. Like others before her, she had never before encountered such a virile man. When it was over she said, 'That was beyond belief. I am yours for ever. I never want anyone else.'

Unfortunately, she paid attention only to François when he was in the inn and refused to go again with the bully-boy. The latter realised that François was responsible and on a pretext of having been insulted, challenged François to a duel.

They met early the next morning with their seconds at a secluded location outside the town. Duels were not prohibited, but who wanted an audience? The duelling procedure was established to avoid fatalities and certain rules laid down: bodies to be covered with the padded tunics used in practice, but without the face masks. The object was to slash the face and the loser was the first to be cut. Such encounters led to interesting scars on the face, but little damage otherwise. The opponents came face to face with drawn sabres, specially sharpened at the tip. It was over in seconds, bully-boy was a very experienced swordsman and François felt a red-hot pain flash down his cheek. Blindly he struck out with his sabre, using the blade and not just the point. His opponent fell to the ground lifeless. The blade had caught him just above the ear and, in fact, gone into his brain. He was indeed dead. This was a serious matter and would have dire consequences for François.

His second said, 'It is better that you leave Heidelberg at once. First, to a surgeon to get your face stitched up and I will try to hush things up.'

When his wound was attended to, François hurriedly packed a few things and travelled on the first coach to Berlin and then on to Tilsit.

His parents were not particularly worried, an accident in a dangerous game.

'However,' Kurt said, 'we must protect you. The best course will be for you to take a commission in my regiment. As an officer you will be untouchable.'

Kurt's *Uhlanen* were now stationed in Potsdam and father and son went to see the colonel. Since François had been a military cadet and a member of the university *Officer Korps*, there was no bar to his entry, particularly with his father's connection, so he was granted the rank of *Oberleutnant*, a step up from the bottom grade. François was more cosmopolitan than most officers, with his French connection, he spoke German, French and had added English at Heidelberg, also he was not so stolid as his Prussian fellow officers. Women had proved to be too troublesome, due to his fortunate/unfortunate physique, so he decided to avoid them, relieving himself when demanding, by the boyhood pastime of masturbation.

On a visit to Tilsit some years later his parents said that it was time he was married.

Kurt said, 'You know our neighbours the Detterling family. Their daughter, Marlene, is of age and, as you will see, not unattractive. The Detterlings have no son and heir and it would be a splendid move to join together our two estates in the future.'

François was agreeable and it was left for his parents to see the Detterlings. An arrangement was reached and the couple who, of course, had known each other as children, met for François to present a formal proposal. Marlene was a very attractive young lady and they were well matched, quite happy to be wed.

Before the wedding, Collette spoke privately with her son, 'Marlene is almost certainly a virgin and after the disastrous experience with the kitchen maid, you know you must be careful.'

Slowly, carefully, François penetrated her and soon they enjoyed a good matrimonial life together.

Marlene was very happy, a lucky woman to have such a wonderful mate. She realised that she had something most women would never know. Very soon Marlene became pregnant and as the time grew near she went home to Tilsit to be with her parents for the birth. She bore a son without any complications, who was christened Otto after Kurt's father, now deceased, and Marlene's father. Kurt, who was now Gräf von Winterstein and Collette the Gräfin, thought, it is likely the baby Otto will succeed me, much better so, as he will be brought up as a Prussian, whilst François is not my real son.

François was very popular in his regiment. At first it was thought that the duelling scar, which gave him a sinister but not unattractive appearance, indicated he was the loser in the duel. He pointed out that this was certainly not so as he had unfortunately killed his opponent, a fact which increased his standing. Now in his mid-twenties and all being acceptable, he was promoted to *Hauptmann* and given command of a squadron. All he wished for now was a chance to see some action, to get away from peacetime soldiering which, with endless drills, guard and ceremonial parades and manoeuvres, was basically quite boring.

Then came the news, late in 1853 that the Russian Czar Nicholas declared war on Turkey and in the first encounter the Russian fleet had engaged and wiped out the Turkish fleet off Sebastopol in the Black Sea. This left the Russians access to the Mediterranean where up to now the British Royal Navy was dominant. War between Britain and Russia became inevitable.

11

The Crimea

Czar Nicholas was ambitious for Russia and became, like others before him, such as Genghis Khan, another easterner, obsessed with expansion. First Turkey, 'the sick country of Europe' and its crumbling Ottoman Empire. His excuse for declaring war on Turkey came when Orthodox monks in Jerusalem were attacked by Turkish police. Palestine was then under Turkish Mohammedan rule and the head of the Orthodox Church, asserted that in the scuffle, several Orthodox Russian monks were killed by the police. Immediately the czar marched into the provinces of Turkey on the Danube. Russia and Turkey were at war.

England was neutral until the Russian fleet had destroyed the Turkish fleet in a great sea fight off Sebastopol in the Black Sea. This gave Russian warships access to the Mediterranean, a nightmare to the British, fearing that the Russians would dominate there, where hitherto the British Royal Navy dominated. The British were obliged to make an alliance with France, although they hated Napoleon III who had seized the throne by a bloody coup and was behaving like a dictator. So as allies, Britain and France declared war on Russia in January 1854. The military men who had been idle for 40 years, since Waterloo in fact, were overjoyed with the prospects of military action. Trumpets were sounding with glory on the battlefield in the background. Others seized the opportunity to offer their services, including François.

François applied to his colonel to be allowed to go as an

observer to the Crimea with the French forces, because of his French connection. The colonel agreed and forwarded the request to the *Kriegs Ampt* in Berlin who authorised François to be appointed to the post, then the War Office would provide the credentials. Moreover, François should be promoted to the more appropriate rank of major.

François travelled across Europe to Marseilles, where the French Expeditionary Force was assembling before embarkation to the Black Sea. He presented himself to the commander-in-chief, who said that as a cavalry officer he would be attached to the cavalry division commanded by General Morris, three brigades of *Chasseurs d'Afrique*, Colonial Cavalry. He reported to the general.

'Major François von Winterstein of the Ulhanen, I am sent by the commander-in-chief as an observer with your cavalry division.'

The general was somewhat puzzled.

'You speak excellent French, major, but your name, François . . ?

François enlightened the general.

'I am in fact French. My father, whom I never saw, was killed in action during Napoleon's campaign in Russia commanding a regiment of Hussars. My mother remarried and I took my stepfather's name, Gräf von Winterstein, retaining my Christian name. I have a son, Otto von Winterstein, who will probably inherit the estate in Prussia, together with my wife's family properties.'

The general said, 'Welcome, you will enjoy being with French officers. My command is three brigades of Colonial *Chasseurs*, mostly Berbers whom I know well from my service in Africa. The Berbers are a warlike people who live along the Atlas mountain range which traverses North Africa. They belong to the same ethnic group as the warrior tribes of the Masai and the Basques, among other groups spread across Africa, from Egypt and even into Spain. They are grand chaps as you will see and redoubtable fighters.'

The British embarked in sailing ships bound on the long voyage down the Channel and across the sometimes more than boisterous Bay of Biscay and into the Mediterranean. They were bound for the port of Varna in Bulgaria on the Black Sea, where they were to relieve Silistra, a Turkish province threatened by the Russians, before going on to the Crimea. The British base was to be at Scutari in Asian Turkey across the Bosphorous, the narrow seaway into the Black Sea. The French infantry divisions rendezvoused with the British off Marseilles. The remainder, including the cavalry, would embark in steamships and travel faster and more comfortably for the precious horses, joining the British fleet in the Black Sea when it was due to sail to Calamita Bay for disembarkation in the Crimea.

With the British fleet the horses, bad sailors in any case, suffered terribly from the hot weather in the Mediterranean. Many, maddened by the heat below decks, had to be shot. As the vessels rolled and pitched, some of the horses went down and other horses, frantic and mad with fright, trampled on them, plunging and kicking: many died. All men and horses disembarked at Varna in a sorry state, only to find that their diversion to Bulgaria was unnecessary. The Turkish Army had already driven the Russians out of Silistra and across the Danube River. The army set about nursing its horses back to health.

Whilst the allies, with part of the French only, were at Varna they were subjected to a serious cholera epidemic, caused by polluted water and also bad food, a fatal disease which decimated the men. In addition, more valuable horses were lost through inadequate planning and provisioning of a reconnaissance in strength, mounted by Lord Cardigan, who commanded the cavalry. They set out across the barren wastes of Silistra to ascertain the whereabouts of the Russians. They failed to find them and were obliged to turn back. The patrol took a terrible toll of the poor horses, suffering from lack of forage and water, unnecessary suffering. Lord Cardigan was blamed. A few days later a small party set out with the same objective and returned in good order, having successfully located the disposition of the Russians who were across the Danube.

The British and French at Varna embarked to proceed to the Crimea and Calamita Bay, which was reported to be clear of Russians, who were known to be to the south across the Alma River. Outside Varna the British and French fleets rendezvoused, the French fleet carrying the balance of their forces, including their cavalry, the *Chasseurs*. The landing was successfully carried out and the armies were assembled for the march to the south, the French on the coast and the British on their left, inland. They set off across a barren land in the midsummer heat, the British riddled with cholera, short of transport and all kinds of supplies. Water was a great problem. The *Chasseurs*, both men and horses, were accustomed to having meagre amounts of water, but for the others it was purgatory.

Laboriously, the armies reached and crossed the Bulganek River, expecting to meet a strong enemy attack by a strong force from Alma. However, apart from Cossack patrols observing them, they were unmolested. No Russian attack took place. The next day they set out for the Alma and that night bivouacked in battle order a few miles away from the river, from where they could see the watchfires of the Russians on the heights above. The Russians had allowed the allies to advance, believing that Alma was impregnable and that a crushing defeat would ensue for the attackers.

At dawn the armies moved, the troops in a sorry condition. Cholera had taken its toll during the night, it was blazing hot, water bottles were empty, the Bulganek River had quickly become a foul muddy swamp and thirst was increased by the diet of salt pork. As they approached the Alma a large force of Cossacks could be seen positioned to attack any infantry formations attempting to cross the river.

The *Chasseurs* were ordered to attack the Cossacks and General Morris lined up two of his brigades in battle array and the other brigade in reserve. The general positioned himself to lead from the front as was the custom, very vulnerable but a splendid example to his officers and men.

He told François, 'You may ride with me if you wish. You will see some action but it will be very dangerous for you, or you can stay behind and observe in comfort and safety.'

François said he preferred to ride with the others and joined the brigade major, the orderlies and trumpeters behind the general. And off they went, a brave and colourful spectacle, a cavalryman's dream of combat: cavalry versus cavalry.

The general, a lone figure, splendidly arrayed, upright in the saddle, sword at the slope, walked his horse steadily towards the Cossacks, the brigades following, anxious to get on with it. British cavalry were seen approaching in a cloud of dust, moving at a fast canter bent on getting at the enemy before the French. The general stepped up the pace and soon the *Chasseurs* were galloping in a furious charge, the brigadiers striving to catch up with their well-beloved commander so that he did not meet their adversaries alone, single-handed. The Cossacks, good cavalry as they were, milled around in disorder, not knowing which way to turn, threatened on two fronts.

Both French and British cavalry struck together in a thunderous clash: flashing swords, clouds of dust, the cries and screams of wounded men and horses, plunging and kicking with pain and fright. The allies were well into the enemy, who had nowhere to run to, hemmed in by the river. The *Chasseurs* broke through like a hot knife through butter, wheeled and countercharged from the river bank and systematically set about finishing off the enemy. François was thoroughly enjoying himself. Although a non-combatant observer, he was obliged to defend himself, cutting, slashing and thrusting, as were all around him. The field was like a busy slaughterhouse, blood and guts.

It was soon over. Some Cossacks managed, or were allowed, to surrender, others tried to escape to the east along the river bank. Most were cut down by the British Hussars, but a few got away inland. Most of those who survived, unless taken prisoner, escaped across the Alma and climbed laboriously up the heights where an easier slope led down to the sea. The path they took was keenly observed by the French command. The cavalry saw no further action in the battle, attending to the wounded and burying their dead, those of Muslim faith being interred with the appropriate rites.

The way now being clear, the British army moved forward to the river. The Russians were massed on the heights immediately above and as the British advanced to cross over the river, batteries all along the heights opened fire. Round-shot tore through the lines. The following battle of the Alma was the scene of one of the most ferocious feats of the British soldier. After a desperate and bloody struggle with many casualties, the British reached the Russian redoubts on the heights.

Meanwhile, the French, aided by the guns of the fleet, attacked from the seaward side, where the Russian cavalry had escaped. The

French infantry gained the heights unobserved at first and then the Russians turned some batteries of artillery on them. The French failed to advance, waiting for support from infantry following them and the artillery having been got up the slope with much difficulty. It was the practice of the French infantry not to advance without artillery support so their attack bogged down.

The British Light Infantry Division pressed on under terrific fire from above and, impossibly, surged up the bank to the steep precipice below the main Russian redoubt. In spite of great gaps being torn in the line, the men of the Light Infantry, heroes of many battles against the French in Spain and Portugal, by a miracle gained the heights and, unbelievably, the Russian guns ceased fire, limbering up and galloping away. The infantry of the Brigade of Guards and the Highlanders joined the Light Division, or what was left of them. The battle was far from over, but now it began to turn in the allies' favour. The French guns were at last in position and together with the British they attacked the massed Russian infantry. With extraordinary courage and firmness the slender lines of the Guards, Highlanders and the Rifles moved inexorably forward, firing their muskets coolly, making every bullet strike effectively. The mass of Russians, enveloped in fire, broke and finally turned and fled, leaving the Alma heights in the hands of the Allies. An extraordinary victory.

François observed the progress of the stubborn British infantry in the seemingly impossible attempt to cross the Alma. The cavalry stood by, champing at the bit, but had no role to play. François reverted to his position as an observer and made copious notes and sketches. When the British gained the heights, he moved up to the area where the French were halted and was able to observe closely the final act and the subsequent retreat of the Russians.

The Allied armies moved towards Sebastopol, the great Russian naval base in the Black Sea, the primary objective. When they arrived on the heights outside Balaclava, its port was the sole lifeline of the army, everything came through there from the sea, food and ammunition, they found the way to Sebastopol blocked by the Russians on the plains of Balaclava. This, it was obvious, was where the critical battle would have to be fought. The road to Sebastopol was denied to the Allies.

Established around Balaclava plain, the Russians had a strong force of some 30,000 infantry and 6,000 cavalry. They were disposed along the Fedioukine Heights to the north and the Causeway Heights to the south, also at the east end of the valley. The valley, over a mile long, was therefore covered by batteries on both heights and at the east end.

Opening the battle, Lord Raglan, the commander-in-chief, ordered the cavalry Heavy Brigade comprising the Scots Greys, the Inniskillen Dragoons and the 4th Dragoon Guards, together with the infantry of the Argyle and Sutherland Highlanders, to attack the Russians holding the heights above the Causeway, who were a much greater force. When they charged, the cavalry were at first engulfed by the great mass of Russians. Astonishingly, the cavalry fought like demons and by the sheer violence of bloody hand-to-hand fights with sword and bayonet, the redcoats forced the Russians to break off and retreat. The batteries on the lower slopes of the Causeway Heights were situated away from the action and remained covering the valley.

It was now the turn of the Light Brigade, which consisted of three splendid regiments of great renown: the 17th Lancers, the 11th Hussars and the 4th Light Dragoons, with some of the 8th Hussars. A message from Lord Raglan which read, 'Lord Raglan wished the cavalry to advance rapidly to the front, follow the enemy and try to prevent the enemy carrying away the guns. Troop horse artillery may accompany. French cavalry is on your left. Immediate.' was sent to Lord Cardigan, the commanding general of the Light Cavalry.

Lord Cardigan said to the messenger, 'Which guns?'

'There are your guns, my lord,' said the messenger, one Major Nolan, who accompanied the subsequent charge against the wrong guns and, like many others, was killed. The guns he indicated were the batteries at the east end of the valley.

Lord Cardigan, a lone figure out front, led the brigade at a walk down the valley, the regiments dressed as for a review. The Russian batteries opened up from both sides, the cannon balls creating great gaps in the ranks which immediately closed up. Still his lordship would not hurry, continuing at a walk, in spite of leaving behind a litter of dead and dying horses and men. As the brigade was near enough, the guns in front joined in and then Lord Cardigan commenced to canter and finally to charge, followed closely by the regiments. They went through the batteries, slaughtering the gunners.

With horror the onlookers watched the Light Brigade vanish into the smoke, pondering whether any would return.

General Morris with his *Chasseurs* remarked, '*C'est magnifique, mais ce n'est pas la guerre* (magnificent, but it is not war).' Then the *Chasseurs* were ordered to attack the Russian batteries on the north Fedioukine Heights and led by the general, with whose staff François rode, galloped over the broken ground, the Algerian horses accustomed to such going in their campaigns in the Atlas mountains. The attack was a complete success. The Russian artillery men and infantry who survived, fled, leaving the guns. They themselves had very few casualties. On the way back through the guns a wounded Russian officer fired at François, the heavy pistol ball hitting him in the face and penetrating to the cerebellum. François fell dead from the saddle. Adieu, François, son of Pierre, also killed in action.

The charge inspired the epic poem by Alfred, Lord Tennyson *The Charge of the Light Brigade*, which opened:

> Their's not to reason why,
> Their's but to do and die.
> Into the valley of Death
> Rode the six hundred.

The remnants, involving a still immaculate and unperturbed Lord Cardigan, rode back down the valley under less aggravation, the artillery behind them and to the north, silenced. Those guns firing from the Causeway slopes were less active, the gunners astounded by the incredible performance by the British Cavalry. The 'reason why', the message was inexplicit; the intention was to capture the guns which remained on the Causeway after the Heavy Brigade and the Argyles' action. The capturing of guns was a confirmation of victory. So all a terrible mistake, wrong guns. Nevertheless, one of the most glorious incidents in the annals of the British army.

François was buried where he fell and his orderly returned to Germany with the reports François had written and his personal effects.

12

Germany

When the sad news reached Tilsit, the families were quite grief-stricken, Collette particularly, having lost her first husband, Pierre, and now her only son, François.

Marlene was shocked and as she and Collette consoled with and comforted each other, Marlene said, 'I will never marry again, there could never be another like him.'

Collette thought, yes and secretly I know why.

They held a council of war and Kurt, who was now looking after both estates, Marlene's parents being now too old, said, 'That clarifies the problems of François succeeding, as Otto will now take over from me, when the time comes.'

Otto, now in his mid-teens, was on holiday from the military academy at Königsberg and would now go on to Heidelberg University, as had his father. During the holiday he had been riding with a young lady, a little older than himself. They were good friends and so far there had been no intimacy between them, until . . . They were passing a field one morning where a few cows were enclosed with a bull for breeding purposes. As they approached the bull was attempting to mount a cow, its forelegs on the cow's back and its great pizzle, at least two feet in length, was prodding the cow's rear to find an entrance. As they watched, the great weapon found its way in, the bull gave a great bellow and with a heave buried it fully home. Otto and his companion, Heide, were visibly affected, she red in the face and fidgeting in the saddle, Otto almost rigid with emotion, an erection trying to burst out of his breeches.

Heide said, *'Mein Gott in Himmel, was ein dinge, so grosse. Komm!'*
She led the way to an empty cottage belonging to her father and without delay into a bedroom.

She lay on the bed and said, raising her riding skirt, 'Come, Otto, do to me what the bull was doing.'

Heide said, *'Nicht so gross wie Herr Bulle, Gott sei Dank.'* She went on, 'but it is enough and, I see, very willing. Come.'

When it was over she told him that she was already betrothed and would soon marry, so never mind the consequences.

'We will meet as often as possible until you go to Heidelberg.'

Otto's mother sensed a change in him but refrained from commenting. Boys will be boys, she thought.

The rest of the holiday was very enjoyable for the awakened Otto: Heide relished a period of extra premarital pleasure, with a very nice young man. All too soon it was time for him to leave for the university. He was well provided with funds from both his grandparents, the gräf and the Detterlings. At Heidelberg, when he was going through the formalities of induction, he got into conversation with another student, with whom he eventually became great friends. Hans told him that he was not going to live in the university but in a private house where his elder brother had also lived, run by a certain *Frau* Winters, a comparatively young woman. Otto agreed to go with Hans to see the house and the good lady before deciding. He was very pleased with the house, where the *Frau*, as she was always called, housed and fed four students.

The *Frau*, somewhat reserved in her manner, in her late thirties, but quite attractive still, agreed that he could lodge with her. Otto found it very comfortable. The *Frau* did not keep a good table but it was adequate. She herself remained aloof and treated the students simply as paying guests, living her own private life. Otto settled down to his studies and sporting activities and also joined the *Officer Korps*. It was a foregone conclusion that he would enter the army, in spite of the loss of his father at Balaclava and grandfather number one in Russia with Napoleon. Otherwise he led a quiet life unencumbered with other activities, but he did, of course, think of the passionate episodes with Heide back at Tilsit.

Coming home one summer evening, he encountered *Frau* just about to leave in her small carriage and she said, 'Would you like to join me? I am just going to the woods to pick some wild flowers. It is a very pleasant evening and you will enjoy the woods.'

Otto was pleased to accept and got into the carriage where he found *Frau*'s young daughter with her, whom they seldom saw about the house, a child of some ten years of age. The *Frau* was very reticent about her private life and her deceased husband.

The drive out into the countryside was very pleasant. The close confines of the carriage lurching over the uneven roads threw their bodies together. Otto made no attempt to prevent this. Some weeks since Heide, he was aroused by the feel of a woman's body and she made no attempt to pull away. They walked in the woods, in which bluebells made a carpet of blue. On the way back again their bodies came together in close contact. Nothing was said but Otto could feel the response in the air. But . . .

That night Otto was awakened to see a figure standing beside his bed, the *Frau*. Not a word was spoken and as she shed her robe, he could see she was naked. She got into the bed with him and commenced a sexual relationship which was to last for several years. The frau was wonderfully experienced and Otto very quickly ejaculated; she clung to him and would not release him and soon he was ready for a more protracted encounter. Her stifled cries indicated her satisfaction. As she left he had a good look at her body. Her figure was pleasing and apart from a little droop in her breasts and buttocks, she had retained her youthfulness.

They became hopelessly in love. She was insanely jealous and kept him sexually satiated so that he had no desire to look at another woman. She had told him that after giving birth to her daughter, she would not be able to bear another child so there was no worry on that score. Poor Otto was a little worn out from so much sex, which sapped his strength somewhat and he recoursed to food and wines which would hopefully see him through. He was so besotted by love that he was always ready when she came to his bed.

When Otto went on vacation, they all remarked how thin and tired he was. He explained that he had been working very hard at his studies and sports. Wise old Collette thought otherwise. Ah, bent on pleasure, I'll wager. She said to Otto with a knowing look, 'Be careful, don't overdo it.'

During the time away from the *Frau*, he missed her terribly and was so glad to return. She likewise had missed him and so they continued their blissful idyll.

The years passed and on his penultimate vacation his grandfather, Kurt, took him to see the colonel of his old regiment of *Ulhanen* in Berlin. The colonel welcomed a former officer of the regiment and also Otto, the son of François, one of the few *Uhlanen* who had been killed in action since Waterloo, more than 40 years ago.

'Yes, Otto would be very welcome when he finished at Heidelberg.'

When Otto returned to Heidelberg he at once told the *Frau* the news that in a few months he would be going to the army. She was absolutely stricken, mind and body frozen, and turned away without saying a word. That night she did not come to his bed, nor ever again. Of course it had to end, but now the time was approaching she was shattered, drained of feelings other than grief, hollow inside. Otto was absolutely desolate. He could not understand why she had cut him off and for some time could barely eat or sleep. The situation was so awful it was literally destroying him so he moved to another lodging, never to see her again, but never to forget the *Frau*, the love of his life.

Otto left the university with a not very good record academically – good only in languages; the *Officer Korps* – promising, but not very active; sport – nothing notable, did not achieve any university teams. He attributed his poor performance to his obsession with the *Frau*. In addition, he did not quarrel with anyone, so no duels, no facial scars. Sadly, he left Heidelberg, going further away from his lost love, although denied him, forever present: a sad affair.

In his absence Marlene's parents, his grandparents, had died, leaving one third of the income to Marlene and Otto, and the balance to Kurt who was now in charge of the von Winterstein-

Detterling combined estates. So Otto was a comparatively rich young man. He had avoided seeing Heide, of the *Bulle*, during previous vacations and now she was married and safely out of reach.

He joined the *Uhlanen* in Berlin as a lieutenant and settled down to a somewhat boring peacetime regimental life. Then in 1861 came the news of the Civil War in America, between the southern secessionists, the Confederates of the slave-owing Southern States, and the Northern Union States whose object was to abolish slavery. He considered applying to go to America as an observer, as his father, François had done with the Allies in the Crimean War, but as an *Oberleutnant* which he now was, was too junior.

He consulted his grandfather, Kurt, who told him, 'If you must go then you will have to purchase a captaincy. Remember, if you do go, you are our only heir and do not involve yourself in the fighting, as your father did. Just observe and report.'

Otto's mother, Marlene, was very upset, having lost her irreplaceable husband whilst also observing with a foreign army. Otto confided in his mother his grief over the unfortunate love affair at Heidelberg. He simply had to get away to a new and absorbing life, hoping to forget.

Marlene said, 'Well, if you must go, take care. You are all I have now.'

Otto saw the colonel and requested his permission to purchase a captaincy and, if granted, to be allowed to proceed to America as an observer. The colonel was quite willing and very soon *Hauptmann* Otto von Winterstein was on his way to the Union army of the north, as the War Office had advised. There were already observers with the Confederates. He paid a farewell visit to Tilsit and departed for America well provided with funds and letters of credit on a New York bank.

13

America

Otto left Hamburg on a steamer bound for New York. There were among the passengers several ladies travelling alone, who cast inviting glances at the handsome young *Hauptmann*. Otto would have none of it. He wanted no other woman since the *Frau*. Uneventfully, in calm mid-summer weather the steamer arrived after just over two weeks crossing the Atlantic, a great improvement on the sailing ship. Otto was met by a colonel of *Hussaren*, the military attaché with the German Ministry in Washington who was in New York on other business. The colonel greeted Otto, 'Winterstein? We have been expecting you. We can travel together by the train to Washington tomorrow.'

On the way to Washington the colonel told him about the Civil War, how hostilities had begun when the southern General Beauregard ordered the Confederate artillery to fire on Fort Sumter. He explained that both armies were mobilised and concentrating on Manassas, which was the main railway junction of the rail network which served the Southern States: a valuable prize to the Federals and a serious loss to the South, if the union army was successful.

The colonel said, 'You will be in time for the first battle. After meeting our minister, Baron Von Richtmann, I will take you to General Irvine McDowell who commands the Union Army of the Potomac.'

The Baron invited Otto to dine with him that evening and Otto turned up, looking very smart in his dress uniform. He met the *Baronin* and their daughter, Heide, a flaxen-haired, blue-eyed young lady, astonishingly beautiful. Otto thought, perhaps I could drown my sorrows in her. We shall see. The baron had also served in the cavalry, the Hussaren prestigious, *Toten Kopf,* black uniformed with a silver skull badge (as were the British 17th Lancers). By chance he knew Otto's grandfather, whom he had met when the *Hussaren* were in the same brigade with the *Uhlanen.* Otto told them about his father, who had been killed at Balaclava when an observer with the French. The baron was quite friendly towards Otto and as they parted he said, 'I hope we shall meet again soon. Please call whenever you are in Washington. We have plenty of accommodation in the ministry and you are welcome to stay with us.'

The military attaché rode out to General McDowell's headquarters, which was on the Washington–Manassas road, a short distance from Washington. Manassas was only 20 miles from Washington, across the border in Virginia. General McDowell was a grizzled old soldier, veteran of the Indian Wars.

He greeted Otto with, 'Welcome, young fella, stick around with my staff and you will see plenty of action.'

Otto found out from a staff captain that they were on the move down the road and expected to meet the Confederates outside Manassas at Bull Run, where they were assembling to protect the vital railway junction.

As the Federals moved down they encountered a roadblock of felled trees and as soon as they started to clear the highway, sporadic musketry fire opened up from the woods across an open area. General McDowell ordered the forward division to spread out through the woods and, when deployed, to advance against the Confederates. So began the Battle of Bull Run, curtain raiser for the Civil War.

From the vantage point they could see the highway with carriages and horsemen swarming down from Washington to see the fun. Otto thought that the German minister and family would be there also. They came as far as the woods where the blue coats were forming up, an open space where little, in fact, could be seen, but it was a perfect summer's day, ideal for a picnic.

Soon the quiet was broken by the rattle of muskets and thunder of guns. Otto could see the lines of the Union army in close formation emerging from the woods towards Bull Run. The fire from the Confederates cut swaths in the ranks of the advancing infantry. Some managed to reach the Confederate positions, but were forced to retreat by the intense fire. McDowell ordered the infantry to attack again. This met with no more success. The Confederates held like a stone wall and the commander of the resolute forward Brigade, General Thomas Jackson, was afterwards given the sobriquet 'Stonewall' Jackson.

About midday when there was a lull in the fighting a servant from the German ministry brought an invitation for Otto to join them for lunch. Otto found the Richtmanns with a splendid repast laid out on a table, excellent cold viands and wines, all around them others doing likewise.

The minister asked Otto how the battle was going and he replied, 'The Confederates are holding on and so far the Federals have been unable to break through.'

After an excellent meal Otto suggested that they might like to take a look at what was going on from the vantage point above, a short walk away.

The baron declined but Heide said, 'I would like to see the fun.'

Otto walked his horse and they went to a position near McDowell's headquarters from where they could see over towards Bull Run. Heide became quite excited as Otto pointed out the positions of the opposing armies, particularly when they could see blue coat soldiers emerging once more in an attempt to break through.

As they watched, intense artillery fire was directed on the stone bridge on the highway below, held strongly by the Union. General Beauregard had brought up all his artillery and reserve troops. Otto could see things were going to hot up and said that Heide should go back. Reluctantly she went with him back down the slope to her parents. As Otto rode back to McDowell's position he thought, 'Well, Heide is quite nice, I wonder . . .'

McDowell ordered the blue coats, those that were still able, once more to move into the attack. As they moved out of the woods they were astonished to see a line of grey-clad figures move out from the cover. Otto watched with amazement as the Confederates advanced at the double, bayonets fixed, through the gun smoke and musket fire, screaming rebel taunts, the mounted officers out front. When they met there ensued furious hand-to-hand fighting with bayonets and even bowie knives. Soon the Yankees, as the Southerners called them, broke away and attempted to form a line further back. There was no stopping the Virginians and Louisianans, their blood was up. The northerners retreated to the trees and, ignoring the exhortations of their officers, did not stop.

Otto realised that the Union army was beaten and retreating so he galloped down to the area where the spectators were gathered, just as the first blue coats burst pell-mell out of the trees.

He told the baron, 'You must leave at once. There is certain to be panic. I will come with you. Let us go!'

In spite of his early warning, others had also left hurriedly. The fun was over. The road became jammed, carriages broke down in collisions with others, and wheels came off on the rutted road. But at last they reached the ministry and the baron invited Otto to stay with them.

'I am sure General McDowell will have his headquarters in Washington, so you can easily keep in touch with him.'

Later, reporting to headquarters, Otto learnt that McDowell had been dismissed and replaced by General George McClellan as commander-in-chief. McDowell's dismissal was routine for a general who lost the battle.

There was no further action until the Army of the Potomac opened up the Peninsular Campaign in the following spring of 1862, meanwhile reorganising, recruiting and re-equipping with the latest weaponry. Otto remained at the minister's residence and consequently met often with Heide. Together they formed a warm friendship which easily led to intimacy. Otto, still burdened by memories of the *Frau* did not press home his suit until, one day walking in the ministry grounds, Heide stumbled and fell against him. Otto was aroused by the close contact and, taking her in his arms, kissed her, to which she responded vigorously. So the affair progressed until Otto, wisely refraining from outright seduction, realised that it would be necessary to marry, although not absolutely stricken with love. So he proposed to her and she accepted joyfully.

Otto approached the baron, requesting permission to marry his daughter, and the baron said, 'I will be happy to have you as my son-in-law. Let us gather together with the *Baronin* and Heide and we will drink a toast to the betrothal.'

The *Baronin* was also pleased and agreed with Otto's suggestion that now they were affianced, he should move from the family home.

Otto said, 'I could find a suitable house in Washington, I have my orderly and can find servants.'

Once installed in a house, he considered it would be very pleasant to bring Heide and perhaps go a little further in their lovemaking.

Together they had been going to the theatre and other functions and Otto said one evening, 'Heide, instead of going to the opera, you have not seen my house. Shall we go there?'

Heide was very willing, realising that they would be alone for the first time. Otto, in anticipation, had given the servants the evening off. They sat together in the drawing room, embracing fervently. Otto released her breasts from her gown, already half-exposed, as was the fashion, caressing them.

Heide was overcome with excitement and readily agreed when he proposed that they go up to his bedroom, telling her, 'We are quite alone, the servants are out.'

Otto, when they were in the bedroom, removed Heide's clothing very carefully. Her body that emerged was very beautiful, delicately formed, small but perfectly shaped breasts, a small waist and her legs white and shapely. All very exciting he thought, I am a lucky man. Maybe this will lay the *Frau* to rest from my mind. He lay her on the bed and she, shyly, watched him undress, astonished at the thing standing up in front of his stomach, which she had never seen before, and admired his athletic figure. Otto was indeed a very handsome man. He lay down on the bed beside her and gently caressed her body. Otto, in spite of being very aroused, controlled his movements, (after all he was not inexperienced) until he could no longer hold back and thrust savagely into her until they climaxed together. A very satisfactory first coupling. They should have a very good sex life together.

Otto had written to his mother informing her of his betrothal to Heide von Richtmann and Marlene replied that she and his grandparents approved. Kurt knew the family and they would all come to Washington for the wedding.

Otto had been sending his reports to Berlin and was now observing the transformation of the army under General McClellan, training, new equipment and particularly weaponry. As a cavalry officer, he was naturally interested in the Cavalry Corps and having met Brigadier General John Buford, who commanded a Brigade of Regular United States Cavalry, suggested that he would like to be attached to the brigadier as observer. The brigadier agreed, telling Otto to clear it with HQ, which Otto did. The cavalry on both sides had taken no part in the Battle of Bull Run.

Otto and Heide continued their tryst at Otto's house. She was very much in love with him and Otto, likewise, was quite happy, but part of him was secretly locked away: his one and only love for the *Frau*. In the early part of 1862, Heide told Otto that she had not had the monthly visitor for two months and was probably pregnant.

Otto was not displeased and said, 'Well, we will get married very soon, immediately my family are here.'

Otto explained to the baron that with the new campaign imminent, it was better to wed before he went off to the war again. All agreed and, allowing enough time for Otto's family to arrive, fixed the date of the wedding.

Otto's family arrived in time for the wedding and all thoroughly approved of his choice. The ceremony was attended by members of the diplomatic corps and the army. The couple left the church under an arch of crossed swords and, as a courtesy the brigadier had provided a guard of honour of officers of the 1st US Cavalry, resplendent in their blue uniforms, gold-braided trousers tucked into spurred Wellington boots and wide-brimmed hats with gold-cord hatbands, knotted at the front. After a grand reception the couple left for a honeymoon in New York, staying at the best hotel, arranging to meet Otto's mother and grandparents there before they went back to Germany.

When Otto said goodbye to his mother, he told her that Heide was pregnant and Marlene said, 'I thought so, you are just like your father.'

They spent a month in New York, during which it was confirmed that Heide was definitely with child. On their return to Washington they moved into Otto's house which, in their absence, had been renovated and refurnished under the directions of the *Baronin*. At headquarters Otto found that things were looking up.

The brigadier told him, 'We shall soon be off and this time we shall crush the rebels.'

The Confederates were quiet, but raids by Jeb Stuart, the southern cavalry commander, even up to the outskirts of Washington, were very successful and causing consternation in the capital.

In the early spring of 1862 McClellan moved the Army of the Potomac southwards. The aim was to take Richmond, Virginia, the Confederate States' capital, 100 miles away as the crow flies. Hopefully, this would put an end to the rebellion. The army crossed into the Peninsular between the York and James rivers, Buford's cavalry leading in the cavalry role of scouting ahead, to see and not be seen and report back. They were not looking for a fight, unless compelled to defend themselves. Buford had four regular regiments, many of the officers and troopers veterans of the Indian Wars and Mexico.

When the leading regiment arrived in view of the York River they saw that the Confederates had pulled back and the rearguard was seen disappearing into Yorktown. Otto, riding with the brigadier, saw the last of the rebels leave and as they watched, gunboats of the US Navy entered the river and commenced shelling the retreating army until out of range. Buford entered Yorktown and reported it clear of the enemy. The Union army crossed over the York and continued its advance to Richmond. The cavalry were in sight of the James River in time to see that the main part of the rebel army was already across.

A considerable rearguard remained to cross, so the brigadier said, 'Right, we will take them.'

He ordered two regiments to attack, led them out at a fast trot towards the Confederate infantry and even a few guns remained with the last of the wagons. Otto rode with him, exhilarated at the prospect of seeing a fight at close quarters. The cavalry broke into a gallop and swept into the mass, struggling to get away. Some infantrymen fired ineffectually and were silenced by the enveloping horsemen. It was over in minutes. The booty was welcome, especially the guns. To capture the enemy artillery was a token of victory.

As at the York River, gunboats went up the James River and, shelling as they went, reached a point only 10 miles from Richmond itself, but were repulsed by batteries on the river bank. The army entered Jamestown and paused to assemble for the battle which would surely come to be.

General Robert E. Lee now took command in the South. He was previously superintendent of West Point Military Academy and a very experienced military man. As McClellan advanced the Union forces, they were checked by Lee and there ensued what became known as the Seven Days Battles, during which the Yankees were again defeated. The cavalry as at Bull Run were not involved but Otto benefited in his role as observer, writing copious reports for Berlin.

McClellan withdrew again to Washington, to reorganise in readiness for the next fray. Otto was pleased to be home with Heide, although, being once more observing the losing side, he felt a little disappointed. Not his war, but still . . . He decided that as Heide was very well and quite proud of her swollen body, he would refrain from intercourse. As a lusty young man he did however look around but decided against making any overtures among their circle of acquaintances and friends. The opportunity occurred when he literally bumped into Heide's maid.

The girl was a daughter of freed slaves, Ashantis from Kumasi, capital of the northern region of the West African Gold Coast. Her parents were taken by slaves when on a visit to Accra, when Comfort was a child. Comfort claimed that her father had been a wealthy diamond merchant and was also related to the Ashanti king and that she would have been the Diamond Princess, and here she was a ladies maid. She was light-skinned, almost golden, her features not predominantly Negroid, her figure elegantly lissom and well-rounded in the right places. In other words, a beauty.

Otto seized the opportunity, provided by their bumping into each other, to clasp her to himself 'in case she fell'. Far from attempting to free herself, she snuggled up to Otto, who felt himself growing and protruding against Comfort. The girl, knowing very well what was happening, released herself and, taking Otto by the hand, led him to her room on the upper floor. When the door was closed and locked, she unwrapped herself from her cloth and stood naked and very desirable. The faint aroma, which all Africans have, Otto found not unpleasant when mingled with her woman's odour. He was beside himself as he had been with no woman other than his one and only true love, the *Frau* of Heidelberg days. Comfort was enthusiastic and experienced. Their coupling was rapturous and Otto was well and truly hooked.

That summer, whilst General McClellan was getting the Union Army in shape for the next move against the South, Otto had little to occupy himself with, until the next battle. His affair with Comfort continued and, not wanting to be found out, he persuaded Comfort to leave her employment. He found a small house on the outskirts of Washington in the direction of McClellan's headquarters and hence could visit Comfort unobserved.

The summer of 1862 passed with Otto enjoying himself with his Comfort, so by name and nature. He became very fond of her and resolved that when he left America he would provide her with sufficient money to set herself up as an expensive courtesan or even to become the madam of a whorehouse. Heide was well and comfortably swollen with child due to be born in October. She had a new personal maid and if she had thoughts about Comfort, she kept them to herself.

In late August, Brigadier Buford told Otto that the brigade was to explore to the south towards Richmond and look out for the whereabouts of General Lee and his rebel army and to do a bit of marauding as opportunity arose. They rode through Maryland into Virginia, the countryside showing a presage of autumn. They were light-hearted and happy to be on the move. Some way towards Richmond they observed the roads cluttered with wagons going north towards New York. Buford concluded that Lee was already on the way north with the intention of invading Maryland and Pennsylvania. When McClellan received the news he set the Union army on a forced march to confront the menace to the most important area of the Federals.

Buford was ordered to shadow Lee and report the Confederate army's movements with the utmost urgency. The cavalry, anxious for the spoils, were given the chance, when it offered itself, to take out stragglers and capture the wagons with their bounty. Otto enjoyed being on this true cavalry operation and, in addition, gaining some information from the captured soldiers and noting their weapons and equipment.

They shadowed Lee and concluded that the Confederate army was heading for Harpers Ferry on the Potomac River, gateway to the North. When General McClellan received the news he placed the Union army to the north of the river. Lee ordered Stonewall Jackson to take Harpers Ferry, which, with his forceful determination, he succeeded in doing without great losses. Lee then attacked McClellan and a bloody battle ensued. The fighting in the Civil War was savage and brutal, each side fighting for a just cause and imbued with hatred for their fellow countrymen.

The Cavalry Brigade were placed to the east flank to guard against outflanking movements and to block any penetration of the Union line; supposedly Jeb Stuart was similarly engaged, unless he was marauding up towards New York. The infantry were engaged at close quarters, hand-to-hand, butt and bayonet; the cavalry were idle until around midday a rebel unit broke through the centre. Buford ordered two regiments to stop the Confederate infiltrators and plug the gap. Otto, with a young man's impetuousness, set off with them, riding with the colonel of the leading regiment.

They galloped through the enemy infantry, tough Virginians who did not give way, fighting back at the slashing swords and trampling horses. Many fell dead or wounded. Some troopers and horses were left behind when the cavalry emerged. The Virginians reformed and faced up to the cavalry which had wheeled round and was charging back hell for leather. In the ensuing mêlée, Otto was dragged from his saddle by a bayonet thrust by a resolute soldier. He had managed to deflect the bayonet from his midrift and it passed through his thigh, literally hooking him like a fish. His attacker picked him up and they joined the remnants who were struggling back to their own lines – an observer who should not have been there.

The men were not a little amused by the officer in the strange uniform, quite a catch. Their officer decided to send him back to Stonewall Jackson. Otto's wound was not very serious, a slash a few inches long, bleeding profusely, but he was able to limp along, after being roughly bandaged and helped by the strong arm of one of his escorts. Stonewall Jackson was very amused.

'What on earth have we unearthed? Who the devil are you young man?' Otto explained that he was a Prussian Officer, a *Uhlan*, and was an observer with the Union Army. The general said, 'You should not have been involved in the fighting; it is against the rules.' Otto was taken to a surgeon to have his wound attended to, the gash cobbled up and bandaged and when he returned to Stonewall, the general said, 'I am going to send you back to General Lee, our commander-in-chief, who I am sure will like to question you.'

Otto was put on a horse and escorted by a mounted orderly to Lee's headquarters.

When he could spare the time, General Lee, an officer and a gentleman, much respected by both sides, spoke with Otto, who explained that he was an observer who had very rashly got caught up in the action.

The general said, 'That was foolish, you should not have been there. Tell me about yourself. I will not ask you about McClellan, I know him and most of the others from my time at West Point.'

Otto told the general about his home in Prussia and his family's military background, his grandfather, Pierre, a Frenchman, Hussar officer serving with Napoleon in Spain and Russia.

'He was killed in action commanding his regiment, at the end of that disastrous campaign.' He went on, 'My grandmother married a Prussian officer, a *Uhlan*. Their son, my father, was killed in the Crimea at Balaclava.'

Lee said, 'An interesting story. Well, young man, "War is Hell". I am going to send you back. Tomorrow you will leave. I will give you a *laissez-passer* and a guide. Very soon we shall be into a bloody battle, Harpers Ferry was only the overture. You can spend the night with one of my staff officers.' Lee sent for the officer and introduced him as Brigadier George Picket. 'He will look after you and see you on your way. Safe journey and give my regards to McClellan.'

Otto spent the evening with Picket, a very dashing flamboyant officer. In the following year Picket was to distinguish himself, perhaps not very favourably, whilst commanding a division at Gettysburg. The brigadier dined and wined Otto too well and the following morning, with a considerable hangover, he set off with the guide.

They rode eastwards round the Confederate position until the guide said, 'We are now out of our area. If you continue north you arrive at the flank of the Union positions. I hope you will be recognised.'

Otto rode on. His wound had become painful and he was glad when he encountered an outpost of blue coats. Fortunately, a junior officer recognised the uniform and knew about Otto. He was taken to the Cavalry Brigade who were not far away and soon presented himself to the brigadier.

Buford said, 'That was very naughty. You are not here to get involved in the fighting. I see you are limping, what happened to you?' Otto told of his meeting with Stonewall Jackson and General Lee. Buford said, 'First go to the surgeon and have your wound checked. Then go and find General McClellan and pass on Lee's message. You will find the general very busy. The Confederates have pulled back to Sharpsburg near Antietam and at this moment a battle is in progress. You can hear the guns.'

The surgeon advised a couple of weeks' rest and then Otto went off to see McClellan.

He found the general very busy indeed, directing the battle with staff officers galloping up continuously bearing information on the situation at the front and dashing off again with orders. In a lull Otto caught the general's attention.

'Sir, I have a message for you from General Lee.'

McClellan's response was, 'Are you mad? Lee is over there on the other side. What the hell do you mean?' After a pause he continued, 'I know who you are, the Prussian observer with Buford.'

Otto hastened to explain with, 'General, I was taken prisoner at Harpers Ferry by the Confederates and taken before Stonewall Jackson and General Lee.'

McClellan asked, 'What does he want, a truce, an armistice?'

Otto replied, 'No sir, he sends his regards and wishes you well. He was very kind, sir, and sent me back.'

McClellan said, 'That's good news when his boys are hammering hell out of us. Get along, young man, and keep away from the sharp end. It is not your war.'

Otto rode back to Buford and told him that he had seen the general who was somewhat angry with him and also that the surgeon had told him to rest his leg for a week or so.

Buford said, 'Well off you go. You will have a tale to tell – "Prisoner of the Confederates for a day. How I met the great General Robert E. Lee".'

Back in Washington Otto found his wife was very shortly to give birth. The next day came the news that the battle of Sharpsburg had ended the Antietam campaign with the bloodiest day of the war with overall casualties of some 12,000. Both sides withdrew and it was a Union victory only in that they stopped Lee's advance.

Otto perhaps exaggerated his limp and drew attention and sympathy from Heide and the *Baron* and *Baronin*, so many acquaintances were very interested in his story and by his meeting with Lee and Stonewall he was a little bit of a hero, having warranted the 'red badge of courage'.

He lost no time in going to see Comfort and when they bedded down she said, 'I will imagine you are my horse' and mounted him astride.

He was very fond of Comfort and the intense pleasure she gave him. Probably she had dallied with others in his absence, but so what? That was her destiny.

In October their child was born, a girl who was named Erika after the *Baronin*. The doctor told Otto that it was a difficult birth and that Heide was very weak from the loss of blood and that it was unlikely that she would bear another child. They settled down happily together, Heide very content to have her true love at home and the, of course, best baby in the world. Otto too had all this and the secret comfort of Comfort as well, since sex, in any case, was off limits with Heide.

In November he went to headquarters and found that McClellan had been sacked, replaced by General Ambrose Burnside. The common practice of relieving commanders because the loss of a battle is attributed entirely to them, is sometimes not only unfair but a too hasty error of judgement. After all, we learn by our failures, or are likely to, and the new general may well be worse in performance. Overall it leads to a wise general not committing his forces until he is sure of winning if his enemy allows him to and does not attack first . . . Hobson's choice. Otto saw Brigadier Buford who said that the army was once more reorganising and they would soon be off again to defeat the rebels. Both sides in the Civil War were beset by the problem of deserters and short-time conscripts. The conscripts generally refused to soldier on and the deserters just wanted to get home. They were mostly small farmers and were compelled to work their farm or be ruined.

By December 1862 General Burnside was ready to go after the rebels. The cavalry established by reconnaissance that the Confederates were concentrated at Fredricksburg, between Antietam and Washington, too uncomfortably close to the capital. A spy brought the information that the Confederate's force consisted of Lee's able General Longstreet, a Corps commander with considerable experience of command in battle. Burnside moved the Army of the Potomac across the Rappahanock River, intending to sweep away Longstreet's Corps and advance on an unprotected Richmond.

Otto had been with the reconnaissance regiments and now the brigade was in reserve, guarding the flank, vulnerable from the east, where a breakthrough could isolate the Union Army from the capital. From an advantage point he watched the massed formations of blue coats advance towards Longstreet's position. As soon as they were within range of the artillery, shells tore through the ranks, cutting great gaps filled with dead and dying.

'That will teach those Yankee bastards! Close up, close up,' officers and sergeants ordered the temporarily broken ranks.

Soon they were within musket range and volleys of balls swept into the oncoming ranks. The slaughter was awful to witness and Otto felt quite impotent. The cavalry were impatiently idle, waiting for their turn which never came. It was not a cavalry fight. The remnants of the attacking formations at last reached the rebels and hand-to-hand fighting ensued with bayonet, musket balls and knives, even bare hands, both sides driven on by an intense hatred for their fellow countrymen. The contest went on for an unbelievably long time, until the tattered, blood-soaked few staggered away back to where they started, defeated. A severe defeat, the Army of the Potomac lost some 13,000 soldiers and, of course, General Burnside was fired. The Confederates were not in sufficient strength to exploit their victory and the Yankees pulled back to Washington. So ended the battle of Fredricksburg.

Back in Washington with the family Otto found little with which to occupy himself once his current reports were on the way to Berlin. The capital was quiet with a subdued air, consciousness of the Confederates not so far away. People could not understand and were shocked by the failure of the army to defeat Johnny Rebel after being engaged in several major battles. He considered taking leave and going with the family to Germany, but little Erika was too young to make the journey, especially in winter with frequent gales in the Atlantic. Replacing Burnside, General Joseph Hooker, known as 'Fighting Joe', was appointed to command the Army of the Potomac.

General Hooker knew that since the beginning of the Civil War the goal of the Federal generals was to capture the rebel capital, Richmond. Only McClellan had come close enough to see the city spires from the James River during the Peninsular campaign. Hooker brought the Army of the Potomac to full strength. In April 1863 he began manoeuvring around the previous scene of a disastrous defeat of Fredricksburg. Lee, Buford's cavalry found, was established at the small hamlet of Chancellorsville and his army of North Virginia much smaller in numbers than the Federals. Hooker manoeuvred his forces to confront Lee to front and rear in a pincer, to be brought together to crush the Confederates. The cavalry were placed as a stopgap between, once more to be onlookers, but from Otto's viewpoint as an observer, an ideal position.

At Fredricksburg, Lee had fought defensively, exhausting the Union troops, who wore themselves out in repeated attacks. Here, at Chancellorsville, Lee forestalled the enemy pincer movement with a vigorous attack. Otto watched with amazement the grey-clad rebels, yelling their customary insults at the Yankees and exhortations to themselves to get at them. Confederate artillery fired continuously, a creeping barrage in front of the infantry. At nightfall the fighting died down and at dawn the Confederates continued the relentless push. Before the day was out Hooker was driven back across the Rappahanock River. And so once again back to Washington; an ignominious defeat, gained by a brilliant display of leadership by Robert E. Lee.

In Washington there was disgust and anger at the poor performance of the army and its generals, particularly when they learned that one Army corps had fled when faced by Stonewall Jackson's irresistible force. Tragically, Stonewall was mortally wounded, a great loss to Lee. Hooker had lost over 17,000 of his army. His generals were very bitter, they had implored Hooker to make a stand and he was also criticised for not using the cavalry effectively, when they could have been harassing Lee's lines. Officers and men were disgusted over the performance of the army and its leaders.

President Lincoln came to Hooker's headquarters at the end of May accompanied by the general-in-chief General Halleck. News arrived that the Confederates were on the move, along the Blue Mountains, going north, arriving in Pennsylvania and the heartland of the north. They soon established that the army was not willing to serve under Hooker. Finally they chose Major General George Gordon Meade, younger and junior to other generals, but who had distinguished himself in the field, showing conspicuous ability in command.

At headquarters, Lincoln met the senior officers and shook hands with Otto, saying, 'Well, Major, you have not seen much so far to impress you with our performance, but I promise you that with God's help we shall do better from now on.'

Meade had very little time in which to pull things together and get the army moving.

Otto went back to Washington for a bit of Comfort and to see his daughter, Erika. The baby was well and thriving under the loving care of her mother and her doting grandparents, the *Baron* and *Baronin*'s first grandchild. Otto had only a few days as Brigadier Buford had told him that the cavalry would move out very soon to shadow Lee's movements. He rekitted himself and his orderly out for what was likely to be a long campaign, said goodbye to Heide and the baby and, of course, taking Comfort on the way, reported back to Buford, now general.

The Cavalry Corps had been regrouped under General Pleasanton and now its two divisions were equal to the Confederate Cavalry of Jeb Stuart. Buford commanded the First Division. The army set out from Washington to move on a line parallel to Lee, south through Manassas and then westwards through Salem and the northerly route to Gettysburg. Although it could not be more than guessed at, Gettysburg was frequently spoken of, obviously on Lee's way to Pennsylvania; none could have foreseen that Gettysburg, that summer of 1863, was to be the site of a major victory for the Union and the beginning of the end for the Confederate rebels.

At the beginning of June 1863 in glorious weather the Cavalry Corps crossed the Rappahanock River, a composite force with its own horse artillery and supporting infantry. The next day they were poised at Brandy Station on the Orange and Alexander Railroad, a few miles north east of Culpeper. The Confederates were known to be in the vicinity of Culpeper and an informer had previously told Buford that Jeb Stuart was there with his cavalry, consisting of more than 10,000 troopers; Pleasanton's combined force amounted to more than 11,000 cavalry, infantry and gunners. Pleasanton's objective was to seek and destroy any Confederate force in the region of Culpeper and stop a raid by Jeb Stuart before it started. The country towards Brandy Station was open, unwooded, ideal for cavalry movement. At dawn the following day Pleasanton sent two cavalry regiments across Kelly's Ford where Stuart's cavalry was known to be assembled; the patrol exchanged shots with Confederate outposts and opened the Battle of Brandy Station, the biggest cavalry engagement of the Civil War.

Stuart responded vigorously to the Union cavalry, and a great fight ensued, a wild fracas of charges and countercharges, whole regiments being involved. Dust and smoke obscured the field. Otto remained close to General Buford, who kept away from the fighting, directing his division. By late afternoon both sides were exhausted and with the approach of the Union Infantry, Stuart withdrew under cover of his artillery. Otto moved closer to the front with the general. The rebel artillery was firing airburst shells and one exploded over the command group and Otto was struck down, hit by a large piece of shell which slashed down his face and buried itself in his shoulder.

Unconscious, he was carried to the casualty station where a surgeon, covered with the gore of the very many wounded men he had attended to, removed the shrapnel from his shoulder and cleaned up the mess of bone splinters and tissue, binding up face and shoulder. There was nothing to do about the eye, it had gone. Otto partially recovered consciousness on the train carrying the wounded to Washington, becoming aware of one eye swathed in bandages and one arm and shoulder likewise, immovable. In great pain he remembered Lee's expression, 'War's hell', and thought, yes, and this war is more hell. He was taken to a military hospital in Washington and sent his orderly, who had insisted on staying with him, to inform his wife, Heide, of his whereabouts.

Heide came to the hospital with the *Baron* and *Baronin*. They were shocked by Otto's injuries, one eye gone and he had a useless arm, but was, nevertheless, lucky to be alive. He was in the hospital for several weeks and then sent home sporting a black eyepatch, a scarred face – not too bad, it might have been a duelling scar from Heidelberg – and his arm in a sling. It would be just possible in time for him to hold his horse's reins. Back at his house, Otto made a slow recovery, coming to terms with his disabilities. Little Erika, a big beautiful baby, was a great joy to him and he would sit for hours nursing her and lost in contemplation. Erika was curious to see what was under the eyepatch, poking at it with her small fingers. Otto restrained her. None should see the horrible empty eyesocket. He often thought of Comfort, what therapy she would be, but apart from sending his orderly to see her and give her the news, he did nothing to see her himself.

In November 1863 the *Baron* came with the news that President Abraham Lincoln was attending the consecration of the National Cemetery at Gettysburg, where the Confederates had suffered a disastrous defeat. He was expected to give an address.

The *Baron* said, 'Otto, I have been invited to attend. Do you feel well enough to come with me? It will be a momentous occasion and I am sure that the President will utter memorable words. Heide can come along to look after you. Gettysburg is not far away and my carriage is very comfortable.'

Otto was pleased to accept. It would relieve the boredom brought on by unaccustomed inactivity.

At Gettysburg they found the cemetery, known as the 'National Cemetery' to emphasise that it belonged to the individual country of America. The cemetery was circular in form with the graves of the fallen radiating from the centre, like the spokes of a wheel. Thousands of the dead of both sides had been collected and reburied in the most impressive resting place. Following the opening oration by a renowned preacher-scholar, Congressman Edward Everett, President Lincoln delivered his Gettysburg Address, which was to become famous.

The address opened, 'Fourscore and seven years ago our fathers brought forth on this continent a new nation, conceived in liberty, and dedicated to the proposition that all men are created equal . . .'

The president continued his brief but memorable address of only some 200 words, to be perhaps the most quoted speech of all time, ending with . . . 'we resolve that the dead shall not have died in vain . . . and that government of the people, by the people, and for the people, shall not perish from the earth.'

The *Baron* and Otto, as were all the gathering, were much moved by the address. Somewhat chastened, Otto thought, there but for the grace of God lie I. However, the outing did him good. When he next called he was surprised to be presented with two decorations, the Purple Heart, the award for being wounded on the field of battle and the Silver Star, the citation of which read, 'for distinguished service at Harpers Ferry on . . .'

The brigadier who presented the medals said, 'I have heard about your capture at Harpers Ferry and your meeting with Lee, not exactly conspicuous gallantry, but you deserve your star. You have been knocked about a bit in our war.'

Well, the baubles would look pretty on his uniform, Otto told Heide.

By the spring of 1864 he was almost his old self and it had been suggested that he could return to Europe but elected to remain in America and even observe more of the war, which continued, seemingly endlessly. General William Tecumseh Sherman, the commander of the Army of the West, named Tecumseh after a great Shawnee Indian chief, whom Sherman's father admired, was beginning the Atlanta campaign, to capture the capital of Georgia from Lee, into which region the Confederates had retreated from Gettysburg. Reluctantly the *Baron* and the military attaché agreed that Otto could join General Sherman if the War Department allowed, which it did.

So once more off to the wars. Heide was very sad: poor Otto so damaged, what next? Before leaving, he went to see Comfort, who was quite shocked.

'Poor Otto, what have they done to you? Last time you came you were my horse and now what? Come to me, I will make it all better.'

And in some way she did.

Otto and his orderly took the train to the west as far as Chatanooga in Tennessee and, buying mounts there, rode into Georgia to Sherman's headquarters.

General Sherman had fought in the Mexican War and as an infantry colonel at Bull Run, his frequent declaration was, 'War is all hell' like his opponent, Lee.

He greeted Otto remarking, 'Dear, dear, you have been knocked about a bit. Trying to catch up with the late Admiral Nelson?'

Otto explained that he had been at Bull Run as an observer and also at Fredricksburg and Chancellorsville and that at Brandy Station he had received his injuries from an airburst shell. He told the general about his grandfather, killed in 1812 in Russia with Napoleon's *Grande Armée* and his father, killed at Balaclava in the Crimea, 1854.

Sherman was most interested in his capture and meeting with Lee and the late Stonewall Jackson and finally told Otto, 'War is all hell. Look after yourself here and stay at my headquarters.'

Just after Otto arrived, Sherman set off with his army, determined to destroy the Confederate army which was commanded by General J.E. Johnston, and to capture the capital of Georgia, Atlanta. Sherman's tactics involved concentrated flanking movements, hooks, which caused the opposition to retreat or be cut off. Before Atlanta at Chattahoochee, the Confederates, supported by another corps commanded by a very able General J.B. Hood, one of Lee's best, mounted a strong counter-attack. Otto watched with astonishment the savagery of the fighting when the grey-clad southern soldiers got in among the Union troops, displaying an unbelievable ferocity against their fellow countrymen. In spite of their determined effort, the attack was repulsed and the Confederates driven back to Atlanta, leaving many dead and wounded on the battlefield. Gore galore.

By July, Sherman was ready to launch an attack on Atlanta and to march to the sea beyond. He determined on a break from the traditional battle form with one side lined up against the other. He reduced his supplies and transport to a minimum, to move rapidly and live off the country, to destroy without compunction whatsoever fell into his hands. Total war. First to take Atlanta.

As a first move, Sherman cut off the Confederate forces from their line of communications from Augusta and the southern heartland, causing a swift attempt by Johnston to withdraw. Exploiting the confusion, Sherman swiftly captured the city and commenced virtually to destroy it.

Sherman's driving principle was that the rebels could only be defeated by laying waste to the Confederacy.

After destruction of the roads, houses and the diaspora of the people. 'Make Georgia heave. Only this will cripple their military resources,' he stated.

By early September, Atlanta was destroyed and the entire population banished. Otto, sickened by the ruthlessness of Sherman, decided he had experienced enough of war and that he would go back to Washington. He remained to see Sherman depart from Atlanta on his swift invasion of the South, a new concept of warfare: lightning strikes and rapid advances, years later to be known as *Blitzkrieg.*

Saying goodbye to Sherman, the general said, 'Well, Major, you have seen something to write about. Your War Office will be very interested in my new principle of war, which, as you can see, is very successful.'

Otto was very glad to be back in Washington with his family. His injuries were troublesome and would remain so for a very long time. War is still more hell.

Heide was, as ever, delighted to have him back, not more damaged this time. Even little Erika cooed or he imagined she did. He spent some time at the War Office and with the military attaché, who agreed sympathetically that Otto could end his duties as an observing officer. The attaché would send for a replacement, but with Sherman campaigning through the South, it looked as if the war would soon be over. Otto said he would be taking a couple of weeks' leave in New York, but meanwhile he would keep in close touch with headquarters to find out all he could about Sherman's movements. The general's novel approach to the tactical side of the conflict was of interest to all concerned.

Next stop, Comfort. After satisfying his needs, he told her that he would be going back to Germany. 'Before I go we will discuss your future, my one and only comfort during this horrible war. Whatever happens I will see you well provided for,' he told her.

The *Baron* and *Baronin* approved of his decision. It was time for Otto and his family to go back home to Prussia. Otto told Heide that he would like to have a holiday in New York and Erika could be left with her grandparents.

Otto left his orderly in charge of the house and they took the train to New York, a second honeymoon, although to himself he wished that Comfort had been by his side – an impossible wish, even in the emancipated North; a Prussian officer and black woman, never.

When they were settled in the hotel, Otto said that he would like to see Chicago, the Great Lakes and Niagara Falls, an opportunity not to be missed as they would probably never again have the chance. Finally, they decided to take the mail coach to Buffalo and on to Niagara Falls where Lake Erie spilled over into the Niagara River and Lake Ontario and the St Lawrence Seaway to the Atlantic Ocean, Niagara a crossroads between America and Canada. Otto had telegraphed a reservation to a hotel overlooking the American Falls and with a view of the more boisterous Canadian Falls.

They were entranced by the scenery and decided not to go on to Chicago, enjoying the second honeymoon, trying hard, but Heide was not to conceive another child as the doctor had advised Otto. He told Heide about the war between America and Britain in 1812 in which the Americans attacked the Shawnee Indians, who were befriended by the British, killing the Shawnee chief, Tecumseh. Further American attempts to invade Canada were repulsed by the British at Niagara. They met an elderly schoolmaster who told them that as a young man in 1812 he had witnessed the events of the war. Did they know that the victorious General Sherman was named after Chief Tecumseh?

Otto told him, 'I have recently been with the general at Atlanta as an observer. I am a German officer and, as you can see, I lost an eye and injured my arm at Brandy Station with Buford.'

They had an interesting talk about history, Otto telling the schoolmaster about his grandfather left behind in Russia in 1812 and his father at Balaclava.

On the American side of the Falls they could stand on a platform jutting out from the cliff face close to the smooth curtain of water, millions of gallons a minute, breaking into turbulence nearly 200 feet below, with a thunderous roar, an awe-inspiring spectacle, an enormous, overpowering vision of the mighty power of nature. When the breeze gusted they were enveloped with a fine spray which, when strong winds blew, blanked out the Falls.

Crossing over the bridge to the Canadian side, they found the scene much more boisterous, the water breaking over a ragged cliff edge and curving out in a great arc; awesome, especially seen from an observation stage reached by tunnels actually situated between the cliff face and the falling water. The noise was deafening. It was useless to try to make any comments on the majesty of the sight, stupendous. Drenched by the spray but exhilarated by seeing close up one of the wonders of the world, they climbed back up the tunnels into the comparative quietness of the town above.

They also ventured on a stout rowing boat propelled by six skilled oarsmen. They were provided with oilskin coats and hats and with the few passengers seated on the thwarts, rowed upriver into the area of the whirlpools swirling round near the falls. It was a trip fraught with danger as boats had capsized and the occupants were inevitably drowned, sucked under by the vortex. But it was especially worthwhile to look up at the vastness of the falling water and they were fortunate to see quite close the spectrum of a vivid rainbow which had formed in the dense mist from the wind blown spray. Fantastic.

The visit culminated in a trip down the Niagara River on a small steamboat which entered Lake Ontario. Crossing over the lake to Toronto, they spent the night at a fine hotel on the waterfront, returning to Niagara the next day. It had been a very memorable holiday and Otto, much recovered, was coming to terms with his disabilities. Their holiday ended after a few days in New York when Otto secretly managed to buy an expensive piece of jewellery for Comfort. He also discreetly enquired of the hall porter the whereabouts of houses of pleasure, *maisons de tolerance*.

On their return to Washington, Otto called at the headquarters to catch up with the progress of the war. He found out that Sherman was sweeping on into the South, apparently irresistible, allowing Lee and his most able Corps commander, General James Longstreet, no respite in order for them to make a stand.

Meanwhile, Heide, with the *Baron*'s help, was making arrangements to travel back to Germany. Otto spent as much time as possible with Comfort who was delighted with his gift.

She told him, 'I will be having a present for you in a few months. Feel my belly, how round it has become. A little Otto.'

He was quite pleased. There was no future for him, but who knows? In any case, he would ensure that she was taken care of financially. He suggested that she should move to New York and set herself up as a 'madam', perhaps buying a share in a house. Since he was certain the embryo was his, their coupling had been vigorous and satisfying, he was not happy that it would be born in a brothel, but it was best for Comfort. Princess she might be, but what else could she do? When he took a fond farewell of her, he gave her his address care of the War Office, from where letters would always reach him.

'Please write to me when the child is born and tell me how you are. I shall remember you for ever and sadly miss you.'

The *Baron* and the *Baronin* came with them to New York to see them safely and comfortably installed in first-class accommodation on the steamship which was bound for Hamburg. The Atlantic was calm and the voyage uneventful. Otto attracted much attention and curiosity from their fellow passengers. How did he come by his injuries? It made an interesting tale, told by a handsome young Prussian officer. The ladies, with the free air engendered by the sea voyage atmosphere, were more than interested but Otto refrained from any offered liaisons. Good boy.

From Hamburg they went directly to Tilsit and home and the warm welcome of Marlene.

14

Germany

Soon after their return from Otto's wedding in America, Kurt became ill and died. He was in his late seventies. The following year Collette followed him. Otto was much distressed. At Tilsit he found the estates of the von Wintersteins' and Detterling families were prospering. Marlene was keeping a careful eye on the two principal managers. In any case, they were long-serviced and trustworthy. Marlene told Otto that she had recently met the new premier of Prussia, Otto von Bismarck, and when she informed Bismarck that her son, a major of *Uhlanen*, was on his way back from America where he had been an observer of the Civil War, Bismarck expressed a wish to see Otto.

'Only by war shall we attain unification of the German states,' he told her.

Currently there was a loose confederation and Bismarck's object was to unite all the states into a German empire. In order to bring this about, the states bordering other countries, Denmark, Austria and France, had to be secured from interference. By war.

Otto duly went to see Bismarck who was quite impressed by the young major.

'You have obviously been close to war. Tell me of your experiences. I am particularly interested in Sherman and his principles of war. How did you receive your wounds?' he asked.

In addition to his eyepatch, Otto carried his arm in a sling to ease the constant discomfort. He was able to hold his horse's reins, however, leaving his right arm capable of using his sword or pistol.

When his tale was finished Bismarck said, 'That was very interesting, young man, we need young experienced officers like you. I shall keep a lookout for your future. Now, in return I shall tell you my plans for a greater Germany.'

Bismarck told Otto how the previous year Prussia had very quickly defeated Denmark in a single engagement and had brought the restless and much disputed state of Schleswig-Holstein under Prussian administration, with the Danish border established at Flensburg.

'Austria is very upset with this move and is likely to declare war against Prussia. We shall win and that will bring the states bordering Austro-Hungary into the German sphere. More, I have in mind. The future will be very interesting for you, as you will see,' he concluded.

Otto reported at the War Office in Berlin and saw the general who had been receiving his reports from America. Again he encountered requests for first-hand information on the activities of the conquering Sherman. It would seem that his principals of battle might well influence the conduct of future tactics in war.

The general told him, 'Major, we are very pleased with your efforts in America. We are, of course, much in need of officers with experience in the field of battle. Now I am going to surprise you. The colonel of your regiment is too old and we propose that you will replace him.' He went on, when Otto had recovered from the effect of this stupendous announcement. 'You will be the youngest colonel in the *Wehrmacht, Oberst* Otto von Winterstein.'

Otto was quite overcome by such a magnificent promotion. To command an élite cavalry regiment was of more importance than being an officer of higher rank in another activity. He wondered how much Bismarck had influenced the promotion.

He went to Spandau and took over from the retiring commanding officer, who was astonished that he was being replaced by such a young man, but impressed by his wounds and medals, then a rarity in the Prussian army. At the formal handing over parade, squadrons dressed, with officers in front, the *Oberstabfeldwebel,* regimental sergeant major, called for three cheers for the departing colonel who then made way for Otto, a gallant figure on his new grey charger, splendidly turned out. When called for, the troopers cheered enthusiastically for the new, young commanding officer. The regiment marched off by squadrons at the trot, Otto taking the salute.

The retiring colonel told Otto that he had a house nearby on Schwanenwerder Island in Lake Havel, which belonged to his family.

He said, 'Schwanenwerder was once the breeding place of the lake's swans and now there were some dozen houses all belonging to senior military or government officials. I am going away to my estate in Prussia and, if you wish, you can have the house whilst you are at Spandau.'

Otto was delighted to accept and it was agreed that he could stay with them right away.

Otto moved in the same day, driving across the short causeway to the island in a carriage which the old colonel told him belonged to the regiment and was the commanding officer's battle wagon, for his use in the field as office and sleeping quarters. Otto was very impressed by the splendid house, thinking, how fortunate I am, Heide will love this.

The colonel introduced him to a young lady, his daughter, Eloise, who with her young baby was staying with him whilst her husband was away with his regiment of *Hussaren* currently serving on the Danish border at Flensburg.

'My wife, unfortunately no longer with us, was French and Eloise is named after her,' and he went on to suggest that Eloise would show him around the house and garden.

Otto found Eloise very charming and friendly, and she said to him, 'I am so glad to see someone new and young. It gets boring for me here. The neighbours are all old and stuffy. My husband has not been back for two months and I feel abandoned.'

The grounds were quite extensive, considering that Schwanenwerder was a small island. They were on the side away from the causeway facing across the lake to the far bank towards Potsdam. She said, 'This is the boathouse and gazebo. We have a small boat which I hope you will enjoy to sail.'

She led him down steps on to a small jetty to see the boat. The lake was deserted. Climbing the steps up to the gazebo she stumbled and fell against him. Otto thought it was by design and held her firmly close to his body.

Eloise said, 'Father told me about your wounds, but you seem all right down here,' inserting her hand between them. 'I believe we have something in common. My mother was French and you told us at dinner about your father, François.' She pulled up her skirt and sprung up, clasping him round the waist with her legs. 'Come on, let's try the bit in common.'

When it was over Eloise exclaimed, *'Gott in Himmel, Das war wunderbar. Du, du . . .'* After they recovered she said, 'I will come to your bedroom tonight and every night until we leave next week. It is too good to miss.'

So a pleasant take-over was accomplished. He was well housed and getting to know the regiment, which he found he had known as a subaltern: well disciplined and orderly, fit for war. Eloise and the colonel departed and shortly afterwards Heide came with little Erika. Heide was delighted with the house and proud of her husband in such an exalted position, an officer of importance. Otto took the regiment on exercises a few times, preparing for the war which he knew from Bismarck was bound to come, the premier's determination to rope in all the states outside of Prussia.

At the beginning of June 1866 Bismarck provoked Austria on the pretext that it was interfering in the affairs of the German Confederation and declared war. Austria and some of the German states opposed the Prussians who were allied to Italy, who had border problems with Austria. So began the next step towards German unification.

Otto moved the *Uhlanen* out on a war footing: the squadrons, attached horse artillery, infantry and engineers. They took the road through Potsdam to Dresden, some 150 miles away, the ways congested with the Prussian army on the move: cavalry, infantry, guns and commissariat wagons with the usual camp followers, wives and whores. At Dresden the cavalry brigade was detached to scout Bavaria's north-east region, Bayreuth, Bamberg, Nuremburg and Würzburg, an area rich in agriculture and forests. Bayreuth was allied to Austria and hence hostile to Prussia. Bismarck had issued clear orders to the generals and down to unit commanders that the doctrine of total war, expounded by the Prussian General Karl von Clausewitz in his masterpiece, *On War*, was to be followed: total war against the citizens, territory and property of the enemy nation. Otto thought to himself, shades of Sherman, who applied similar strategies. In the event they found the Bavarians most cooperative. Whatever soldiery they had was off with the Austrians and the regional governors all expressed willingness to submit to Prussia.

On leaving Dresden, the Cavalry brigadier despatched the three regiments in different directions, Otto's orders were to sweep the area to the south-west of Dresden down to Würzburg, a distance of some 300 miles, reporting on any opposition they encountered. After three days' uneventful march they reached Bavaria proper and Otto ordered the squadrons to be on the alert, from here they could meet resistance and even run into Bavarian forces, whose whereabouts at that time were unknown. They passed through the village of Gelsenhausen and followed the road through a copse which had been left when the land was cleared for farming. Without warning, shots rang out on both sides and several troopers fell and horses were wounded.

Otto, with the leading squadron, ordered the men to fire their carbines into the woods and then dismount and carefully enter the trees. He ordered the two other squadrons to surround the area and some 20 men were in the bag and surprisingly three obvious women in men's clothing. He ordered the prisoners to be taken to the village square and the squadrons to line up around. In the centre the six dead troopers and an officer were laid in view of the assembled villagers. Then Otto decided to teach them an unforgettable lesson á la Clausewitz.

The village carpenters were rounded up to build a gallows to accommodate four unfortunates at one go; no platforms, they would stand on a large farm cart. So the troopers placed the first four on the wagon, roped with hangman's knots over their heads and at a signal from Otto, the cart was drawn away from under them. The trooper-hangmen pulled down on the bodies to make sure they were dead. The villagers, hitherto silent, broke out with cries of protest, the women weeping, begging for mercy.

Ruthlessly, the hanging continued until there were only two of the ambushers left, youths, almost boys. There were spared, but tied to the cart wheels, shirts torn off their backs and flogged until they were unconscious. Otto ordered the women to be stripped of their attire and sent naked back to the wagons. The men could use them as they wished. He thought that they would not last long.

Finally, he ordered all the villagers rounded up and sent down the road, men, women and children, all of them utterly dismayed. It all seemed very hard, but some of them, now punished, had killed some of his men. The horses, cattle and livestock were sent back to the wagons. That will feed the regiment for a while, he thought. Next, he burnt Gelsenhausen to the ground. Otto thought to himself, I suppose I may be known as Sherman von Winterstein in future. Whatever, there was no further trouble in Bavaria. Word got round very quickly.

After three weeks on the road and having successfully carried out the mission to Würzburg, they joined brigade at the rendezvous near Plauen and proceeded to the main body which included the Italians, and was poised on the border with Bohemia at Toplice, the spires of which they could see across enemy territory. All was ready and the commander-in-chief sent the cavalry over the border to find the Austrians.

'Your joyride is over,' he told the brigadier. 'Now get on with the war.'

The cavalry found that the main body of the Austrians was in the area of Sadowa, where they had some advantage in position on high ground facing the open country over which the Prussians were expected to appear. The Prussians and their Italian allies duly arrived at the area in front of the Austrians and and dressed for battle. It was a clear midsummer day and soon after dawn the artillery on both sides opened up a continuous bombardment. At a signal from the commander-in-chief, and after the guns had thundered for an hour, the order was given for the massed infantry to advance. The infantry, all armed with breech-loading Mauser rifles and, above all, superb discipline, were more than a match for the Austrians, mainly furnished with old muzzle loaders and less well drilled than the Prussians.

The cavalry were ordered to approach along the high ground

on the left flank and be ready to strike when the infantry were engaged at close quarters. Otto, from the front of the regiment, kept his eye on the brigadier who, with his orderlies and staff officers, was nearest to the Austrian flank position, where could be seen the guns, now silent, some infantry and a bunch of cavalry waiting, like themselves, to join the fray. When the signal came from the brigadier to advance, Otto moved forward: walk, trot, canter and finally gallop into the somewhat disorganised cavalry. Otto was not alone. Because of his disability, it was necessary to guard him carefully and stout troopers stayed with him in close attendance. Nevertheless, managing the reins with his only partially effective left arm, he struck out at the nearest opponent with pleasing success. The cavalry were soon swept away and the *Uhlanen* were in among the guns, the crews running away, attempting to surrender and mostly being slaughtered. They turned the enemy flank coinciding with a breakthrough by the infantry. That was too much for the Austrians who broke and fled in disorder, leaving much booty on the field, including guns. To capture the enemy's artillery was sure confirmation of victory.

So ended the battle of Sadowa, Austria suffering a decisive defeat. The remnants straggled along the road to the capital, Prague. The cavalry were ordered to chase and harass the retreat. Two regiments with the brigadier penetrated the region towards Prague, laying waste to anything of use en route and generally marauding, picking up much loot. The remaining regiment nibbled away at the rearguard. Before what was left of the Austrians reached Prague, collapse was complete and they surrendered. So ended what became known as the Seven Weeks War.

At the former royal palace, Hradcany Castle, Bismarck dictated the terms of the Treaty of Prague. The Emperor, Francis Joseph, was to be eliminated from all German affairs and in addition the state of Hanover, Hesse, Nassau and Frankfurt were to be ceded to Germany. The Italians gained Venetia. Bismarck had achieved the second stage in the validation of the German states and the creation of the German empire. His master, Kaiser Wilhelm I, was delighted with his increased domain.

Otto had been invited to the castle with other senior officers to attend a meeting after the signing of the treaty to be addressed by Bismarck. He thanked them for their success in the recent conflict and the demonstration of the superior Prussian arms. On leaving, he stopped to talk to some of the officers and Otto was easily recognised.

Bismarck said, 'Winterstein, our man of American experience. I heard about your exploit in Bavaria. It was very creditable and may well have saved lives from continued resistance. Moreover, you carried out my orders to conduct total war. It will not be forgotten.'

Later on Otto was awarded the Prussian Order of the Black Eagle.

On his way out of the castle he encountered a young lady walking in the grounds and in passing bade her good day.

She smiled at him and said, 'A brigand Colonel,' (referring to his eyepatch,) 'fancy you being here, but you Prussians are all the same. ' They walked together and she introduced herself. 'I am Countess Olga Masaryk, my husband, the count, was killed at Sadowa leading his cavalry regiment. Maybe you were responsible.'

Otto offered his condolences. She said, 'Oh, I am not sorry, he was a beastly man. I hated him, so good riddance.' She went on, 'Prague is the most beautiful city of Europe, so many splendid buildings. If you like I can show you round, my carriage is outside.'

First of all she showed him round the castle. 'Hradcany was formerly our royal palace, the most famous building in Bohemia.'

Olga took him to the cathedral of St Vitus with the tombs of St Wenceslaus and several kings and emperors. From there to the archiepiscopal palace, the church of our Lady of Victory where she showed him the said to be miraculous statue of the infant Jesus of Prague.

She said, 'You see what magnificence there is of the Middle Ages. Enough for today. If you are free tomorrow we can see some more.'

Otto told her the regiment was on a few days' leave so it was not a problem.

'I shall be delighted, you are most charming and it is so kind that you take the trouble.' They drove to her house, near the centre of Prague. It was small but there was evidence of wealth. She invited him to dinner and he was pleased to accept, thinking, this is a good thing. I wonder what's for supper?

After a sumptuous dinner with lots of wine, she said, 'I would like to celebrate my widowhood and it would be nice to do so with you, the conqueror. Please take me to bed.'

Nothing loath, Otto followed her up the stairs and into a magnificent bedroom. There was little sleep for either of them that night. The spoils to the victor.

That day Olga showed him the palaces Waldstein, Schwarzenberg and Czernin, telling a little of their history. Otto was very impressed and even more so when they crossed the Moldau River on the famous Charles Bridge, one of many bridges. On the other bank they saw the University of Prague, or Charles University, named after Emperor Charles IV, who in the eleventh century created the splendour of the city. The tour concluded with a visit to the Old Town Hall and Tyn Cathedral, finally across Wenceslaus Square and to Olga's residence.

At dinner Otto told her about himself, the French connection, his home in Prussia and his experiences in the American Civil War and the making of his unfortunate wounds. When they went to bed she stroked his damaged shoulder and her finger traced the scar on his cheek and touched the eyepatch, which he refused to remove. It was hideously unsightly.

Her fingers traced the scars on his thigh and she said, 'Lay back, you deserve a treat.'

In the morning they said a loving farewell and she told him, 'We were good for each other. It is a pity you are married. However, you never know, I may see you in Berlin. It is not far away.'

Otto told her he would be parading the regiment on Wenceslaus Square the following day, prior to leaving for Germany.

She promised to be there, and, 'I will wave to you.'

The parade was inspected by the commander-in-chief. It was a glorious midsummer morning and the troops gathered in the sunshine, a splendid army, horse artillery out front with Otto's

Uhlanen on the right of a battalion of guards. The general rode along the ranks, accompanied in turn by each of the regimental commanders. The inspection over, the general stood in front of the spectators' stand and took the salute as the units marched off, cavalry first followed by the guns and then the goose-stepping infantry. As Otto led the *Uhlanen* past the saluting base, he spied Olga standing on the dais provided for prominent citizens and slightly inclined his sword towards her, to which she responded with a wide smile. The following day the brigade set off for Berlin.

At the house on Schwanenwerder, Otto found all in order and Heide pleased to see him return from the war with no further injuries. Little Erika, now three years old, had been coached by her mother to say, 'Daddy, I am so glad to see you back from the horrible war. I hope you are well.' She was very fond of her father, as girls usually are. The *Uhlanen* settled back into barracks at Spandau and commenced a period of training and the use of new types of arms, carbines and revolvers. Otto called at the *Kriegs Amt* to renew his acquaintance with the generals and staff officers he knew. It was hinted that he could look for promotion to command a brigade or join the staff. He let it be known that if he were needed he would have no choice. In the event, they let him be.

The year followed with intensive training and drills, in spite of the fact that the troops had just returned from a successful campaign: regimental exercise, brigade and corps manoeuvres, the latter across the Rhine to the west. Otto remembered Bismarck's remarks about German unification, Denmark finished with, Austria now out of the way, that left France . . . The troops, dressed in the new, less conspicuous field-grey uniforms, accepted enthusiastically the harsh discipline and a splendid army was created by Bismarck's iron determination to succeed with his scheme: to create a great and glorious fatherland.

Comfort had once written to Otto from New York. She was prospering with her business and her partner, the madam, was now retired. 'How lovely it would be if we could meet but you must be very busy,' she wrote. 'I read about your war with

Austria and hope you did not collect any more nasty souvenirs.' The following midsummer of 1868 she wrote, 'I am coming to Germany, I have an introduction to someone in Hamburg who has houses in the Reeper-bahn. Hope we shall meet.' As Otto knew, the Reeper-bahn was the notorious red-light district of Hamburg. Comfort would do well there.

In due course Comfort wrote to say that she was installed in the Reeper-bahn. 'Please come soon, I am so looking forward to seeing you.' Without telling Heide where he was going, after all he was so often away on duty, he took a week's leave of absence and took the train to Hamburg. His journey was exceedingly smooth. In Bismarck's new army, a colonel was god-like to civilians. He went to the Four Seasons Hotel and that night changed into mufti and set out to find Comfort in the Reeper-bahn.

He found the bordello at the address Comfort had given him. The house was unpretentious on the outside but, passing through the hall, he entered a splendid lounge, ornately furnished, where quite beautiful and very elegant girls were seated. One young 'lady' seated him at a corner table where he could see all that was on offer and asked him what he would care to drink.

He declined the offer and said, 'Give my regards to the madam and tell her Colonel von Winterstein is here.'

Comfort came at once from her private quarters and without much fuss in front of the girls took him to her quarters. Once they were alone she was ecstatic in her greeting.

'Otto, my love, I am so glad to see you. It has been too long. Let us not waste any time, my best friend must be hungry.'

She led him into the bedroom and with her skilful lovemaking took Otto through a wonderland of sexual satiation. She had learnt much in her time managing the business.

She told Otto when they were resting, 'I have done very well thanks to you, and am now quite prosperous. Perhaps I may soon be able to return to my homeland.' When he left, Comfort told him, 'When you come this evening I will have something special for you.'

That evening Comfort took him to a room where there were two very young girls, quite beautiful, with the figures that females have only in their youth, lost forever as they grew older.

Comfort said, 'Twins, not quite virgins but fresh from the country. They will entertain you very well, natural whores who are very enthusiastic, liking the work. I will leave you to it. Enjoy yourself. It makes me quite jealous but you deserve something extra.'

The girls undressed Otto, chattering away like a pair of schoolgirls, laid him on the outsize bed and, removing their robes, revealed outstandingly lovely, small pert breasts, contoured buttocks and elegant thighs, all very exciting. When they had finished, Comfort came into the room and shooed the twins out.

'I have been watching you from a secret spy hole,' she said. 'I am quite excited and now you can pleasure me also.'

So the week passed and all too soon a more than satisfied colonel of cavalry was on his way back to who could guess what.

15

Into France

In the middle of the year 1870 Bismarck commenced the conspiracy to bring France to declare war against Prussia. His object was to end France's hegemony in Europe and to bring the French-influenced German states into the German confederation, thus creating the German empire. The Emperor of France, Louis Napoleon Bonaparte, Napoleon III, a ruthless dictator and consequently unpopular, was confident that his army could easily defeat the Prussians and such a victory would restore his popularity in France.

In July Bismarck sponsored a move to place a Prussian Hohenzollern prince on the throne of Spain. The French, in response to the despatch informing of the impending combination between Prussia and Spain, were infuriated and there ensued a general clamour for war. By mid-July France had declared war. The Prussians were ready, their offensive already planned by the able General Helmut von Moltke. So began the Franco-Prussian War, the outcome of which was to cause an uneasy peace between the European powers for the next 40 years.

By early August the German army had crossed over into France, sweeping any resistance aside. Von Moltke knew that he had to secure the great fortresses of Metz and Sedan which were guarding the way to Paris, his ultimate goal. The *Uhlanen* Brigade, still an independent unit, was reconnoitring towards Metz when the leading squadron reported a French cavalry regiment coming their way, obviously also scouting. The brigadier ordered Otto to go to hell for leather and cut the French off from behind. So Otto led the regiment at a furious gallop and was in position before the enemy, ambling along in the summer's sun, in their bright blue uniforms and glittering brass helmets, were fully aware of the trap. The rest of the brigade swept forward and the French cavalry were caught in a pincer movement. The *Uhlanen* very quickly crushed any fight in the French, savagely cutting down any resistance. A few miles along the road to Metz they arrived at Mars-la-Tour and could occupy the high ground beyond Marshal Bazeine's army, thereby denying him the road to the fortress.

Marshal Bazeine had some ten divisions of infantry, two cavalry and artillery, around 130,000 strong. Von Moltke had a much smaller force of five infantry and two cavalry divisions and less artillery support. So began the first battle of the Franco-Prussian War, the Battle of Mars-la-Tour. The German advantage lay in the iron discipline of the troops and superiority of equipment, particularly Krupp breech-loading cannon and Mauser rifles. The new weapon, the rapid firing machine-gun, was in its infancy and all were subject to stoppages, French Hotchkiss and American-manufactured Browning and Gatling Guns. The *Uhlanen* Brigade approached Mars-la-Tour and found that the French were falling back from Metz towards Verdun. Von Moltke's Corps commander, General Alvensleben, with 30,000 men, only a quarter of the French force, blocked Bazeine's route to the west by placing his Corps in front of Mars-la-Tour and across to Vionville. The battle opened on 12 August 1870 with the artillery pounding away at the infantry divisions with considerable effect. Then, under a creeping barrage, the Germans moved forward, a solid phalanx of grey-clad men, rifles with gleaming, saw-edged bayonets at the port, the Prussian steam-roller, the endless command to 'close-up', to fill the gaps caused by enemy shells. The ground was littered with dead and dying but press on regardless.

The cavalry, two divisions and Otto's brigade were in the rear when two French cavalry divisions appeared on the French right, obviously bent on outflanking the Germans. The Corps commander ordered the German cavalry to intercept and there followed a rare major cavalry fight. The *Uhlanen* Brigade took the centre, Otto's regiment leading, the heavy squadron in front, and Otto behind with the other two squadrons, all in a tight vee formation, stirrup to stirrup. The whole brigade rode full tilt at the French centre, driving a wedge between the two enemy divisions, with a terrific impact. Pandemonium ensued, unseated riders, horses knocked down kicking and screaming. The *Uhlanen* wedge burst out and they spread on either side, creating havoc. Meanwhile, the two German divisions advanced at a gallop to either side of the French, like the horns of a bull, shades of Genghis Khan. Both sides hacked away at each other until the French gave way and began to withdraw. The cost of the action was terrible, the ground strewn with dead and wounded, men and horses both German and French, but the flank was secure. Otto's regiment suffered heavily, being first in, but he came out bloody but unscathed.

The infantry had pushed on against twice their number, ensconced on high ground. In spite of great losses, they drove the French from their position and soon they were hastily retreating towards Metz. Alvensleben broke off the engagement. Dusk was falling and his sorely tried troops were exhausted after the long day's fight. It later transpired that the Corps had lost over 15,000 men, half their original strength; the French casualties were about the same. Until von Moltke sent more troops, they could not pursue Bazeine.

A few days later, a reconnaissance by the *Uhlanen* brigade discovered the French on a line of high ground beyond Gravelotte and stretching to the village of Saint-Privat-la-Montague, a few miles from Metz. Von Moltke had arrived with the rest of the Germans and had taken over the direction of the following action, the Battle of Gravelotte. Whatever the outcome, Bazeine was denied his line of retreat. The two sides now were even in numbers but the French had an advantageous position.

The *Uhlanen* found that the right flank of the French was approached by easier going and, moreover, their old adversary, or what was left of them, the enemy cavalry, were right there at Saint-Privat. Von Moltke decided to make his main attack, a right hook round Saint-Privat and infiltrate behind Bazeine. The *Uhlanen* supported by the guns of the Horse Artillery and accompanied by a brigade of Prussian Guards, were to lead the field. Otto's regiment, having the honour to be the first in, the troopers muttered, 'What, us again? What about someone else?' The *Uhlanen* moved out at first light, the Guards hanging on to the stirrups. When close enough, the cavalry paused and the guards moved to the front and poured a withering rifle fire into the opposition. At the right moment, the French in disarray, the *Uhlanen* swept forward and, scattering the opposing cavalry, were through, out behind the French lines. This was the beginning of the end. The German infantry divisions poured through the gap and the French, after a day of hard fighting, were retreating to Metz and the great fortress. The struggle around Saint-Privat was especially vicious and both sides suffered heavy losses: in all, the Germans over 20,000 men and the French some 13,000. Von Moltke left some of his forces to lay seige to Metz and proceeded to the next obstacle before Paris, Sedan. So, in four weeks since the French declarations of war, the Germans had bottled up the enemy field army in Metz and the morale of von Moltke's troops was consequently very high. Now the main French army, commanded by Marshal MacMahon, accompanied by the Emperor Napoleon, a force of some 120,000 troops, moved to relieve Bazeine. The German troops, now reinforced by the 3rd Prussian Army, were more numerous, amounting to more than 200,000 and so far had proved to be superior in battle.

At the end of August the *Uhlanen* reported three French units of considerable strength guarding the approaches to Sedan across the River Meuse. These were removed in three short, sharp engagements and at the beginning of September 1870 MacMahon had been foiled in the attempt to relieve Metz and was, in fact, encircled outside the fortress of Sedan. The French fought desperately to break out of the trap, employing their cavalry in fruitless charges, which resulted only in costly casualties. In addition, Marshal MacMahon was severely wounded, causing confusion in the French command and resulting in the added disadvantage of the emperor assuming command.

At dawn on 2 September the German artillery pounded the main French position throughout the whole morning and then the attack by the German cavalry and infantry commenced. The

Uhlanen charged with great determination into the French cavalry and since there was no place to retreat to, they were forced to surrender. Poor Otto, recipient of so many wounds, received a slash from a French sabre which laid open his thigh down to the bones. Very soon Napoleon III surrendered, the situation being hopeless. He was taken prisoner, with more than 80,000 soldiers. The French casualties were some 35,000 killed and wounded and the German much fewer than 9,000. A resounding victory.

'Paris here we come.'

Otto was taken to a casualty station that the surgeons had established at a convent some miles outside Sedan on the banks of the Meuse. The added advantage was that the nuns were proficient in nursing the sick and injured. The mother superior was most helpful with Otto, poor, gallant, wounded officer, one eye gone, a useless arm and now a terrible wound in his previously damaged thigh, a present from the American Confederates, giving him a very pleasant room overlooking the river. The surgeon cleansed and stitched the terrible wound. 'You are fortunate, colonel,' he said, 'it will heal if you lie quietly here for a few weeks. It is better to remain here in the convent, where I shall stay until all my wounded are well enough to move on.'

The mother superior told him about the convent.

'Colonel, you poor man, you really have been knocked about. War is terrible.' She continued, 'We are fortunate in being well endowed and, in addition, there is a school for the girls of the local gentry, which brings in a good income.'

Two novices were appointed to take care of Otto, feed him, bathe and take care of his body excretions, the latter an unpleasant task causing him initial embarrassment to perform in the presence of young women. The novices always visited him together, never alone, but one day Otto was left alone with Claire whilst the others went away to fetch something. Claire, Otto could see, had quite a beautiful face and he suspected that all else was equally desirable under the all-enveloping dress.

She told him, 'I am in the convent because my mother caught me making love with a neighbour's son. I hate it and would escape if I had somewhere to go.'

Bed-bathing their patient one morning, modestly covered by a bed sheet, Claire inadvertently, or otherwise, brushed her hand against his penis and kept it there, feeling it grow hard under her touch, saying, 'Well, what have we here!'

Several times Claire came to his room at night and contrived to satisfy him. Otto, needless to say, was delighted, thinking, I am very lucky, someone always turns up at the right time.

Otto wrote to Heide in Berlin of his forced incarceration in the convent and said that it would be unwise for her to attempt to visit him there, as there was still a war on. In October came the news that Bazeine had capitulated at Metz. Paris remained under seige. A leading French politician, Léon Gambetta, escaped from Paris in a hydrogen-filled balloon and formed a new government in the south. In addition, he organised the raising of a new French army. The balloon was a new concept in communications and the beginning of aerial warfare. It was used to observe the besieging German forces. The new government sent an emissary to negotiate a peace with Bismarck. German demands for Alsace and Lorraine to be ceded to them were unacceptable, so negotiations were broken off and Paris remained under seige.

At the convent, the inevitable occurred: Otto and Claire were found out and poor Claire was expelled.

The mother superior was very angry, telling Otto, 'I don't blame you entirely. Claire would never have made the grade and you men are all the same. Anyway, very soon you will be fit to leave.'

Before Claire left Otto told her, 'You are a very enthusiastic young lady and a natural with love. I am sure you do not want to go home to your parents and I have a good friend in Hamburg who will help you.'

So it turned out. Otto provided her with funds and a letter to Comfort and off she went. Nun to whore, what a transition; farewell to Claire.

Early November, Otto rejoined his regiment which was stationed at Pontoise, to the north-west of Paris. They were very pleased to see their colonel back, not too much the worse for wear. Otto, fortunately, had a remarkable physique which could take much punishment and still carry on, apparently unaffected.

Being in France and not fully occupied, Otto thought about his French connections and his grandmother, Collette. He was familiar with her background and considered the possibility of visiting her former home, near Caen in Normandy, less than 200 miles from Pontoise. He proposed to the brigadier that his regiment carry out an exercise into the countryside; they were getting slack, away from home and idle. Much to Otto's surprise, the brigadier agreed.

The *Uhlanen* set out in holiday mood, enjoying the fine late autumn weather, the countryside in the post-summer glory of golden browns and the all-pervading scent of burning leaves and stubble. Otto planned the route through Nantes and on through the Bocage countryside to Evreux, Lisieux and Caen, part of the route taken by Pierre, his grandfather, when recruiting for the French Hussars, some 60 years previously. The people they encountered on the way were astonished to see the strange, foreign troops, but were not at all hostile. The newly-formed French army was located well to the south, nevertheless the war was still on. There had been no declaration of its cessation, in spite of the defeat and collapse of the French main forces.

When after several days of leisurely travel, enjoying the ride, they arrived at the village outside Caen, Otto sent his adjutant to enquire of the whereabouts of the Flamand family. The family, it transpired, were still at the chateau. Otto left the regiment to settle down outside the village and rode alone to the chateau. His arrival caused a flutter. The woman who answered the door was astonished at encountering the strange officer and called her employer, a man of about the same age as Otto. There was even a resemblance in their appearance.

Otto said, 'I suppose we are distant cousins. My grandmother was Collette who was the wife of Pierre Flamand who was killed with Napoleon in Russia.'

Jacques Flamand, as he introduced himself, said, 'Well, yes, of course, I remember. Collette remarried a German officer she met in Paris after the battle of Waterloo.' Otto was invited to stay and was made most welcome. 'One of the family, well, well!' Jacques told Otto, 'You must visit Collette's family, the Armands. Like ourselves, they are still at the same house, our neighbours.'

It was a tremendously enjoyable encounter, the French and German branches of the family meeting with complete amiability.

'It is not us but our rotten governments who make us enemies.'

The troops equally enjoyed the holiday and many a village maiden would live to regret their encounter with the dashing, easygoing cavalrymen. All good things come to an end, however, and they set off to return to the boredom of the seige of Paris.

Inside Paris, the occupants were having a dreadful existence: cut off except by balloon and near starving, reduced to eating rats even. Towards the end of January 1871, the city surrendered and an armistice was declared. The peace settlement was ratified a month later and, more formally, in May 1871 by the Treaty of Frankfurt. The harsh provisions of the treaty gave Germany Alsace and Lorraine together with Metz. In addition, France had to pay an enormous indemnity and Germany would remain in the northern region of France until this was paid: a very severe punishment which was to smoulder resentment for the next four decades, culminating in the First World War in 1914.

The most calculated insult to France came when the Prussian king was proclaimed Kaiser Wilhelm I, Emperor of the German Empire, at Versailles. Versailles was the palace of the former kings of France. The ceremony took place, planned by Bismarck, a major triumph for the conniving statesman, in January 1871, as soon as the peace settlement was agreed. In the future, the Germans were also to be humiliated at Versailles.

When the proclamation of the Kaiser took place at Versailles, Otto's regiment was detailed as the sovereign's escort, one squadron leading the procession and two following behind the royal carriage, all in dress uniforms. Otto himself rode alongside the carriage. It was a very splendid affair and the French officials and personages who were obliged to attend at the palace looked very miserable and downhearted. Afterwards, the Kaiser held a medal parade, when he presented decorations to senior officers. Otto received the Prussian Order of Merit, the highest award. Bismarck saw Otto afterwards and congratulated him.

'You have earned the honour, Winterstein, a small consolation for your injuries.'

Soon after Versailles there was a victory parade by representative German military forces, cavalry artillery and infantry. The parade was led by the chosen cavalry regiments, including the *Uhlanen*. As they entered the Champs Elysée, Otto was unaware that they passed the building that housed Collette's couterie so many years previously. They proceeded up the Champs Elysée, lined by infantry to control the crowds, towards the Arc de Triomphe de l'Étoile, built to commemorate Napoleon's victories.

Halfway up the Champs Elysée, a woman broke through the line of soldiers, running towards Otto, who was riding alone in front of the regiment.

She pointed a revolver at him, held in her outstretched arm and crying, 'filthy German,' fired three shots before being cut down by Otto's second-in-command, who spurred forward.

Poor Otto stood no chance. She had approached him from his blind side. One bullet passed through his temple and into his brain and Otto fell from the saddle, dead. The body was quickly removed and the charger led away. The parade continued on its way. Otto's soldiers were very angry but showed restraint.

Shame. Poor Otto, after all a gallant soldier, undeserving of such an end. But he had had a good slice of the cake. War was indeed hell, but assassination worse. The assassin had lost her husband, killed at the Battle of Sedan. She died almost immediately from the savage cut to her head by the sword of Otto's major.

A few days later, a funeral procession took place, the cortege following the same route along the Champs Elysée. Otto's body, now embalmed and sealed in a magnificent coffin covered by the Prussian flag, was mounted on a gun carriage, drawn by troopers on foot. The Champs Elysée had been cleared and pedestrians were forced to stop and watch. The gun carriage was preceded by a squadron of *Uhlanen* and followed by Otto's charger, black plumed, led by his orderly, Otto's jackboots reversed in the stirrups. The other squadrons followed and behind them a battery of horse artillery and a battalion of the Prussian Guard. The parade dispersed at the Place de l'Étoile. Otto's remains were sent back to his home in Prussia for burial. Farewell Otto.

16

Germany

Bismarck had now achieved his aim, by successive wars, to unify the German states and create the German empire. Immediately following the conclusion of the Franco-Prussian War, Bismarck was elected chancellor, later to be called the Iron Chancellor.

Heide received many letters of condolence, from Bismarck and, incredibly, one from the Kaiser himself. Otto was very well regarded and had served Prussia honourably, a distinguished officer. Other letters poured in from senior officers, comrades and neighbours. One unusual letter was from Hamburg, signed by a princess, who said she was on a trade mission for her West African country. She had seen the sad news of Otto's death in the Hamburger *Zeitung*. She wrote that she had met Otto when they were on the same ship from New York to Hamburg. She would like to visit one day to pay her respects.

When the coffin arrived, it was interred in the family burial ground at Tilsit, now becoming more like a war cemetery. Otto was placed alongside the grave of his father, François, and both were below a memorial to Pierre, his grandfather, lost in Russia. All their men fallen, Heide moved in with her mother-in-law, Marlene, and together the two war widows consoled each other, concentrating on the running of and improvement to the great estate and their workers.

In due course, Comfort paid a short visit to Tilsit, in response to the invitation she received. Heide was astounded by the elegant beauty of the African princess, the like of which she had never imagined. She could understand that Otto had befriended her and it did cross her mind that perhaps there had been something more. Never mind, it was ended now, whatever. She showed Comfort the graves and told her briefly the stories of these, the fallen in battle. Comfort shed a tear, as women will. She told them that some of the men of her family had been slain in fighting against the British on the Gold Coast.

'I am on a mission to stimulate trade with our capital, Kumasi, where we have gold and diamond mines. At home I am known as the Diamond Princess. Not quite true, but it was a good cover story and, in fact, she was helping Ashanti at every opportunity through her clientele.

They parted firm friends, Heide begging Comfort to come again. They loved her unique foreignness, a welcome touch of colour.

Little Erika was now growing into a beautiful young girl, nearly ten years old and well taught by a governess who was permanently living with them. Marlene considered that Erika should not be a lone pupil and so they invited neighbours to send their young children. At present there was a class of six children, boys and girls from good families. Erika had become very friendly with a boy a little older than she, Paul von Ritter. Erika and Paul played often together, particularly at doctors and nurses, as children often do, as an excuse to examine their very different parts, the wee-wee hole and the winkle. This child love was to blossom in years to come, the first and never forgotten.

When Erika was 16 she went to a ladies' finishing school in Königsberg. Paul von Ritter was already at Heidelberg with his elder brother. They did not meet at Tilsit until two years later when Erika emerged a very beautiful and accomplished young lady. Many men tried to improve their acquaintance, but Erika was keeping herself for Paul.

When they met it was quite obvious to others that Erika and Paul were entranced with each other. Marlene and Heide were secretly pleased. Paul was a studious young man, unlike many hard-drinking, boisterous undergraduates. They thought that when, rather than if, they married, Paul would take over Tilsit. It was time there was a man about the place. Paul was indeed very reserved and it must be said that Erika, gay and high-spirited, led him by the hand up the path to intimacy. Once more the gazebo came in useful. Erika led Paul there and embraced him fervently.

"Now we are grown up, we should remember being sweethearts, when we were children,' she said. 'I have never forgotten my first and only love.'

After a close encounter, Paul said, That is as far as we should go now. Later, when we are betrothed, we shall see.'

During Paul's next vacation their betrothal was announced, with the approval of both families, the Wintersteins and Ritters. The Ritters were pleased that their youngest son would be off their hands and with an assured future. The marriage would not take place for another year as Paul wished to continue his studies at Heidelberg. He was taking philosophy under Friedrich Engels, a renowned social philosopher and an associate of Karl Marx, whose revolutionary ideas were to have far-reaching consequences in the future.

Although Paul would have liked to continue at the university, he was obliged to leave when, soon after returning to Heidelberg. Erika wrote that she was expecting a child. Once they were affianced, Erika, being of an amorous nature, lost no time in resorting to the love nest, the gazebo.

'Now you can have me,' she said to him. 'Come, my love, I have waited so many years for this.

And so he did, with more enthusiasm than might have been expected

Paul arrived back in Tilsit, much to the surprise of Heide. He explained that Karl Marx, Engel's friend, had died in England and Engel had gone there for an indefinite stay to clear up Marx's affairs. So the wedding arrangements were put in hand at once. It was a grand affair and although the Iron Chancellor could not attend, he sent a lavish wedding present with his best wishes. After the reception, the newly married couple left for a honeymoon in Italy, a friendly country which had been allied to Prussia when Bismarck was carrying out the second part of his plan to create a German Empire, against Austria.

They followed part of the route taken by Otto and his *Uhlanen* in the war, to Dresden on to Mernick and across the Alps to Milan and thence to Rome. They had an introduction to a German archaeologist, Professor Pulver, who had made his home in Rome, who to augment his means ran a pension. The pension was converted from a splendid house, formerly the Villa Corsini, on the west banks of the river Tiber, not far from Vatican City.

The professor showed them the Colleseum, round the Vatican City with the splendid St Peter Cathedral, the Castel St Angel and many fine palazzi and then left them on their own. They preferred to sit in the garden overlooking the busy Tigris, enjoying the warm sunshine, so different from the northern clime and, moreover, to drink the fine Italian wines and choice foods and make frequent love as newly-weds will. Two months later they were back at Tilsit, sun-tanned and very happy together, a good start to their married life. Heide scrutinised her daughter very closely for signs of pregnancy, but it was not until over three months, when she was showing, that Erika declared that she was with child. All were overjoyed. They now not only had a man to take care of things but perhaps his successor on the way.

When Erika gave birth, a bit prematurely it was considered, it was indeed a boy, who was in due course christened Karl, after Paul's father.

Karl, unlike his father, grew up to be boisterous and wild and when at Heidelberg given to wine and women, a bit of a rake. He naturally joined the University Officers Corps and showed an aptitude for things military, all for the best with Germany building up its armed forces. His close friend's father commanded a crack cavalry regiment and said that he himself would be joining the same unit.

'Perhaps you will join with me, Karl.'

The opportunity came sooner than expected. Karl was sent down from Heidelberg. He had usually assuaged his sexual appetites with the girls to be easily had in the taverns with no strings attached. However, he had become involved with the wife of a professor. She was much younger than her husband and, although considerably older than Karl, a very interesting lady and good in bed. It was their habit to meet at the professor's house when he was away on university affairs, which was fortunately frequent. Unhappily, the old man returned unexpectedly one night and found the pair asleep, entwined in his bed. So Karl was obliged to leave Heidelberg, not really in disgrace; after all it was a bit of a lark, a not uncommon display of high spiritedness.

Before he left, his friend said, 'Look, I am fed up with life here, I will go with you and we can join my father's regiment together.'

Karl returned to Tilsit and informed his parents that he had left Heidelberg and intended to join the army. He told them that he would have to purchase a commission, and that even though his friend's father was the colonel of the regiment, it would be expensive. Paul and Erika accepted that it was probably for the best, suitable to Karl's character. In any case, Karl now had a brother and a young sister. Karl told them that the regiment he intended to join was the prestigious *Toten Kopf Hussaren*, the Death or Glory cavalry boys, their badge a silver skull, the uniform black with silver trimmings. They were the flower of the German cavalry, brave, fine horsemen, bold, dangerous and rash, utterly reckless. Their counterpart in the British Army was the 17th Lancers, who distinguished themselves in the Crimea at Balaclava.

Whilst Karl was growing up many changes had occurred in Germany. Wilhelm I died and Wilhelm II was the Kaiser, Emperor of Germany and King of Prussia, a grandson of Queen Victoria of England. His overbearing character had clashed with that of the Iron Chancellor, Bismarck, whom he dismissed. The Kaiser appointed General Paul von Hindenberg as chancellor, which suited Wilhelm's naval, military and colonial aspirations. His plans considerably antagonised Britain, France and Russia. He particularly hated Britain as when he visited Queen Victoria, she treated him like a child, calling him disparagingly 'Little Willie'. He was also envious of Britain's enormous Empire, the map of the world coloured red, and of the supremacy of the Royal Navy.

So Germany was prepared to fight on two fronts: against France to the west and Russia in the east. The spark which was to ignite the war situation arose in Bosnia at Sarajevo, plotted by the Serbs as a move to liberate the Serbs under Austro-Hungarian domination.

17

Europe on Fire

The match was struck in the Balkans at Sarajevo in Bosnia, a region of Serbs, occupied by Austro-Hungary, as part of the attempt by Serbian nationalists to liberate their compatriots. On learning that the Archduke Ferdinand, heir to the Austrian Emperor Francis Joseph, was to visit Sarajevo at the end of June 1914, on a military inspection, the secret society, Union or Death, plotted his assassination, leading to the end of 40 years of uneasy peace.

On 28 June 1914 at Sarajevo, the Archduke Francis Ferdinand and his commoner, morganatic wife, Sophie, whilst driving in their open carriage, were shot dead by a Bosnian Serb, Gavrilo Princip. The Austrians immediately presented Serbia with an ultimatum the terms of which were so unreasonably harsh and unacceptable that war would inevitably follow. Austria already had Germany's support if it should start such a war and would also deter Russia, an ally of Serbia, from interfering. As Serbia's reply to the ultimatum was unacceptable, on 28 July 1914 the conflagration that was to set Europe on fire commenced with the Austrian artillery bombarding the Serbian capital, Belgrade.

The nations of Europe were allied in two potentially hostile groups: one Germany and Austria, with Turkey later on, and the other France, Britain, Russia, Italy and Japan, with the United States of America joining in 1917.

Russia ordered general mobilisation and Germany declared war against Russia in accordance with its treaty obligations to Austria. France rejected a German demand to remain aloof and then declared war against France. On 3 August Germany moved troops into Belgium and on the 4th, Britain having treaty obligations with Belgium, declared war against Germany. The stage was set for the Great War which was to last for four shocking years and cause the death of millions of soldiers and civilians.

Gräf Alfred von Schlieffen, a German field marshal, chief of the general staff, had already developed the Schlieffen plan in case of war with France. The plan called for an overwhelmingly strong strike through Belgium, capture of the English Channel ports and a sweep down onto Paris. At the same time, a weaker attack was to be mounted along the Franco-German border to keep the French occupied to the south.

The German army had been massed, ready for the off, along the borders of Belgium, Luxembourg and the Ardennes and Lorraine, from Aachen down to the Swiss border, concentrated on the north in accordance with the Schlieffen plan. At dawn on 2 August the Germans moved into poor little Belgium. The Cavalry division of General Kluck's First army crossed the border between the great fortress of Liege, mighty and important, and Maastricht, spearheading the push to capture Brussels. *Hauptmann* Karl von Ritter, now second-in-command of a squadron, was up front with the leading regiment, the *Toten Kopf Hussaren*. The sleepy border guards were swept aside like fallen leaves before a gust of wind and the cavalry pressed on at a smart pace. The die was cast. Britain, in accordance with the treaty with Belgium, immediately declared war against Germany.

A few miles on after passing through Tongeren, Karl's squadron spotted an enemy cavalry patrol crossing a ridge in front. Spurring on, the Hussaren pursued the patrol and upon reaching the crest observed a group of Belgian Dragoons, estimated at brigade strength, on the move towards the advancing Germans. The major sent Karl back to alert the brigade. Both forces met on the crest with a great clash of weapons. Karl was in great form. Here it was at last, what they had trained for in the years of soldiering. Karl's first blood came when confronting a dragoon officer: to parry his thrust and run him through his midriff, in, out and on to the next foe. The Belgians were no match for the élite Hussaren and gradually gave way. The

German cavalry would not disengage and literally ran their opponents into the ground. It was all over in a few hours of fighting. The Belgians, though half of their original number remained alive, surrendered. The German casualties were light. Next stop a short fifty miles away to Brussels.

Delaying tactics by the Belgians proved of no deterrent and in two weeks since crossing the border the Germans were in Brussels, which was to be theirs for the following four years, and had advanced beyond, southwards towards Paris.

Whilst the Germans were moving towards the French border, the small British Expeditionary Force was landing in France and moving up towards Belgium to the north of the French armies. Their object was to intercept the German advance. As soon as Britain declared war on Germany, the regular army began transportation to France. The army was highly trained and many soldiers were battle-experienced veterans of the South African War at the turn of the century, a great advantage over the Germans who had not been involved militarily for 40 years.

Before the end of August the British had reached Mons, an important town some 25 miles inside Belgium. Mons was situated at a junction of La Condé – Centre Canals which were the shipping route for the nearby coal mining district. Throughout previous centuries it had been repeatedly attacked in several wars. Now it was to host the first British-German battle of the Great War, the one to end all wars.

The German cavalry division leading General Kluck's First Army in the successful occupation had advanced from Brussels, through Halle and Waterloo, the scene of the Battle of Waterloo, when in 1815, Napoleon was finally defeated. At that time, the Prussian army, under General Blücher, were allied with the British, commanded by the Iron Duke, the Duke of Wellington. Beyond Soignies approaching Mons, they could hardly believe their eyes, but there in front, clearly visible through binoculars were to be seen khaki-clad horsemen, the British; the khaki uniform replacing the red coat during the South African War, the officers distinguishable only by the Sam Browne belts instead of webbing and riding boots, and the troopers' puttees. In a remarkably short time the expeditionary force had moved across the north of France:

Through the heavy August weather
The horse, the foot, the guns together,
and here they were, opposing the way into France, out in front of the La Condé canal.

The German brigade, comprising the *Toten Kopf Hussaren* and two *Uhlanen* regiments, paused to realign, the three regiments abreast, and then advanced somewhat cautiously towards the British. They could see the enemy cavalry coming up at the trot and were taken by surprise when at 1,000 yards they came under intense, accurate rifle fire. The British cavalry, comprising the Scots Greys and the Bays, with a long history of battle honours, had advanced with an infantry battalion, the Green Howards, the men clinging to the stirrups.

On the order from the British brigadier, 'Stand fast the Greys, stand fast the Bays and let the Green Howards go through,' the cavalry halted and the infantry deployed in front, lying and kneeling load.

The marksmen of the Howards were encouraged by their officers. 'See that Boche officer there in front, a shilling if you bring him down.'

Karl's major, felled from his horse by a bullet through his chest, was one of the army officers who earned a shilling for the riflemen. Karl took over the squadron and the brigade, overcoming the shock of the encounter, shook itself out and broke into a gallop to meet the British cavalry now advancing in front of their infantry.

Just before the stupendous clash of arms, Karl picked out the British Officer who, like himself, was leading a squadron. The officer was a captain, quite young, certainly a product of an English aristocratic family, as their cavalry officers inevitably were, and most likely in his first fight. Karl had the edge over his opponent, having bloodied his sword on Belgian dragoons. All around was the furious turmoil of a cavalry battle, men and horses vying with each other. Karl without hesitation slashed through the other's raised sword arm, causing the arm to fall uselessly, the sword hanging down by its knot. By an astonishingly swift movement, the officer grabbed his revolver hanging on its lanyard and fired at Karl. The bullet from the

Webley forty-five, of which it was said that it would bring down a running horse, struck Karl on the sword arm, smashing the humerus near the shoulder joint. Before he could deliver the coup de grâce with a further bullet, he was cut down by a hussar, who was alongside Karl. In great pain and with the shattered arm, with the now useless sword hanging on by the knot, causing unbelievable discomfort, he carried on with great courage. Controlling his horse with his knees, he drew his Mauser automatic pistol and carefully selected the targets offered, of which there was no shortage. He was closely supported by two of his men. The fight raged on, it seemed interminably, but in fact only a few hours, the contest split up into individual groups or single combatants, the field littered with the dead and dying, men and horses. In the end, the remnants of both sides were exhausted and by mutual consent withdrew: a draw to probably one of the last cavalry versus cavalry actions. The machine-gun and improved artillery weapons were to render the cavalry useless.

Karl at the end was in a sad state, exhausted and faint from loss of blood. He had continued to command the squadron to the bitter end, his orderly putting fresh magazines on the Mauser pistol, which was a deadly weapon at close range, semi-automatic and easy to use. He notched up quite a few of the enemy. The regimental surgeon dressed his arm and immobilised it against his chest. Then began the interminable journey in a motor ambulance, the way Karl had ridden full of expectancy of glory; a bumpy road to Brussels.

The Germans had commandeered all the hospitals, which were filling up with their wounded. The Battle of Mons had continued after the cavalry action when the main German forces arrived on the scene. Massed formations of infantry stormed up to the La Condé Canal. The British resisted with great courage and ferocity, the light Lewis machine-guns creating havoc on the packed mass of soldiery, more fodder for the already blood-soaked ground, or Brussels's hospitals. By the end of the day, the retreat from Mons had begun. The British fought a stubborn rearguard action but were forced back as the French, on their right, were retiring in disarray.

Back in Brussels, the surgeons removed Karl's arm. The humerus was shattered and beyond repair, close enough to the shoulder joint to make the attachment of an artificial limb impracticable.

The surgeon told Karl that he was sorry that the arm had to come off, 'But in a few weeks you will be fit enough to go back to the army. I am sure you will find a useful job away from the fighting.' He went on, 'To cheer you up, the Kaiser is paying us a visit next week and may even speak with you as an officer of one of his favourite regiments.'

The Kaiser came, splendidly dressed in a magnificent uniform from gold-embossed *Pickelhaube* helmet to shining black riding boots with gold spurs. He was accompanied by General Erich Ludendorff, the chief of staff to Hindenburg and, incidentally, the brains of the army. The party came to the room Karl shared with another officer and an aide introduced him to the emperor.

'Major Karl von Ritter, Iron Cross, first-class.'

An orderly handed the decoration to the Kaiser who carefully pinned it to Karl's chest, stepped back and saluted.

'Congratulations, major, a small compensation for the loss of your arm.'

Well, Karl thought, promotion and the Iron Cross, that's something to write home about. A major at 24 but perhaps unfit for anything but a desk job.

Karl's companion in the hospital was a Guards officer who had been wounded in the fighting which followed the cavalry action at Mons, his foot blown off by a Mills hand grenade. After a month they were allowed to go out into Brussels for short periods, a sorry pair, one on crutches, but nevertheless smart young German officers of élite regiments. A friendly doctor had told them to take a cab to a certain address where they would find all they were likely to want: wine, girls and food. The *maison de tolerance* was in the residential district not far from the hospital. They entered a splendidly furnished salon where scattered around were very decorative young ladies.

The madam greeted them with, *'Pauvre gentilhommes, blessé dans la guerre, c'est horrible. Quel dommage.'*

She sat them comfortably with glasses of fine French wine and told them that as they would both need some help, she would give them two of her best, willing girls.

'Afterwards you may care to dine, we have a marvellous cuisine.' Whilst sitting with their wine, a girl at the piano was playing a very popular song, others singing the refrain:

> *Après la guerre finir*
> *Soldat Allemand partir*
> *Mademoiselle mit Kind*
> *Après la guerre finir . . .*

and so on.

Karl and his companion had an unforgettable night and arrived back at the hospital satiated and very happy. They would certainly go there again.

Karl had carefully followed the progress of the war. By the end of August the Germans had advanced across the north of France and were a mere 25 miles from Paris, on the River Marne but within range of the great artillery piece, Big Bertha, which was mounted on a special railway truck. The British Expeditionary Force, having endured a spectacular retreat from Mons aided by the 6th French Army, brought up by taxicab from Paris, a theatrical but successful manoeuvre, dug in their toes and halted the German advance.

The Battle of the Marne was fought with great stubbornness by the Allies. The cause will never be known, certainly the German army was extended, with difficult lines of communication, but whatever, after a few days the Kaiser ordered a withdrawal. The news from the Eastern front was very encouraging. Since Germany declared war on Russia at the beginning of August 1914, the Russian 'Steam Roller' had waltzed through Poland into Prussia itself. Ably conducted by General Ludendorff, the German army defeated the Russians at Tannenberg at the end of August. The Czar's army never recovered from the crushing blow and thereafter it was a war of attrition, in which the Russians were relentlessly driven back, with enormous losses. The eastern front was a problem and the conflict ended in 1917 with the Russian revolution and overthrow of the Czar.

In France, the Allies, taking advantage of the German hesitation in fully carrying out the Schlieffen plan and their withdrawal, managed to stabilise a defensive line of up to 50 miles back from the furthest penetration of the Germans towards Paris. The line stretched from the Channel coast just inside Belgium and down through France along the Aisne River, by Arras, Soissons, Rheims, Verdun and on to the Swiss border; henceforth the war would be fought on territory in blood-soaked Flanders, already the scene of many previous conflicts throughout the ages.

In October Karl was discharged from hospital and ordered to report to the *Kriegs Ampt* in Berlin, to General Hans von Brausch, director of tactical planning for the Western front. The return journey was made easy as the mainstream of travellers and goods was in the other direction and there was no shortage of help for a wounded Hussar major sporting the Iron Cross. Karl was saddened to be leaving the action to ride the war out from a desk, but, who knows? In spite of his disability he might still get back into the fight.

Karl found General von Brausch to be an elderly officer who had seen service in Bismarck's campaigns against Denmark, Austria and France, very experienced and responsible. The general was directly under the command of Ludendorff, who was virtually second-in-command to Hindenburg. The general greeted Karl warmly.

'Ritter, I know your family well. Your maternal grandfather, Otto von Winterstein, was with me in the *Uhlanen* and we both had houses in Schwannenwerder, where I still live. Otto was a fine officer and his death at the hands of a mad French woman undeserved.' The general went on, 'I expect you feel disappointed at missing the fighting, but at least you took part in a spectacular cavalry battle and distinguished yourself. There will be no further role for the cavalry on the Western front and that is where the war will be fought. The east is a backwater and you are better off here. In any case, you are, unfortunately, no longer able to ride and fight well enough with one arm.'

Karl said he was pleased to be joining the general and would take up residence at Schwannenwerder where the family still kept the house.

'Meanwhile,' the general said, 'take a couple of weeks leave to see your family and then report back to me. I look forward to having you as my aide-de-camp.'

Karl went to Tilsit where Heide and Paul were so glad to see their son again.

Heide said, 'It is awful to see you like this with one arm missing, and the right one too, it must be very awkward. But we are lucky to see you at all. The family has been so much hurt by senseless wars.' She recalled, 'Your great, great grandfather, French Pierre, was killed in Russia during Napoleon's campaign of 1812. Then your great grandfather, François, was lost in Russian Crimea. Grandfather Otto, my father, was shot down in Paris. At least you are safe now.'

Karl told them about the posting to General von Brausch and that he would like to use the house at Spandau, on Schwannenwerder. His mother was enthusiastic and said that when Karl's leave was up she would return with him to put the house in order and engage servants.

'Also, it will be interesting to meet the general again. I knew him as a young girl when he was serving with the *Uhlanen* with my father. We were living at Schwannenwerder at that time.'

18

Hell on Earth

When Karl reported back to the general, he told him that he was moving into the house on Schwannenwerder and his mother, Heide, was helping him.

The general said, 'I remember your mother. I will ask you both to dinner, say tomorrow. Meanwhile, I have ordered a car with a driver for your use and an orderly from the *Toten Kopf's* depot. Now I will bring you up to date with the situation at the front.' Crossing to a map, the general pointed to Ypres, just across the French frontier into Belgian Flanders, and said, 'We are thrusting towards the Channel coast, to secure Dunkirk and Calais. The enemy in this section is the British Expeditionary Force and they are resisting very forcefully.'

The general said that he did sometimes visit the front but now the conflict was confused, with the action surging back and forth, very mixed up. He explained that whatever the outcome of Ypres, the German army was determined to hold on to the gains it had made so far. A system of trench warfare was being planned, a defensive line stretching from the Belgian coast, through France to the Swiss border. The continuous trench system, the trenches sufficiently deep to cover a standing man, were to be lined on the forward parapet, with sandbags and protected by barbed wire, entanglements in front: 'no man's land'. Dugouts would provide shelter for rest and side trenches for latrines. Communication trenches led to the rear for supplies and also connected to a support system of trenches for reserves, to fall back to in case of a successful enemy attack. The army engineers were responsible for the construction and provision of duckboards for a walkway along the bottom of the trench, as it was anticipated it would be continually wet and muddy in the inclement weather of the Low Countries. A continuous fire step would stretch along the side towards the enemy with duckboards and either sandbags or timber reveting, linings or supports as required. Strongly protected machine-gun emplacements were to be positioned so that the fields of fire from each one covered the area to the next emplacement.

The general pointed out that the conduct of the war had changed. Mobility and manoeuvre, the realms of good generalship, had been displaced by the emergence of rapid-firing artillery and the machine-gun. The British at Ypres were attempting to restore mobility, but so far, at enormous cost of lives, had failed to do so.

He said, 'We consider that static war is inevitable, so have developed the trench system. Let the enemy batter themselves against it and when they are eventually exhausted, we shall emerge from our fortress and destroy them.'

'As for your duties,' the general told Karl, 'I will send you to the front personally to assess the situation on the ground and the implementation of our planning.'

Karl was to go to the *Wehrmacht* headquarters at Brussels where, as the general's representative and therefore indirectly to Ludendorff, the great conductor of the war, he would be given every assistance. The general himself would occasionally go to the forward areas himself.

Karl and his mother went to the general's house on Schwannenwerder, which was near to their own.

The general greeted Heide with, 'I remember you as a young girl, when your father, Otto, was here, commanding the *Uhlanen* at Spandau. He was a fine man and a very good officer. A pity he met such a sad end.' He introduced the young lady with him. 'This is my daughter, Eva. Unfortunately, my wife died two years ago, but Eva looks after me very well.'

Eva was in her early twenties, perhaps two years younger than Karl and apparently unmarried; quite beautiful, well formed and attired, a very desirable young woman.

It was quite obvious to both the general and Heide that the young pair were immediately attracted to each other. And so it came to pass. They met as often as possible and very shortly Karl asked Eva to marry him. Such hurried betrothals were common in wartime, but theirs was different in that Karl would not be departing for the front and, as it was happening, to almost certain death, such were the casualty rates. The general gave his consent with pleasure: two fine, landed, Prussian families cementing their birthright.

They married in January 1915 and had a short honeymoon at Tilsit. There was nowhere else they could go outside of Germany. Battles were in progress all around. Italy was with the Allies and Turkey had joined Germany.

Before the wedding, in December, the general sent Karl to Brussels to visit the front and report on the consolidation following the inconclusive end of the Battle of Ypres. After three weeks of heavy fighting with considerable losses, both sides were digging-in. Karl reported at headquarters, Brussels, and was handed over to a staff colonel, who put him in the picture.

The colonel said, 'Following Ypres, there is very little activity, occasional shelling and the enemy have introduced aerial warfare in the form of small aircraft armed with machine-guns, in order to strafe our lines. In addition, they have observation planes which drop small, hand-held bombs on likely targets. In this new form of warfare, no place is safe. Even our headquarters in prominent chateaux are targets.'

Karl found Brussels teeming with soldiery, the Belgian civilians moving around somewhat furtively, a little quiet and ashamed, suffering from the ignominy of their swift defeat and surrender. Although Karl was newly affianced to Eva, he decided to pay a visit to the *maison* he had used when hospitalised in Brussels. The madam was genuinely pleased to see him.

She said, 'The girl you had before has gone, but I have a new, very young girl, almost a virgin and very pretty.'

So Karl found, to his pleasure, that she was indeed very young and inexperienced. Karl thoroughly enjoyed her, thinking that this was how Eva would be: a tight encounter.

The staff colonel told Karl the next day that he had arranged for him to visit the Prussian Brandenburger Division, one of the best groups in the *Wehrmacht*. The Brandenburgers were holding the line in front of Ypres and divisional headquarters was at Passchendale. A car would deliver Karl there and the Brandenburger general would look after him.

'I suggest you spend a week with them. You should be able to visit the front line and see the situation for yourself.'

The drive of some 50 miles through the wintry, wet Flanders countryside was slowed down by the volume of traffic on the roads, which were becoming worn and potholed by columns of heavily-laden infantry in full marching order, all kinds of motor and horse-drawn transport, supplies and equipment for trench construction, ominous groups of ambulances, empty out, laden coming away from the front, jolting uncomfortably over the uneven carriageway, all wet, muddy and miserable.

At the divisional headquarters of the Brandenburgers, in a magnificent chateau, Karl presented his credentials to a staff colonel, introducing him as an emissary from General Brausch of Tactical Planning on a tour of inspection.

'Ritter,' said the colonel, 'I know your family. It is a good time to visit the front as "Tommy" is, like ourselves, entrenching.' He went on to say, 'I see that riding up to the communication trenches would not be easy for you, so you can use one of our new motorcycles with a sidecar.'

Karl spent the evening in the mess, which was lavishly furnished and where the regimental silver trophies were on display and on the walls tattered battle standards. In the ante-room, before dinner, Karl met the major general commanding the Brandenburgers. The General was a splendid figure of a soldier with a chest covered with medals and decorations, a typical Prussian Officer of the old school. Karl thought, yes a fine man, but too old for the new kind of static war and different armaments.

Karl found the motorcycle waiting for him in the morning, with a smart corporal rider and his orderly, who could ride pillion. The sidecar was comfortably cushioned and there was a machine-gun mounting in front. The machine-gun had been removed. The going was quite good, the roads less congested as they approached the front. Less than ten miles from Passchendale, they reached the headquarters of one of the Brandenburgers' brigades, which was at a farmhouse, very close to the lines. The brigadier, who turned out to be an elderly Prussian officer of the old school, said that Karl could go that afternoon to one of the regiments, accompanied by a staff captain. The line was quite close, a mile down the communications trench.

He went on to say, 'A raid is laid on at nightfall so you will see some action.'

The staff captain guided Karl and his orderly along a communication trench, where Karl first experienced the awful, chalky mud of Flanders which covered the duckboards. To slip off the boards meant probable immersion up to the knees in a gooey mess and to fall down; to say the least, very uncomfortable. Karl, without one arm, found keeping balance difficult. His orderly, well aware of the problem, kept a hold on his belt in case he slipped. They were obliged to make way for parties going the other way: injured men, runners and returning carriers of food, ammunition and water, the latter a constant flow, the only way to supply the huge numbers of troops in the trenches.

On arrival at the front line, all was quiet, one could hear the bird-song and the infrequent clatter of arms and utensils and quiet voices, even from the enemy lines a few hundred yards away. They reported to the regimental command dugout, a substantial affair, well shored up and faced with timber. The colonel turned out to be a younger man than his superiors and more adaptable to the new form of conducting a war. He suggested Karl traverse the regiment's part of the line; he could observe over the ground, which was no man's land, through the frequent periscopes. Off they went, passing the soldiers squatting against the trench walls, all ready for any action. Occasionally there were snipers, marksmen, on the fire-step, protected by sandbags, alert for the slightest movement above the enemy trench. The guide said that the snipers' score was quite high; men could not resist the temptation to have a look. At intervals there were Maxim machine-gun emplacements, their interlocking fire covering the whole front. Karl found it weird to look out through a periscope across the strip of land between the contestants, barbed wire strung out in front of both sides; shell holes filled with chalky rainwater, discarded arms and equipment; some corpses being consumed by rats, which swarmed over the battle zone; a kind of hell, but at present deceptively quiet.

In the evening, after dusk, Karl watched the raiding party consisting of a lieutenant, a sergeant and ten men, clamber out of the trench. They were carrying only essentials to facilitate stealthy movement, nothing to make a rattle. They disappeared into the muck and mud, silently towards the enemy trench. There was no warning, no shots rang out and after less than one hour they were back, bringing six Tommies, a corporal and five privates. The Brandenburgers had been lucky. They did not have to go into the trench. The prisoners were a wiring party, caught in the open. One had resisted forcefully and was quickly despatched by a single thrust of a trench knife. There was no fire as both sides were out there together, but, later, flares went up, turning the night into day. A salvo of artillery shells followed, high explosive bursting and shrapnel whistling in the air; as it happened, quite harmlessly.

At dawn the following day, the British guns from the artillery lines behind the front line opened up a barrage of shells falling just in front of the Brandenburgers. Some shells exploded in their trench and close by Karl, who, rudely awakened from his slumber in a dugout, witnessed a direct hit in the trench a few yards further along. Men, weapons and debris were flung into the air, a frightful shambles. There were a dozen blown to bits and as many wounded. Through a periscope, Karl saw a line of khaki-clad figures emerge from the British lines and immediately the Maxims chattered and rifle fire cracked from the Brandenburgers' manned fire-step. It appeared to be an attack limited to a brigade front as the lines to the north and south were quiet. The advancing figures were mown down by the intense small arms' fire and the German artillery added to the slaughter. Still, a few very brave men came on and even reached the Brandenburgers' trench throwing hand grenades, only to be very quickly despatched.

It was soon over, a strike that fizzled out with a terrible loss of life, totally wasted. Karl considered the awfulness of 'going over the top', out in face of an appalling hail of fire with little chance of survival. What a display of unbelievable courage, and what a waste, with nothing gained. Stretcher-bearers were out, safe under the Red Cross flag, retrieving the wounded and the dead and those wounded who had drowned in water-filled shell holes. Unbelievable hell. The Brandenburgers were busy clearing up and repairing the damaged shell-torn trench. Karl spent a few days at brigade and visited the front daily, where all was quiet as though nothing had happened and there was no war on.

Karl went back to Berlin and reported to the general. Eva was blooming and excitedly she told Karl she was pregnant. They shared the great joy the news gave them but decided to keep it to themselves until it was obvious.

Allied offensives continued throughout the spring of 1915, all wasted, costly efforts. The Germans sat firm, holding their line whilst the enemy battered futilely against it, not an inch of ground gained. Towards the end of April, the British mounted a full-scale operation, involving special corps, the second Battle of Ypres. Coordinated by General Brausch, Tactical Planning had developed, with German scientists, a secret weapon, gas. The poison gas chosen was chlorine, its fumes, greenish yellow, its odour suffocating, heavier than air, destroying the lungs. It was contained in steel cylinders for transportation to the front. Phosgene, a gas with similar lung-affecting characteristics, was also to be used, contained in artillery shells. The Allies' push had been anticipated and, combined with observations from the front, reports from spies had indicated the Ypres area. Gas was to be the surprise countermeasure.

When Karl returned from the first visit to the front he discussed with the general the supply of rations to the forward areas. Currently the soldiers existed on tinned *wurst*, black *brot* and potatoes, sugar and condensed milk, coffee, which as the war went on, increasingly was mixed with acorns, sometimes tinned peaches were on the menu. Cigarettes, cigars and pipe tobacco were rationed; there was a daily issue of cognac, *Weinbrand* and sometimes a bottle of *Steinhager* gin. Karl suggested adding onions and garlic, cheese and jam to the issue and more tinned fruit and vegetables. The general leant on the supply services and in subsequent visits to the lines, Karl noted a marked improvement in the soldiers' material lot.

Apart from gas, weaponry had been augmented by the trench mortar, which could throw bombs right into the opposition's trenches, and a small quick-firing cannon which could deliver shells over open sights from front line emplacements.

The British attack was preceded by several days of artillery bombardment, which gave the Germans ample warning of the assault. When the British infantry emerged from their positions, they were mown down by machine-gun and rifle fire. The day's casualties to the enemy were the heaviest they had sustained so far. Karl was at the front to witness the use of the poison gas, which came as a complete surprise to the Allies.

Steel cylinders containing the chlorine were placed at suitable intervals along the trench parapet. The soldiers handling the cylinders and those in the vicinity were equipped with gas masks, covering the nose, mouth and eyes. The contaminated air filtered through a canister filled with activated charcoal, just in case the prevailing wind, which was towards the British lines, veered round. When the second wave of infantry appeared they were allowed to come well into no man's land. As the cylinder valves were opened the visible cloud of gas spread over the oncoming troops. Watching from the flank through binoculars Karl witnessed the shattering effect of the gas: men coughing and choking, eyes streaming, rendered almost helpless. He saw some men cover their faces with handkerchiefs or pieces of cloth wetted with water, or their own urine. This was partially successful against the gas and some very brave soldiers reached the trench and captured a gas cylinder and masks. The Allied attack was a complete failure. The men who survived were to live out their often short lives in agony, with constant bronchitis and continuing disintegration of the lungs.

In the coming months the Germans introduced new types of chemical warfare weapons, which even more reduced men's appetites for fighting. Mustard gas, so named because of its mustardy odour, was a colourless oily liquid compound of carbon, hydrogen, chlorine and sulphur, product of the brains of I.G. Farben, the great German chemical firm. Mustard gas vapour attacked the mucous membranes of the respiratory tract, destroyed lung tissues, blistered skin and caused conjunctivitis. Horrible. The countermeasures required that no body areas be exposed. Lewisite, equally nasty, also attacked the skin, so that soldiers encumbered with additional gear to their already heavy equipment, had to struggle on. 'Go over the top,' or be shot for cowardice in face of the enemy. These new weapons were making hell on earth even more diabolical. In due course, the Allies responded with similar chemical weapons.

The von Ritters in the course of time were rewarded with the birth of a son whom they named Kurt. Both families were overjoyed.

The general soon after the happy event, told Karl, with a twinkle in his eye, 'I am making you up to *Oberst*. You deserve it for the good work you have done for the planning department and in any case, Kurt should at least have a colonel as a father.'

So life, in spite of the war, looked rosy for Karl and Eva.

The Allied offensives carried on throughout the winter of 1915, with freezing cold and snow added to the burden of the miserable men in the trenches. Early in 1916 the general told Karl that the High Command had decided to carry out an attack at Verdun, where they had been successful in 1870 and incidentally had taken prisoner the Emperor Napoleon III.

'Your grandfather, Otto von Winterstein, was there commanding his regiment, the *Toten Kopf Hussaren*,' the general remarked. Karl was to go to the Brandenburger Division. 'You know them well and it is best that you observe their activities,' said the general.

In late February Karl was at the Brandenburgers' divisional headquarters, when the heaviest artillery bombardment so far experienced in the war began on the front opposite Verdun. The French trenches and barbed wire were destroyed and under a creeping barrage of shellfire, the German infantry advanced the first day some two or three miles. They had broken the static war situation. Before the end of the month the Germans had captured all the forts around Verdun and were attacking on both sides of the River Meuse. Paris, a mere 100 miles away, was in sight. Karl kept up with the progress of the battle from advanced brigade headquarters, very close to the actual fighting. Although the Brandenburgers continued to advance, French resistance was very stubborn and on both sides the casualty rate was horrendous, the wounded coming back from the front, stumbling along or stretcher-borne in pathetic columns.

The German offensive was slowed down by diversionary attacks on the Russian front and the Italians on their front, both requiring removal of troops from the western front. In addition, General Pétain took over command of the French, inspiring new efforts to save Paris. Nevertheless, the German advance crept forward throughout the coming weeks until the British opened up their offensive on the River Somme. Thereafter the intense struggle at Verdun died down and the Germans ceased to send further reinforcements to the sector.

The Battle of the Somme began at the beginning of July, preceded by a week of artillery bombardment, which gave the Germans ample warning of the event. The Brandenburgers had been pulled from the line to replace their numerous casualties and recoup for the next round. Karl was back in Berlin to report to General Brausch, who told him to take a few days' leave and take Eva and the baby Kurt to Tilsit to see their parents.

The general told Karl, 'We are anticipating a major attack on the Somme. Our spies report the unconcealed preparations in that sector, held by the British. I have planned a surprise for the Tommies. When their artillery barrage falls on our front line it will be empty, except for a few observers. Our troops will be safe in a second line to the rear, ready to counter the assault. As soon as you return from Tilsit you will go back to the Brandenburgers to observe the result of this manoeuvre.'

Karl returned to the front, feeling somewhat sickened by the thought of seeing once more the seemingly endless, futile conflict, in which both sides were so far only losers. He had seen in Berlin many ex-soldiers displaying their terrible wounds and almost beggared. Conditions among the civilian population were not too good. There were inevitable shortages, caused by the blockade of supplies from abroad by the Allied navies, in spite of the activities of the U-boats of the Kaiser's High Seas Fleet, and the *Kriegs Marin*.

At the front Karl found that the British had already started the massive preliminary bombardment. It was known that 11 British divisions, some 100,000 men and 5 French divisions to the south, were in place ready for the attack. The Germans were safely ensconced in their concealed positions whilst their old front line was continuously pounded by heavy shells and mortar bombs. After a week of shelling the British emerged from their trenches, confident that no man's land would be secure from the German defenders, or what was left of them. The 60,000 attacking infantry were allowed to move forward unmolested almost in symmetrical parade formation. Karl watched with amazement the mass of men slowly advancing towards the German lines. Then the German machine-guns opened up and the enemy were mown down in masses. Still they came on and reinforcements followed, more 'cannon fodder.' At the end of the day the British had suffered the heaviest day's loss ever sustained by a British army. The generals sat back in comfort, urging the troops on to more sacrifices, no more leading from the front like kings and queens and generals in former times.

The Brandenburgers' brigadier, whom Karl by now knew very well, was paying a visit to the front line on the second day of the battle and met the colonel and his second-in-command in their dugout for a conference. There was desultory shelling but for the moment the scene was quiet. The brigadier and the colonel, with his staff officer, were drinking coffee laced with cognac and the air was thick with cigar smoke. By unlucky chance a shell had their names on it. The projectile tore through the blanket-covered entrance and exploded in the crowded space. All inside were blown to bits. A tremendous loss. Karl was in the line, luckily outside in the trench. He was horrified; such a shocking, sudden loss, indeed hell on earth.

Karl left on one of his periodic visits to Berlin and told the general about the battle.

'Your plan to empty the front line trench was totally successful. The Tommies were literally slaughtered.'

The general said, 'It is not yet over. Haig, their commander, will keep them fighting, regardless of losses.' He went on, 'I heard about the tragic loss of the brigadier. So many of our senior ranks are being lost by such mischance. It may surprise you that I am going to recommend that you take over the brigade.'

Karl was astounded.

'General, I am much too young for such a command and, in any case, I have only recently been promoted. There must be others more suited.'

The general replied, 'It will be considered to be nepotism, but it is not the case. We need young blood in this modern war. You have seen action and have closely observed events at the sharp end. We will see what the powers that be decide.'

The brigade, without a leader, was temporarily parcelled out among the other two units until a new commander appeared. Karl had a few days with his family, until the general informed him that his appointment had been approved. He was to take a very short staff course and, immediately following, take over the brigade.

It was a great surprise but his acquaintances told him, 'Well, promotion in wartime is quick if you survive. Into dead man's shoes, if you are lucky.'

Haig's next move was against the southern sector of the Somme battlefield. This time the British were partially successful. With enormous loss of life, they took the German front line position, but were unable to exploit this gain, foundering against stubborn resistance. So it continued throughout the summer of 1916, the British making small gains at great cost to both sides, but serving no purpose in winning the war.

Karl duly completed his course and was gazetted Brigadier-General Karl von Ritter. His mother, visiting Schwannenwerder at the time, was very pleased.

'Well done, Karl, we have not had a general officer before in the family. Although I believe your grandfather, Otto von Winterstein, my father, was offered promotion, but preferred to remain with his regiment.'

Karl told her, 'I am lucky, that is all. The brigadier of the Brandenburgers, whom I have been observing, was killed at the front.'

His mother said, 'You must take great care. Surely nowadays a general does not have to actually engage in combat.'

Karl explained, 'Mother, I will need to show my face in the front line sometimes, but I will take care. My predecessor was unlucky.'

Karl took over the brigade when it was out of the line, resting at the rear. He sensed some opposition from some of the older senior officers, but never mind; at this stage of the war, all were only concerned with staying alive.

The British were now also using poison gas, although it was proving to be more of a nuisance than an effective weapon. The wearing of gas masks was another burden for the suffering troops, in addition to the interminable wet, muddy trenches, lice and monotonous rations with leave to go home if you survived or were severely wounded. Gas could only be used if the wind was in the right quarter, which favoured the Germans, but could also veer round and blow back over the users.

In mid-September the British launched their secret weapon, the tank, or land battleship. The first tanks to appear, untried in battle in their developing stages, which would have lost the advantage of surprise, were the Mark I, known as 'Little Willie'. This massive machine, propelled by 'caterpillar' tracks, 28 tons weight with a speed of less than four miles per hour, had a protective shell of half-inch thick armour plate. The armament was considerable, two six pounder artillery pieces and four machine-guns, a veritable land battleship. The crew of eight, tank commander, engine mechanic, gunners and steersmen, the tank was steered by applying a brake to either track, operated under a tremendous strain. Inside the hull, in effect a small room with a height that did not allow a man to stand upright, the noise was so great that speech was impossible and communication was by signs. In addition, the temperature rose to tropical heights and the crew suffered from thirst and became sick and feverish from the engine fumes and, even worse, from cordite when the guns were fired.

Some 50 tanks took part in the first assault, preceded for several days by a heavy bombardment of the German lines, who were, of course, warned of a forthcoming attack. About a third of the cumbersome vehicles broke down before reaching no man's land. More ended up bogged down in shell holes. From the front line the Brandenburgers observed with amazement this strange apparition and an urgent message was sent back to Karl at advanced brigade position. Karl, seeing the observation slits in the armour plate, diverted snipers to fire at them, in the hope of wounding or killing the crew. It was noticed that the special, steel-cored bullets used by the marksmen actually penetrated the armour and caused injury or damage inside: an anti-tank weapon besides the artillery.

A few tanks broke through the German defences, causing the occupants to withdraw under the hail of fire from 6 pounders and the machine-guns. The attack soon fizzled out. Those few tanks that broke through reached the limit of their range, some 20 miles, or broke down with mechanical failure, ending in their capture.

So a new terror weapon was introduced. The German High Command examined the captured tanks and decided that such a weapon was not viable. Look what happened to their initial employment. The high morale of the German troops, and the future embodiment of close support artillery in an anti-tank role, would counter the threat. The Brandenburgers had enclosed the small gain in a ring of steel and prevented any further attempt by the British infantry. Karl felt some pity for the exhausted crews who emerged from the tanks and invited a major, apparently in command, to have refreshments at brigade. The major, without disclosing any secrets, told him quite a bit about the new weapon. The French were also producing their own tank, a Renault of much lighter construction than the British monster. This was not to be used in action until mid-1917.

In November the rains literally turned the battlefield into a quagmire: waterlogged trenches, no man's land a muddy swamp, practically impassable; lines of communications unable to supply an army in battle. So ended the Battle of the Somme, which cost the Allies more than half a million casualties and the Germans about the same: a miserable failure for the Allies except that it diverted a possible German success at Verdun and beyond.

In early 1917 the Germans withdrew to the Hindenburg line, a carefully prepared fortified position, stretching from the Belgian coast to the Swiss border, through Belgium and along the French borderlands. It was considered to be impregnable. The Allies could wear themselves out with the continual offensives. The Brandenburgers were in the line where most activity took place, on the British sector to the north. Karl had a more permanent brigade headquarters and life was not unbearable. He looked after his men and spent more time in the front line than most generals.

On a short visit to Berlin, he very much enjoyed seeing Eva and their son, Kurt, who was by now walking and talking. Their lovemaking was very vigorous, spurred on by the general desperation of the war, which was affecting everyone, particularly the civilians. Before Karl went back he suggested that Eva should leave Berlin and return to Tilsit. The British had commenced bombing raids over Germany in response to the Zeppelins dropping bombs on London.

Better be away from the danger if they reach Berlin, he decided.

The Allies continued their attacks in 1917 at Ypres, Arras, Messines, Passchendale and Cambrai. At Cambrai, the British employed a formidable formation of over 400 tanks which carried out a surprise attack on the Hindenburg line. There was no warning artillery bombardment to alert the Germans. The tanks advanced behind a ferocious creeping barrage of shells and, simultaneously, the rear areas were bombed and strafed by an aerial armada, all the planes that could be assembled. The tanks penetrated the so-called impregnable line over a length of some 20 miles and to a gain in depth up to 10 miles, the greatest move since the stalemate in 1915. The Germans were driven back to the final prepared line of defence where, by heroic action and much loss of life, the advance of the tanks was held. Brave men clambered on to the monsters and threw hand grenades down the hatches. A new weapon using petrol, a flame thrower, was most effective, setting fire to the tanks, which roasted the crews or blew them up if the ammunition exploded. The Brandenburgers suffered heavy casualties and the division was withdrawn for reforming. Karl had a short leave and found that Eva, not unsurprisingly, was pregnant.

The population was becoming dissatisfied with the war, which seemed to go on endlessly with more and more shortages and bereavements. Most families had lost someone at the front.

The Allies were in a similar state and at the front the British army was practically worn out, having borne the brunt of the fighting. So many of the original force had been lost and the remainder, mainly conscripts, were not of the same mettle: 'the best have gone before you'. However, the Australians and Canadians were showing sterling strength and drive. In April 1917 the Americans declared war on Germany, angered by the sinking of their ships by German U-boats. This event was the turn of the tide, fresh troops with the latest equipment. Nevertheless, the Germans fought on. In November the Russian revolution put an end to the war on the Eastern front, with consequent extra troops for the Hindenburg line.

On leave in Berlin, Karl visited his father-in-law and former chief, General Brausch, who intimated confidentially that with the Americans joining the Allies, the war might go badly for Germany. He also suggested that Karl could very well be promoted to major general and take over a division. There were some commanders too old and worn out by the constant fighting. Karl said that he preferred to remain with his brigade of Brandenburgers, of much more use to the emperor than commanding a probably weaker division of second line troops.

Karl kept the house on Schwannenwerder open for his use when in Berlin and employed a discharged wounded soldier and his wife to look after the premises as manservant and housekeeper. The poor man had received a terrible head wound and was not entirely capable. However, his young wife was able to look after him and put him to work on cleaning and gardening. One night Karl was awakened by shrill cries and he went to the attic where Emma and her husband slept. Entering, he found Emma struggling to hold her husband, who was thrashing about violently on the bed.

'He is having a fit,' she explained, 'it is his poor head. It occurs sometimes but he soon recovers and falls asleep.' Karl helped her to restrain Rudolf and soon he did indeed fall asleep.

Emma said, 'I am sorry, general, thank you for your kind help.'

Karl noticed that her nightdress was ripped open, revealing a considerable amount of flesh. She noticed he was looking and hurriedly tried to cover herself, blushing coquettishly.

She said, 'Shall I make you some coffee, general?'

Karl said, 'Please. You can bring it to my room.'

When Emma came back with the coffee, she had tidied her dress but without delay Karl reached out for her and pulled her on to the bed, exclaiming, 'Never mind the coffee, I want something else.'

He had abstained from sex with his wife Eva whilst she was pregnant and found Emma very willing and satisfying. That was one problem out of the way. No conscience, he thought, when the urge drives.

19

The Final Act

In the spring of 1918 Ludendorff opened an offensive aimed between the British and the French sectors. Karl's brigade spearheaded the thrust to break through the weak area. They succeeded in establishing a bulge several miles in depth, a considerable achievement. Karl moved up his headquarters and, supported by the rest of the division and other troops, held on to their gain for several weeks, a thorn in the Allies' side. Ludendorff's plan was to make a breakthrough from the advantage point gained and possibly end the war. The gunners launched the offensive, for the first time using a German tank which had been secretly developed, known as A7V. The tanks advanced, with Karl's men close behind, forerunners of the Panzer Grenadiers. The advance was very successful, much ground was won, until countered by a force of the new British light Whippet tank. A tank versus tank battle ensued, the first of its kind and quite like the cavalry battles of former years.

The tanks, more mobile than the original heavies, buzzed around like angry hornets, guns blazing at each other, and soon the area was a cauldron of knocked out flaming tanks. The crews baled out or were roasted to death. The brigade was obliged to retire and Karl ordered them to dig in behind the tanks, observing the furious engagement with amazement, a new method of conducting war. He thought, if the tanks could break through they could reach Paris. In the end the Whippets were more numerous and gained the ascendancy. Taking advantage of the situation, the British tanks advanced swiftly, closely followed by a massive formation of infantry. The Germans were forced to pull back and, unable to halt, returned to their original line before the offensive. So ended Ludendorff's spring attack, both sides suffering heavy losses to no purpose.

The division was relieved, having borne the brunt of the fighting for several months, to reform and get in shape for what must be a final effort to defeat the Allies. Karl returned to Tilsit for the birth, which was overdue. He found that Eva was having problems. The baby was reluctant to appear and the doctors considered force to be unwise. Soon after his arrival, a great tragedy occurred. Wakened in the night by terrible screams, he went to their bedroom. The doctor and a midwife were bent over Eva, who was writhing in agony. The doctor hurried him out of the room.

'It will be all right, general, a difficult birth. The baby is very large. I will come to you when it is all over.' Eventually the screaming ceased and the doctor appeared dishevelled and spattered with blood. 'I am sorry,' he said, 'your wife is no longer with us. She suffered an enormous haemorrhage. Regretfully, the baby, a boy, was no longer breathing, strangulation caused by the convulsions of the mother. A terrible blow for you.'

Karl was by now well acquainted with blood and gore and sudden death and although he was terribly upset by the tragic loss, quickly recovered. His mother Erika was very considerate.

'You will have to go back to the awful war, I know,' she said, 'but you can leave Kurt safely with me. He is growing into a fine boy, the Prussian air suits him.'

Karl said, 'Mother, I have thought carefully about it and I would like to take Kurt to Schwannenwerder. I have a good manservant and a housekeeper and, above all, I want my son to go to the old school at Spandau. The school for officers' children has served our family very well and it is a good start in life.'

Reluctantly Erika agreed saying, 'I am managing very well here as you can see; the agent is a very experienced man.'

Karl thought that perhaps the man was also experienced in other activities; he was a quite handsome, well set up fellow and his mother was only in her early fifties.

She continued, 'One day, when the war is over, I am sure you will return to take over the family estates. I pray always that you will be kept safe. You will, I hope, come when you are able, bringing the boy with you.'

When Karl went to Schwannenwerder there was another surprise. Emma told him that her husband, Rudolf, had gone out of his mind as a result of his head wound and had to be admitted to an asylum.

The doctors told me,' she said, 'that it is unlikely that he will recover and be able to leave the institution.'

Karl said, 'I am terribly sorry for you. We have both suffered terrible losses. We must comfort each other.'

Emma replied, 'I will always stay with you so long as you want me, general.'

Karl said, 'You must call me Karl, at least when we are alone. I am more than fond of you and we are good for each other in bed, which is, after all, very important, and I am happy that you will take care of Kurt when I am away.'

That night Emma came to the bedroom and, standing in front of the bed, took off her clothes slowly. Karl exclaimed, 'Come here, you lovely thing,' thinking, well, Emma is truly lovely. I am well satisfied. Farewell to the old and into the new.

Before going back to the front he made financial arrangements for Emma and with the officers' school for Kurt. He told her to engage any servants as she thought fit.

'If you wish to have your family visit, that will be all right,' he told her.

She said, 'I am an orphan. My father, a sea captain, was lost in a storm in the Baltic when his ship capsized. My mother was with him and so I was brought up by an aunt, who is now dead. I married Rudolf when I was working in the hospital where he was being treated. Probably I do not love him, but it was expedient for me to marry.'

Karl went back to France and rejoined the brigade, which moved with the division to the area in the Ardennes near Soissons, a hitherto quiet sector. The divisional commander outlined the plan which was to make an all-out assault into the Marne region towards Chateau-Thiery, from where Paris was only 20 miles away. The Brandenburgers climbed out of the trench with other divisions on both flanks. The attack had been preceded since midnight by a massive bombardment of high explosive and gas shells. The night sky was a sheet of flame. The projectiles could be heard, a sibilant swish as they passed overhead. At the receiving end, the trenches only a short distance away, they could feel the earth shuddering under the avalanche of explosives.

Poor fellows, they are getting a terrible hammering. There will be nothing left for us.

So it was. There was little opposition to the German push, the weak defence and the sector occupied by second-rate French divisions collapsed. The Brandenburgers moved rapidly across a hitherto undisturbed area and by dawn the next day were at Belleau Wood near the objective, Chateau-Thiery. Karl had moved his forward post behind the brigade and at daybreak could observe that the advance was held up. He went forward with his orderly and found the brigade gone to ground.

The colonel of the leading regiment told him that when they reached the position in front, just beyond the wood, they came under a hail of bullets and bursting shells from close support French 75s, a formidable artillery piece. In spite of the storm of fire, the Brandenburgers, even though these days weakened by the new replacements, older men and almost young boys, the Fatherland having suffered so many casualties was now forced to conscript men hitherto not soldier material, fought on and reached the enemy trench. Hand-to-hand fighting took place and in the end the Brandenburgers were driven back into the wood, finally managing to hold the present hastily dug line.

'The enemy,' said the colonel, 'were troops we had not met before, young, fit and well equipped. I realised that the Americans had arrived.'

The next day the Brandenburgers were to stand to before dawn when, covered by an intense barrage, the Americans poured out of their trenches. The Brandenburgers met the attack with a murderous fire from the Maxim machine-guns and rifles. Still the Americans advanced, in spite of heavy losses. Close combat ensued, bayonets and pistols. The enemy pressing with the vigour of fresh troops, forced the Germans to withdraw to hastily prepared positions some miles back, much of the previous gains lost. The division was pulled back to rest as they had, as was usual for them, borne the heaviest combat and consequent losses.

The Germans managed to hold on to the bulge throughout the months of June and July, but the drive to reach Paris was foiled. The Allies in August mounted a full-scale attack from the Retz Forest, along the front between Soissons and Chateau-Thiery, aimed at driving the Germans out of the bulge and back to the Hindenburg Line and, who knows, even beyond? The Brandenburgers were in the line in front of Vierzy, where Karl had his brigade headquarters, some few miles behind the front. The Americans, who were attacking, were cut down by a murderous hail of fire, literally mown down. Still they came on and by nightfall had gained considerable ground. The Brandenburgers had been driven back to a line just in front of Vierzy, forced to retreat when enemy tanks joined the battle.

In the early morning the enemy came on in strength regardless of casualties, which reduced their number to a few stalwarts, who reached the Brandenburgers' position. The Americans held on gamely in close combat; fresh and fit, young men, more than a match for the Germans, although outnumbered. Very soon they were joined by a fresh wave of troops and the Brandenburgers were forced back out of the trench into the town. Systematically, the Americans advanced. The house-to-house fighting was bitter and many fell on both sides. Houses were cleared by hand grenades thrown through open doors and shattered windows. Karl, at a house near the further edge of Vierzy, decided that advanced headquarters had to move or be captured.

Out in the open they were caught in a burst of fire from a flank position. Some of the enemy had broken out of the town. Several of Karl's men fell and he himself received a bullet in his leg. His orderly, who was unhurt, applied a tourniquet, using his belt and literally dragged his brigadier back to the second defence line. Karl was put on a stretcher and taken back to his rear position where he handed over to a staff colonel: his number two. He was seen by the surgeon at a first aid post and started on the long road back.

At the casualty clearing station, Karl was treated by the surgeons, his leg set, the wound dressed and the whole limb cased in plaster. He recovered consciousness and found himself on a cot in a large tent. There was another occupant, who was sitting looking at Karl. Seeing that he was awake, he got up and approached him, his hand swathed in a cocoon of bandages, unsteady on his feet. He spoke to Karl, 'You have just come from the front. I was commanding the 10th Wurtenberg Division when I was wounded by a long-range shell on my headquarters. The Wurtenbergers were counter-attacking. What happened? Did they succeed?'

Karl had no idea but told the colonel, 'Yes, they were on our flank and held up the American advance. The Brandenburgers were driven out of Vierzy and I was hit.'

It was not true. The 10th had also been forced to retreat, but did it matter?

The general exclaimed, 'Thank God, they held, I knew they would.'

Clinging to the tent pole, he swung round and collapsed heavily on the earth floor. Karl called for help and when the orderly came he pronounced the general dead.

Karl was taken to hospital in Brussels, where he had been in 1914. On his morning rounds the officer recognised Karl.

'You were here after Mons. I was your surgeon. You were a captain and now brigadier. Such is war. I am also promoted to the command of the hospital, from surgeon lieutenant to colonel.' He went on to say that there was nothing they could do for him. The clearing station had done a good job. 'When you are recovered and fit for the journey, I will put you on the train to Berlin.'

Karl in the coming days thought about the brothel, but no chance.

Karl arrived at the hospital in Spandau, weary and in considerable pain from the interminable train journey. The permanent way was in a poor state, there being insufficient labour to cope with the heavy wear from the troop and supply trains, the carriages jolting and swaying alarmingly, with frequent halts. The system was falling apart and Karl thought, what else? Germany is also in a poor state. Are we lost?

At the hospital the plaster was cut off, with great discomfort for Karl. The stench from the rotting wound made him physically sick. The surgeon found that both leg bones, tibia and fibula, were fractured. Reset and plastered, Karl was at last put to rest in a comfortable bed in a single room for senior officers. Others were in cramped wards. At last he could rest peacefully, away from the constant alarms of the front, the noise and tumult of war.

The general came to see him.

'Well, Karl, it is good to see you back. At least you will survive the war.' He brought Karl up to date with the events. 'A combined American Australian corps has retaken our ground gained in the Saint Michel Sector in the south and we are so far holding them in the Hindenburg Line.' He continued, 'The British, aided by hundreds of their own and French Renault tanks, are making a determined assault in Flanders. Between us, I must tell you that we are finished. We have no more reserves of manpower and our resources are coming rapidly to an end. The cupboard is bare.'

Karl was not altogether surprised by the general's words and said, 'General, it is so sad. We have fought so hard over the past four years, lost so many good men, the flower of Germany. All for nothing.'

Emma came to see him with little Kurt. It was obvious to Karl that the boy was accustomed now to regard her as his mother. They came, Emma with Kurt holding her hand, with fondness and confidence. That is good, thought Karl, we both like her and she is obviously kind to the little one and will bring him up well: a true surrogate mother. Karl called for the nurse, asking her to take the boy for some refreshment, 'whilst I talk with his mother.' When they were alone, Emma took his hand in her hands, kissing him gently on the mouth and murmuring, 'Darling, it is wonderful to see you again and, although sad to see your awful wound, I am so happy you will be away from the awful war and perhaps we can be together. I love little Kurt and will look after him as I would my own son, if you will let me.'

Karl told her, 'I love you, Emma, and although we cannot marry, as your husband still lives, we can be together. Things have changed. People no longer care about the proprieties of such matters, since the war began.' When she left, Karl was happier. 'Please come every day.'

At the beginning of October 1918, the general informed Karl that President Hindenburg had secretly made overtures to the Allies for an armistice. The Allies called for complete surrender, which was not accepted. Soon after Ludendorff resigned, leaving the *Wehrmacht* headless. Another blow fell when Germany's only friend, Austria-Hungary, surrendered to the Allies, driven by open revolt in Vienna and Budapest.

'It will not be long now,' the general predicted, 'we are finished. A terrible shame after we have fought and sacrificed so many lives. Betrayed by the Americans. If they had not joined in we would have beaten the rest. Our spring offensive this year would have succeeded.'

At the same time, Karl was released from the hospital. The surgeon told him that the plaster must remain for several more weeks.

'I will fit a walking iron, but you will find it very difficult to get about with one crutch or a walking stick. You can also have a wheelchair, which will have to be pushed.'

Karl was delighted to get home to the house on Schwannenwerder and to his beloved Emma and son, Kurt. There were shortages of foodstuffs and other necessities but the larder was well stocked and they would manage. When it was over they could return to Tilsit, away from it all.

November saw the end. Revolution broke out in Berlin. Angry crowds, many of them led by armed ex-service men, former front line soldiers, joined in, clamouring for an end to hostilities. The Hindenburg Line was still holding, although partially broached by the earlier British assault. On 10 November the Kaiser fled to neutral Holland, where he had an estate at Doorn, deserting a sinking ship. On the 11th Hindenburg accepted the Allies' conditions of total surrender and an armistice was signed. The tumult and fires of war were quenched, 'O'er dune and headland sinks the fire.'

The general told Karl that under the terms of the armistice the armed forces were to be disbanded.

'Conditions here will become intolerable,' he said. 'I have my staff car and can find a few lorries with drivers from my estates. We must leave before the thousands of soldiers return from the front. Then the situation will become much worse.'

Karl agreed at once and within a day or so they were on the road. Karl was told at the hospital that he could have the plaster removed at home.

'It will be all right,' the surgeon said, 'but you will walk with a limp, possibly forever, when the plaster is off. Good luck, general, or should I now call you Herr von Ritter?'

Taking with him as much as could be loaded into the lorries, the convoy left early in the morning, skirting round Berlin to avoid possible interference from the mobs. On the journey to Königsberg the countryside was quiet. The unrest had not yet spread from the capital. Arriving safely at Tilsit, Karl's mother, Erika, was overjoyed to see her son, home at last and safe. The war was over, no further harm to him. She was upset over his wounded leg.

'It will be all right, Mother,' he assured her, 'as good as new, when the plaster is off.'

He introduced Emma whom, he said, was his housekeeper and that her husband was in a mental hospital following a war wound to the head.

'Emma has been caring for Kurt and, as you can see, they get along famously. She has been a godsend.'

Whatever Erika thought she kept to herself, but thinking, well, why not?

20

A Fragile Peace

At Tilsit, in the beginning life was much the same as before. There were few shortages and little disaffection. From Berlin came stories of near famine, the collapse of the mark, the paper money practically worthless. A sackfull was needed to purchase a loaf of bread and notes of one million marks' denomination were printed and barter became the norm. Karl gradually took over the management of the Winterstein and Richtman estates. His own Ritter family properties were in the care of his elder brother. Early in 1919 Karl's plaster was removed and he could walk almost normally with the aid of a stick.

The situation in the cities remained tense. There were considerable hardships but by 1921 things were seen to be moving towards better times. Nevertheless, since the end of the war, Germany was beset by political agitation, nationalist and communist, mass unemployment and inflation, which totally diminished the nation's wealth. The conclusion of the armistice came in June 1921, by the Treaty of Versailles: a humiliation for Germany, recalling the former treaty in 1871 when they were the victors following the defeat of the French in the Franco-Prussian war. The terms of the treaty were very harsh: reparation payments, Alsace and Lorraine returned to France, parts of Prussian Silesia to Poland, German colonies were mandated to the newly inaugurated League of Nations, and demilitarisation of the Rhineland under Allied occupation. Although Germany signed the treaty, the Allies little realised that its harsh terms sowed the seeds for future upsets. One probable mistake was to allow the new Weimar Republic, constituted under President Hindenburg, the rebirth of the German Army. Although limited to a strength of 100,000 men without artillery, tanks and aircraft, it was a beginning. Unlike their Allies, they were not hampered by obsolete military hardware, a great advantage to begin afresh.

The news of the formation of the new army roused intense emotions in the returned, old soldiers, thoughts of revenge for the betrayal and the defeat. Karl was approached by a workman on the estate, a former sergeant.

'General, we are thinking of forming a branch of *Die Alte Kamaraden Verein* for ex-servicemen. Would you consent to be our patron?'

Karl was willing, also considering that such an association could help those in need, of whom there were many in these barren times. Karl was told that they already had obtained a suitable hall in the village which was offered free of cost by the pastor of the church.

'If a meeting is arranged will you be so kind as to join us?'

So Karl went on the evening of the event, finding the hall prepared with long tables and chairs and in one corner a bar with several barrels of beer arranged behind. About 100 old soldiers were present, all very excited at being together once again, meeting old comrades and wearing their decorations and medals. One man confronted Karl.

'General, I served with your brigade in France and am so very pleased with having the honour of meeting you.'

Karl was brief in welcoming the inauguration of *Die Alte Kamaraden* branch, ending, 'I am sure we can all be of service to ourselves and particularly to those of us in need of help. I see we have plenty of refreshment, so when we are all served, we will drink a toast to the greater Reich.'

So that was the beginning of a long and fruitful association. They carried on well into the night, drinking and telling stories from the war days. They sang the old songs beloved by soldiers, marching melodies, some bawdy as become the rude licentious soldiery. Even the Tommies' 'Long way to Tipperary,' and its parody, 'It's a long way to tickle Mary,' was surprisingly popular, as in future years, 'Lili Marlene' was to become the favourite of all sides, good rousing songs. The event was a good start, a resurgence of the old patriotism, love of the country, making a man feel proud once more. Karl was very happy and drove home in his specially adapted car, erratically steering from one side of the road to the other.

By 1925 Germany had achieved a miraculous economic recovery by dint of hard work and without the burden of spending vast sums on defence. Some of the former Allies saw it as a Germany once again overshadowing Europe, but there was little they could do to prevent this. The Americans who did not sign the Treaty of Versailles because the terms were thought to be too hard on a fallen foe who could no longer be of harm to them, the Americans were far away from events across the Atlantic. In fact, they were largely responsible for Germany's rebirth by loans which helped to pay the heavy reparations.

At Tilsit life went on smoothly, remote from the doings in Berlin. There were significant changes. Emma's husband had died at the asylum. Karl and she had carried on their liaison and now were free to marry. The announcement came as no surprise to Erika, who was quite aware of the situation between her son and his housekeeper. Kurt was now at preparatory school and would eventually go to the military academy at Königsberg, following the family tradition.

The new German army, a small but élite force, was determined to benefit from the events leading up to their defeat and clandestinely set about acquiring its own tanks. A secret arrangement was made with Russia, the Soviet Union, to establish a Panzer school deep inside that vast country at Kazan, inside the remote Tartar province. The Russians obligingly purchased a British light tank from which the Germans developed the first of their breed of *Panzerkampfwagen* the Pzkw Mark I. This secret addition to the military arm was under the guidance of General Guderian, who became the expert on armour and mechanisation.

The recovery was halted by the great depression which began in America in 1929 and spread all over the globe. Germany, with the collapse of the monetary system, was thrown into near bankruptcy.

This situation was exploited by a relative newcomer, Adolf Hitler, the *Führer* of the National Socialist movement, the Nazi party. Hitler, an Austrian, was then 40, a malcontent following his early years of the utmost poverty and rejection for which he blamed the Jews. His violent anti-Semitism began in his early years before the war. In 1913 he enlisted in the German army and became a corporal, was wounded, gassed and received the Iron Cross for bravery. Following the war years, Hitler became involved in politics and led what became known as 'the beerhall *putsch*' in Munich. This coup d'etat was put down by the army and Hitler was sent to prison. In prison he wrote *Mein Kampf* (my battle), which became the bible of Nazism. Released early, he set about building up the party, blaming the ills of the depression on the Jewish capitalists, communism, the Treaty of Versailles and the opposition party, the Social Democrats. At the time he gained spectacular growth for the party. His magnetic personality and rousing oratory, loaded with promises, gained him many supporters, including some of the great industrialists, such as Krupps and I.G. Farben, who saw him as a tool to their own ends. Backed by General Ludendorff, he established his own private army, the Brown Shirts, and under his propaganda chief, Goebbels, a powerful press. In 1932 he lost the presidential election to Hindenburg, but the National Socialists gained overall majority in the *Reichtag*, the parliament. Hindenburg appointed him as chancellor the following year, beginning a virtual dictatorship. To further establish his position, he accused the communists of setting the *Reichtag* building on fire, although it was thought by most that the fire was, in fact, started by the Nazis. In 1934 President Hindenburg died and the *Reichtag* voted Hitler dictatorial powers. Hitler then grasped the power and cemented his position by outlawing communism, taking charge of all state activities, establishing the very important youth movement, the Hitler *Jugend*. Anti-Semitism became law, and concentration camps were established for the enemies of the regime. Hitler's position as the *Führer* was confirmed by a vote of confidence in which nearly 90% of the voters favoured the union of president and chancellor in the person of Adolf Hitler, in consequence virtual master of 80 million subjects. The Allied powers were disparaging in their comments about Hitler. It was wishful thinking. The former Austrian corporal was, as the future revealed, *Keine Kleine Mann,* no small man.

In Italy another dictator in 1935 carried out a successful action against Ethiopia, colonising the country, adding to their already successful occupation of Libya. The rest of the world, represented by the League of Nations, barely protested. This was Hitler's chance to repudiate the Treaty of Versailles and in 1936 he began intensive rearming and occupied the Rhineland without opposition by the French. The same year the German army paraded three Panzer divisions, equipped with Mark II tanks, and the Mark III was in production. The Mark III was to prove superior to any other tank in service, with an astounding speed of 20 miles per hour, a 37 millimetre cannon and three machine-guns, the bullet-proof armour nearly one inch thick; a formidable weapon, developed secretly in Russia.

Karl followed these developments with professional appraisal. He soon formed the view that Germany was bent on another world war. Kurt, having graduated from the Königsberg Military Academy, was now at Heidelberg, following his family footsteps. As a cadet he had avoided the Hitler *Jugend* and now had joined the University Officer Korps. Karl, in principle, supported Hitler's regime. After the ignominious defeat and harshness of the immediate post-war years, Germans could feel proud once more.

So far Hitler was encouraged by the attitude of France and Britain. His aggression had been met with appeasement and conciliation. Continuing his plans to resurrect the Fatherland, in 1936, Hitler sent German troops into Austria and, the successful *putsch* recaptured Austria. Another milestone passed. So it went on. Unopposed in early 1939, Czechoslovakia was his. The Sudaten Germans living there were back in the homeland. In April, following Hitler's example Mussolini annexed Italy's neighbour, Albania, causing only weak protest from them.

A visit to Hitler by the British prime minister, Neville Chamberlain, resulted in a vague agreement that Poland's sovereignty would be respected, although it was made clear that Britain would not use military intervention.

A pathetic, umbrella'd Chamberlain came down the steps of the aircraft at Heathrow waving a piece of paper and declaring, 'Peace in our time.'

In the Spanish Civil War, which raged from 1936 to 1938, both Italy and Germany sent troops and aircraft to assist their brother dictator, Franco, to defeat the Spanish communists. It was a wonderful opportunity to try out new weapons of war and also against the Russians, who were in some measure aiding Franco's opponents, the communists. German aerial bombing was particularly effective. The defenceless town of Guernica was bombed to ruins with great loss of life. The action caused widespread indignation and inspired Picasso's famous painting of the mural, 'Guernica'.

Later, in 1939, the world was astounded when Hitler by concluding a non-aggression pact with Stalin, to the dismay of communists in other countries, seeming to be their betrayal. In August 1939, further encouraged by his new friend, Hitler invaded Poland. France and Britain declared war on Germany. Very rapidly poor Poland was overcome. The German *blitzkrieg*, armoured columns supported by Stuka dive-bombers and followed by motorised infantry, smashed any resistance, the Polish cavalry opposition going down bravely in a welter of blood. The Russians also advanced from the Ukraine and the two Allies met halfway and divided Poland between themselves.

Kurt von Ritter was now 23 years of age and had graduated early from university, convinced that there would be a war and wishing to join the army as soon as possible. So, at the outbreak of war he had already been a soldier for two years, serving with the prestigious regiment, *Erst Panzer Hussaren,* the new armoured cavalry. Owing to the rapid expansion of the *Wehrmacht,* Kurt was already a *hauptmann,* second-in-command of a squadron of Mark II Panzers. Kurt had devoted himself to study and only infrequently satisfied his sexual appetite with prostitutes. He was the apple of his grandfather Ritter's eye. The eldest son had not produced an heir and it was quite obvious that Kurt would inherit the estate, in addition to the Winterstein properties. The family von Ritter had adopted a young lady, Elsa von Schramm, who was orphaned when her father was killed in the Great War, her mother dying soon after from grief, tragically by her own hand. Elsa was, in fact, a protégée of Kurt's grandfather. The couple almost grew up together and it was inevitable that they became betrothed. Kurt was obviously fond of Elsa and happy that she would become his wife. Elsa, on her part, was besotted with her handsome young officer. It was decided that the wedding ceremony would not be rushed. The war would be over in a few months, better to wait. Kurt did not anticipate the wedding night, perhaps wisely foregoing the pleasure, although Elsa showed signs that she would have welcomed a coupling of their bodies.

Kurt was on a short home leave when Hitler invaded Poland, his regiment was not involved. When the arch enemies of the *Reich*, France and Britain, declared war on Germany, Kurt was immediately recalled. His farewells were sad, he himself raring to go to the war, as young men do, surrounded by weeping women. Grandmother, Erika, stepmother, Emma, and fiancée, Elsa, were all tearful.

His father, Karl, said, 'You must understand, my boy. Look at myself, one arm gone and a gammy leg, not funny.'

He went on to remind Kurt, that his grandfather, Otto, had been assassinated; his great grandfather, Pierre Flamand, and great-great grandfather, François, both killed in action.

'Now you are off to what may turn out to be a worse war than mine. Look after yourself and may God keep you safe.'

21

Into France

Kurt's Panzer battalion, the *Erst Hussaren*, with the *Erst Panzer* division, was marshalling in the Rhineland on the border of Luxembourg, a pleasant farming area. They were part of General Guderian's 19th Panzer Army, Guderian, a master of tank strategy. The well-rehearsed tactical move was to follow the Schlieffen plan that failed in 1914 due to hesitation by the general staff. This time, Paris or bust. Kurt's unit was equipped with the new Mark III and were to spearhead the thrust, following the recce battalion detachment: rapid moving troops in armoured cars and BMW motorcycles, some with sidecars and machine-guns, in constant communication with the advancing tanks.

In September 1939, they expected to go, charging at the bit, but nothing happened. In Poland, the army had taken Warsaw after a massive aerial bombardment and by the end of the month it was over. The *blitzkrieg* series of engagements of encirclement, with speed and determination proved to be overwhelming, especially when preceded by Stuka dive-bombers. Pockets of resistance by the brave but weak Polish army were simply bypassed, to be cleared up by the following infantry, a perfect demonstration of the new form of warfare, the *blitzkrieg*. A similar plan had been considered by the British General Fuller as early as 1919, after the war: air strikes followed by medium and heavy tanks, but this envisaged an assault on a fortified position, trench warfare, not the swift advance through and behind the enemy. Aerial reconnaissance revealed that the French army, considered to be the most formidable in Europe, was tucked behind the redoubtable Maginot Line. This line of fortifications, concrete and steel with fortresses at suitable locations, was equipped with heavy artillery and with underground facilities for men and ammunition. Impregnable, but of course, the guns were all facing across the border towards Germany. In 1939 the line stretched from the Swiss border to just short of Sedan, where France bordered on Luxembourg. From there on it had been previously considered that Belgian defences would suffice. When the war broke out there was some hasty rethinking. Remembering 1914, poor little Belgium could not hold out against the mighty *Wehrmacht*. So the British Expeditionary Force were put to work, expanding the Maginot Line to the Channel, some 300 miles of fortifications.

By the end of 1939, Russia had occupied the Baltic States, Estonia, Latvia and Lithuania, without much protest from others. Russia also attacked Finland and met strong resistance by their redoubtable Marshal Mannerheim. By March 1940, the brave Finns were obliged to sign a treaty with the Soviets which ceded parts of the border regions to Russia. Later, in 1941, the Finns joined Hitler in his Russian adventure. Germany was not idle. Following the successful occupation and division of poor Poland, Hitler, perhaps not quite sure of his military strengths, suggested peace terms with Britain and France. These were rejected outright. Early in 1940, Hitler occupied Denmark and Norway without much trouble. Britain did send an Expeditionary Force to Norway, but in a very short time it had to withdraw. The 'phoney war' went on in the west. *Was gibts Neues? Im Western Nichts,* nothing new in the west, all quiet on the western front, as Erich Maria Remarque wrote about the other war. The British sang their somewhat ridiculous marching song, 'We're Going to Hang out our Washing on the Siegfried Line', the German equivalent to the French Maginot Line. The Panzers also had their own refrain:

> *Über die Scheldt, das Elbe und der Rhine*
> *Panzer rollen im Europa Vorwärts,*
> *Das ras von de Kessel das drone der Moteren,*

Panzer rollen im Europa Vorwärts,
Hussaren das Führer, Hussaren in Schwartz,
Über alles die Panzer Korps..

Over the Scheldt, the Elbe and the Rhine,
Tanks roll forward in Europe,
The noise of the tracks, the drone of the engine,
Tanks roll forward in Europe
Hussars of the Führer, dressed in black,
Over all the Tank Corps.

A favourite on drinking nights. There was little else to do but eat, drink and wait. No leave, trained to the hilt and ready to go.

Meanwhile, in Poland the German occupation was carried out with ferocity, a display of *schadenfreude,* malicious pleasure in the torment of others, encouraged by the Poles' previous mistreatment of Polish citizens of German origin, persecution of them, and a denial of any citizen rights. The situation had worsened when some 1,000 Germans were shot down by Polish soldiers on the pretext that they had been shot at. So it went on and many more ethnic Germans were literally murdered. With the defeat of Poland, Hitler put his Storm Troopers, the SS, to work, to revenge the German dead. Thousands of Poles were sent to Germany for work on farms. It was worse on the Soviet side. Nearly two million Poles were deported to Russia to work as slave labour and 15,000 Polish officers were rounded up and shot and burned in the forest at Katyn. In Poland the Germans created a concentration camp at Auschwitz where prisoners were used as slave labour and executed at will. This was to be the pattern for the other countries occupied by Hitler.

Hitler, since the outbreak of the war, had told the OKH, *Ober Kommando Heer,* the German Army High Command, that he intended to attack in the west to protect the all-important Ruhr and its manufacturing industries. The OKH were reserved about this and Hitler had not made up his mind, still hoping that Britain and France would accept his occupation of Poland and talk peace. This proposal was rejected by the Allies, so Hitler ordered Field Marshal Halder and General Brauchitschh to prepare a plan for an offensive into France.

On 10 May 1940, the balloon went up, nothing still quiet in the west, Five Panzer Groups attacked simultaneously, directed against Holland, Belgium, Luxembourg and France, 16 divisions of the latest armour and all highly trained. Each division comprised a reconnaissance battalion, a Panzer regiment of three battalions, a rifle regiment and an artillery regiment, all mechanised. The German airforce opened the conflict by heavy strategic bombing. Rotterdam was severely damaged and extensive raids were carried out along the French and Belgian defensive lines and major cities along their borders. After five days of bombing raids, the Dutch capitulated and the Panzer Group in the north was unhindered to move into Belgium.

The southernmost group, Panzer Guderian, at dawn on a fine spring morning crossed into Luxembourg. Luxembourg, a tiny country, no more than 50 miles long and 30 miles at the widest point, had a population of mainly German or French-speaking citizens of around 400,000 in number, prosperous and peaceful. The Panzers moved swiftly up to the border strung out on minor roads, reaching the Luxembourg border near Dietrich, some miles north of the capital city, Luxembourg. The division was fielded in three prongs, led by the three battalions. Kurt's company, equipped with the very new Mark III tank, was in the lead, headed by a few motorcycle scouts. When they reached the border, Kurt ordered his driver to go on without slackening speed. The astonished border police at once raised the barrier and scattered. Kurt ordered his gunner to put a round through the border hut as they passed, destroying any communications to the interior. The column crossed the South Ardennes mountains, inevitably slowed down, but at nightfall were halted on the border with Belgium. Luxembourg was occupied by Hitler and the head of state, the Grand Duchesse Charlotte, fled to London. There was no resistance. It would have been futile.

At dawn the following morning, the Panzers pushed on. Kurt, in the lead, sped through the barrier, again shelling the posts, and on into the Belgian forest of the Ardennes, which the French considered unusable by armour. The Germans proved that it could be penetrated in force, and with overwhelming speed. The route took them along the rides to the south of Bastogne. They encountered no resistance until they reached the French border crossing in front of Sedan. The motorcycles reported that the post was guarded by a few light tanks and some infantry.

Kurt led the company round the bend of the road from where he could see through his binoculars six Renault tanks lined up in front of a wood; no cover. Stupid fools, he said to himself, they've had it.

Over the radio he ordered his Panzers to fan out and as soon as they were in range, 'Wait for me to open fire and then hammer them.'

The French tanks were outgunned and their projectiles coming back were harmlessly spent when they reached the Panzers. Very soon all six were blazing and ammunition exploding. Some of the crews were baling out and were machine-gunned before they could reach the safety of the woods. The border guards and some infantry also perished, under a hail of fire from the Spandau machine-guns. Kurt was very satisfied. The event proved the superiority of the Panzers and reflected the training of the crews, particularly the all-important gunners. He was to be awarded the Iron Cross for this action.

The Allies expected the main attack to be in the north and concentrated their armies along and across the Belgian border. Instead, Guderian pressed on and three days after the beginning of the offensive his three prongs had cleared the Ardennes forest and were on the River Meuse near Sedan, well into France. Further north, the Panzers of von Kleist had also reached the Meuse, so that five Panzer divisions and three motorised divisions, a truly formidable force, were poised to cross the river and break through into the interior. Without pausing, the Panzers assembled at the crossings and watched with awe as the French infantry on the other bank were also subjected to an air bombardment such as they had never imagined. The Stuka dive-bombers, gull-winged and quite graceful, streaked out of the sky, engines howling in a nerve-rending scream, releasing their bombs a few hundred feet from the ground, a terrifyingly effective weapon. In spite of the blitz, the French put up a stubborn resistance and some of the crossings were denied to the Panzers.

The Panzer regiment, equivalent to a brigade, assembled on the west bank of the Meuse and the CO at an order group told them that the commander in the west, von Rundstedt, planned to blitz through to the Channel coast to the Boulogne-Calais area and cut off the main French and British forces in the north. The battalion colonel put the company officers in the picture.

'Let's get on with it, full speed. God with us and we shall win.'

In the region at that time were two French armoured divisions which were in a position to intervene, but the High Command seemed not to be aware that a large German army was, so soon after the commencement of the battle, already into France. Consequently, orders were muddled and the two divisions were not committed to the fight and subsequently were swallowed up in the chaos which ensued.

They set off on the 400-mile journey to the coast, Kurt's company in the lead of the regiment, following elements of the recce regiment, who were the pathfinders. The planned route was to avoid major cities and skirt any known defences, bypassing Charlotteville, Le Cateau, Arras, Lens and on to reach the coast in the Pas de Calais at Abbeville, west of Boulogne. Guderian's Panzers raced past Charlotteville and on towards Le Cateau without opposition, barely stopping to rest. At this point Kurt's company were brought to a standstill by the road being jammed by refugees fleeing out of Belgium and in northern France: lorries, buses, cars, carts and bicycles, even wheelbarrows, pedestrians loaded with whatever they could carry. They could not go back and now they were faced by the enemy from another direction. It was inconceivable that the Panzers should be held up. Within the hour Stukas, with the new terror device added attached to the propeller to add to its unearthly howl, and Mg109 fighters were clearing the roads using bombs and machine-guns. Many refugees fell dead, others scattered abandoning their possessions. The road was then passable for the Panzers.

So it went on, and on 20 May, ten days only after the start, Kurt was looking out over the English Channel. Many Panzers had been lost through mechanical failure, none by enemy action, but the great flanking operation had encircled the Allied armies in Belgium and the north of France. Two other Panzer armies had blitzed through Holland and were driving the Allies out of Belgium. The British made a stand on La Bassé canal but were driven back, retreating ever further westwards. Soon there would be no place to go.

The British had a strong base at Arras and from there counter-attacked with a mixed force of Matilda infantry support tanks, slow and lumbering and lightly armed. However, they took a division of Panzers commanded by Major General Rommel by surprise. Rommel was leading a thrust up the centre, paralleling Guderian. In the tank versus tank fight that ensued the Panzers eventually won the day and only a few Matildas got away and they were soon to be abandoned in the general retreat. Some Panzers were hit and destroyed by the Matilda's guns and caused the German High Command to put a brake on the advance. This gave the British time to form a perimeter, a ring of guns from where they could evacuate their army from Dunkirk and Calais. In spite of aerial and artillery bombardment against the crammed area, the enemy managed to ship out in an armada of small boats, a third of a million men, British and Allied. Almost a miracle, perhaps a Matilda miracle. By the end of May, a short three weeks, France was alone with Hitler well inside the door.

The Panzer armies fanned out into France, went to Cherbourg and Le Havre, south to Paris, Orleans, Dijon and the Swiss border. Guderian was ordered to proceed westwards to the ports of Cherbourg and Le Havre. The Panzers, after the hard usage, were in poor shape, particularly the older Mark IIs. Kurt was quite excited that the route would take them through Evreux and the home of his French forbears, the Flamand and Armand families, being aware that his grandfather, Otto, had visited them in the previous war. One column took the coast road to Le Havre and Kurt's regiment proceeded south to Rouen and into Normandy. Before Rouen, cresting a hill, Kurt saw a column of tanks coming along the road towards them. They could only be French. Several Panzers deployed on either side of the road. Kurt ordered them to fire when the range was certain to knock out the last tanks and thereby block the escape of the others. When this was done, the French column came to a grinding halt and Kurt shot up the leading tank. The remainder surrendered very hurriedly and were taken over by the Panzer Grenadiers coming up behind the Panzer company. The roads were now clear of refugees. There was nowhere to go. The German advance had been too swift.

After Evreux, on the way through the country to Caen, Kurt enquired in several villages and eventually found someone who knew the Flamands.

'The whole family left at the outbreak of war, last September. I believe they went to Canada.' And the Armands? 'They also left. Many of the rich families cleared off.'

So that was that, a link severed. On to Cherbourg, which very quickly surrendered leaving the Germans with all the Channel ports in their hands.

After the beginning of June, the British had gone and half of France was Hitler's. By the middle of June, the French sued for an armistice and this was agreed and signed at Compiègne in the same railway coach in which the Germans had capitulated in 1918. In order to avoid the complications and high costs of occupying the whole of France, Hitler decided to stay on the present line and the remainder of France continued unoccupied under an approved government. So Vichy France, under General Pétain, renowned for his stand against the Germans at Verdun in the previous war, took over as head of the new government. Hitler was still intent on coming to terms with Britain. He had other plans and approaches were made in Switzerland and Spain by the German ambassadors. Churchill was now prime minister, replacing poor Chamberlain, and the overtures were rejected outright. 'We will fight them on the beaches,' etc.

When France was defeated, the Italian dictator, Benito Mussolini, joined Hitler and the Axis was formed. Balkan states, Hungary, Rumania, Slovakia and Bulgaria were also drawn in. Italy had occupied Albania but was repulsed in Greece. Hitler was practically master of Europe and the British were almost alone in their defiance.

There was a victory parade along the Champs Elysée, an, awe-inspiring procession of armour, motorised infantry and artillery, passing interminably in front of the crowds held back by the firm lines of infantry. Kurt, leading his company of Panzers, thought of his grandfather, shot down in the Franco-Prussian war, riding at the head of his cavalry in another victory parade. The people of Paris crowding the scene were very subdued and ashamed by the swift defeat of their grand army, Napoleon turning over in his tomb at the scene of the foreign soldiers marching by the Arc de Triomphe, monument to his glorious victories. Hitler took the salute, standing prominently on the podium, with the generals ranged behind. As the Panzers approached, the turrets were traversed and the guns aligned on the saluting base and dipped in salute. The Panzer commander, head and shoulders outside the hatch, also saluted.

The *Erst Panzer* Division were ordered back to Germany to be re-equipped with the latest Mark III Panzers and a few of the Mark IVs, a Panzer which was to be the main battle weapon in the coming years. The Mark IV was a very advanced Panzer, far superior to any other in service in any army at that time. Its 75mm gun, with an assortment of projectiles, armour-piercing high explosives and smoke, outgunned any other. Weighing over 20 tons and with a speed of 25 miles per hour and over two inches of armour plate, it was practically invincible.

The division was ordered to proceed to Poland, much to everyone's surprise. They had been expecting to join the activities in the Balkans, Greece, and perhaps to move to Libya where the Italians were confronting the British across the sandy wastelands. There was some leave and Kurt went to Tilsit, where all were overjoyed to see him safe and sound. General Brausch was not particularly optimistic about the future.

In confidence he told Kurt that, 'Hitler is preparing to have a go at Russia. I hope we do not follow Napoleon and underrate the Russian steamroller and the appalling winter climate.'

The general went on to say, 'Our *Führer* is in command now and the generals are obliged to go along with him, or else . . .'

21

Operation Barbarossa

With breathtaking speed Hitler had reversed the ignominious defeat and surrender of 1918. He was bathed in power and glory and indisputably master of a united people. The few who dissented, mainly communists, were dealt with as was the Jewish 'problem', which had now been solved. The OKH, the High Command, was his toy and he alone controlled the strategic conduct of the war. After all one must agree, *Keine Kleine Mann*, no little man.

As soon as the conflict in the west was over and only Britain remained resolute across the Channel, Hitler announced to the High Command that he was going to abandon the non-aggression pact of 1939 with the Soviet Union. He ordered the commander-in-chief of the army to examine the Russian problem. The outcome was code-named Operation Barbarossa. Khair ad-din Barbarossa was an Algerian pirate, scourge of the Mediterranean in the thirteenth and fourteenth centuries. Allied with Turkey, he defeated the Venetian fleets and put most of the North African countries and Cyprus under Turkish domination.

The directive issuing from the Chief of Staff emphasised the use of the Panzers: 'The bulk of the Russian Army stationed in the west of Russia will be destroyed by daring operations led by deeply penetrating armoured spearheads.' So preparations began for a pre-emptive strike against the Soviet Union to rid the world of the Bolshevik menace and, of course, to allow Hitler to pursue his strategic plans for world domination, unhindered by the Russian bear and free to solve the problem posed by Britain and America.

The Officer Korps, having a long tradition of anti-Semitism and a belief that Bolshevism was Jewish in conception, were more than willing to realise Hitler's dreams. The Panzer Korps, following the enormous success of the armoured *blitzkrieg* in France, were further encouraged by the new Panzer which was appearing in selected units, the Mark IV, a great advance on previous models, which was to become the principle battle tank. The Panzer Mark IV was made of 21 tons of armour more than two inches thick with a 75 millimetre main gun, high velocity and versatile, with two machine-guns and a speed of 25 miles per hour, a formidable weapon.

Kurt found himself the proud commander of a company of the new Panzers and quite overwhelmed by being promoted to major. Since the regiment was not apparently destined for service in the Balkans or Africa, rumour had it that something was brewing in the east. At home on leave he spoke about coming events with his grandfather, General Brausch, who was no longer on the active list, but kept in close touch with military matters. He told Kurt that he did not share the Officer Korps support of Hitler's dreams and that any attack on Russia would be compromised by the primitive road system and the Russian snows and freezing cold.

'Your new Panzer is a fine weapon, but I am getting reports of a new tank which the Russians have been secretly producing for the past two years.' He went on, 'The Mark IV is not equipped for winter warfare in a vast territory with poor communications. Perhaps Hitler should look at Napoleon's experience in 1812.'

Kurt's father, Karl, and his stepmother, Emma, made a great fuss over the promotion and the Iron Cross. Karl remarked that it would be a long war. 'Germany has many enemies and probably America will join them. So you may even end up as a divisional commander. I agree with your grandfather. If we are going to tackle Russia it will not be a pushover.'

Kurt's betrothed, Elsa, made it very clear that even if their marriage was to be delayed until after the war, they could still make proper love. He was held back, although not unwilling. What if Elsa became pregnant and he was killed? Unthinkable for a von Ritter.

Back at the regiment, he found preparations for an unhurried movement to the east, into occupied Poland, further evidence of an impending attack on the Soviets. There was much discussion about the new Russian tank, the T34 which, unbelievably, outperformed the Mark IV Panzer. The T34 weighed 28 tons, was capable of a speed of over 30 miles per hour, had broad tracks for better going on snow or mud and a superb 76.2mm gun.

'We shall see. After all, we have better experience and outnumber Ivan with over 3,000 Panzers to his mere 1,000. He cannot cover the whole of the vast front,' was the general view.

In early winter 1940, the regiment set off on its tracks to cover the 300 miles to their destination; no hurry, conserve the mechanical condition of the Panzers and improve the crews' performance, however, with a spirit of forwards against the foe, the *Hussaren* were elated. The weather was good, the people in the villages very friendly and showered them with gifts of food and tobacco. When they camped by night, many a local lass was to regret her submission to a handsome, young Panzer soldier, but it made for more healthy babies for the *Reich* and Mother money from the state, an encouragement initiated by Hitler himself, fine children for the future glory of the Fatherland.

The crews were in great form, 'bright, clean and shiny', glad to be on the move, away from the barrack square and into a different discipline. Kurt's own crew was the original one from France, with the addition of a co-driver, who also used the machine-gun located in the front of the hull. With Kurt in the turret was the gunner and wireless operator/gun loader. They were all correct in their relationship to an officer, but inevitably there grew up a camaraderie. After all, in the field they were closed in together in the Panzer, ate and drank together. Fortunately, the wireless operator was a good hand with the rations, a godsend, and they slept together on the ground, rolled in blankets and waterproofs. The officers and sergeants commanding the company sections were all carefully selected, proud to be fighting men of the *Erst Panzer Hussaren*. So far there were no misfits and most had been with the company in France.

They crossed into Poland over the river Oder at Frankfurt-on-Oder and into Slubice. Here they found a different atmosphere, the few Poles in the streets sullenly ignoring the passing of the hated enemy. They moved by easy stages on the byroads, through plain farmlands and woods, the latter perfect for ambushes, but the Poles were so stunned by their defeat and occupation by Germans and Russians that the Panzers moved, unhindered. Skirting Poznan, they continued on the way to Warsaw. Before reaching their destination, Plonsk, they encountered heavily fortified areas, the woods concealing military installations close to the Russian/Polish border. It was an extraordinary feat of military engineering, carried out in such a short time by plentiful slave labour drawn from all over Europe.

On the journey to Plonsk, the attached Panzer Grenadier Company travelled with the Panzers, practising the role of close support in action and as guards to the Panzers, which were, under certain circumstances, vulnerable to enemy infantry. The Grenadiers were very fit, young soldiers, well-armed and tough. They marched or trooped behind individual Panzers or rode packed together behind the turrets on the engine cover. Stout fellows, they had already proved their worth in France. The Grenadier captain and Kurt were great friends and he always rode behind Kurt on a small seat welded on the outside of the turret. Close cooperation.

The regiment was situated in a vast forest region, the companies spread out, housed in huts with the Mark IVs parked among the trees. Of course, the Russians knew they were massed on the frontier, but could do little about countering the threat. They had too few resources and their only strategy was to guard the approaches to Moscow, Leningrad and Kiev. They were already moving the war industries to safe areas to the east, behind the Urals and beyond any conceivable German advance.

It was a fine life, out there in the woods, well supplied with the good things plundered from the occupied countries. The company officers' mess, a hut by itself, was comfortably furnished and the bar stocked with fine wines and cognacs, with no shortage of good food and tobacco. A good life, fattening them up for the kill, but not their kill, others were intended victims. For gunnery practice they were taken to a range some miles to the west on the way to Torun. The villages around were still occupied by Poles who were in a pitiful, near state of starvation. This was a blessing to the soldiers, who could easily find a willing girl to bed for a few cigarettes, the universal currency, or a little coffee or tinned meat. A good soldier's heaven, in bed or out of barracks. The sergeants and corporals messed together and the other ranks were also well taken care of.

Kurt had a run-about general purpose car turned out by the Reich Volkswagen enterprise by the thousand, the *Kriegswagen*, rugged and without frills, but ideal for the going away from the roads. The winter of 1941 was mild and spring came early. There was little snow left in the woods. Kurt took to exploring the endless miles of forest rides, often encountering not a soul, in spite of the enormous concentration of troops; the forests were vast.

Driving one day near the camp, he met a horse and rider coming suddenly out of the trees in front. Kurt stopped and went to help the rider. The horse had shied violently, threatening to throw her and bolt. Kurt grabbed the bridle and very quickly steadied the horse.

The young woman dismounted and Kurt exclaimed, 'What on earth are you doing here? This is a military area, civilians are strictly not allowed.'

The woman, Kurt could see, was in her thirties with light brown short hair and cornflower-blue eyes, not particularly beautiful and typically German. She hastened to explain that she was living in a nearby cottage, once occupied by a gamekeeper.

'It is a long story, but the general in the big house knows about me. Please walk with me. It is not far and I will tell you about my situation. My name is Sasha Grudzyn, my mother German and my father Polish.'

Kurt introduced himself, saying, 'Kurt von Ritter, I am camped nearby with my company.'

So they walked the horse back along the forest path from where Sasha had emerged. Sasha told Kurt that she had been governess to the count's children at the mansion, which was now occupied by the general and his officers.

'The count went away with his regiment of Polish Lancers. My father was an officer in the Lancers and since last year nothing has been heard of them, but we presume they are all dead. My mother went back to Germany and I moved to the cottage. As I told you, the general knows about me and allows me to remain.'

When they arrived at the somewhat derelict cottage she led the horse to a ramshackle stable where there was another horse.

'I love riding and "reserved" them from the count's stables.' She invited Kurt in for coffee, 'Or what passes for coffee these days, probably dried acorns.'

She explained that she could obtain some essentials from a village outside the military area. 'But there is very little to be had and in any case my money is running out so I shall have to leave or eat my lovely horses.'

Kurt was quite attracted to Sasha. Her story was so typical of the times and she was a good companion. Also Kurt enjoyed riding. It was a heaven-sent opportunity.

'Look, Sasha,' he said, 'I can help you. We have plenty, the army is well provided for. In exchange, I would like to ride with you, or at least have the use of one of the horses.' In his mind he probably thought, and maybe the use of something else. She is, after all, quite bed-worthy. Aren't I lucky? We shall see, no hurry.

Kurt told his company quartermaster sergeant to make up a box of rations. The QS understood at once. Lucky sod, he thought. Drink from the mess was simply a matter of signing a chit. Heigh ho, off we go, none but the brave deserve the fair. Sasha was delighted.

'A veritable cornucopia!' she exclaimed, 'now I can be easy in my mind and stay with the horses. You are too kind. Shall we go for a ride? I know some lovely glades and forest streams. It is beautiful country.'

Kurt asked for a saddle bag and put in two bottles of wine, some chocolate and biscuits.

'We will have a picnic.'

They rode for an hour, encountering no-one, quiet astonishing as there were so many troops around.

She said in answer to his remark, 'The woods are vast and can easily swallow up whole armies. Also, I know my way around. We are, in fact, on the fringe of the soldiers, towards Warsaw, some 50 miles to the south and, it is said, strictly out of bounds.'

At a green-grassed glade by a small stream they tethered the horses and sat with backs against a fallen tree trunk. Kurt opened the wine and he told her about himself, his home in Prussia, university days and the war in France. He spoke of his father, a brigadier who had lost an arm in 1914, and his mother, who had died and how he had been raised by his stepmother, who had been very kind and loving.

Anticipating her curiosity he said, 'I am not married. I am, however, affianced but it is more of a family arrangement, a convenience.'

They finished the wine and he turned to her, gathering her slim body in his arms and laying her down on the soft grass.

She said, 'Please take me.'

And so Kurt did, very satisfyingly for them both.

He said, 'Sasha, we seem to be very suited to each other. I hope we can continue to be together whilst I am here. One day we shall be moving on, until then . . .'

He was indeed a 'lucky sod', but their affair inevitably blossomed into love. Kurt spent all the nights with her and days also, when he was free. Leave was possible but he had no inclination to go home. He had never been happier. The *Hussaren* were honed to a fine edge and raring to go. It would not be long now. Early summer and the enemy harvest to be interrupted and destroyed. One morning Sasha brought his coffee to their bed, as she always did before he left to take the early morning parade, and sometimes to jump in with him for a bit of love. This morning was different. She was dressed in his uniform, a little oversized but she looked very smart.

She said, 'Soon I won't be able to get your breeches on. I will be too big. I am pregnant.'

Kurt was taken aback and, quickly recovering, said, 'That is wonderful. We get on so well together, complement each other, I cannot think of life without you. I will think of something and we will talk it out tonight.'

Sasha produced a camera and said, 'Please take my picture as I am now. You can carry it with you to remember this morning.'

When Kurt came that night he brought a bottle of very old,

Author's note:
In case the reader does not believe it happened.

special fruit-flavoured, Polish vodka.

'We will have a last drink together, to toast our baby, and then no more for you until it is over.' He told her he had very carefully thought things over. 'I want to marry you. Will you have me? We will be so good for each other.'

Sasha, of course, was more than willing. 'But how can we here and what about your fiancée?'

Kurt explained that he had already written to Elsa von Schramm breaking off their engagement, and also to his parents.

'Even if you did not want to marry me, I could never love anyone else.'

He told her that he would see the general.

'He served under my father in the Brandenburgers in the last war. He will help us and, when the time comes, aid you to go to my parents.'

They had their drink of the precious vodka and so to bed.

'We must be careful,' he said, but of course they were not and perhaps even the baby enjoyed it.

Kurt drove up to the mansion to see the general, 'on private business'.

The general said, 'Ah, Kurt von Ritter, *Erst Hussaren,* I know your father well. What can I do for you?'

Kurt explained that he had met the girl in the cottage and had been living with her for several months.

The general said, 'You young devil. Yes, I remember her, Sasha something, mother German. I allowed her to stay there.'

Kurt told him that he wanted to marry her and eventually send her back to Prussia.

'You are serious,' the general said, 'well, I hope you know what you are doing. The padre here can perform the ceremony and I shall be a witness. Afterwards, I will give you a small reception. Not too much fuss, it's not entirely regular.'

So Kurt married his beloved Sasha.

'Sasha von Ritter,' said the general, 'it suits you better than Grudzyn.'

The general promised that before the balloon went up he would provide her with a *laissez-passer* for her to travel to Germany. Of course, the company heard about it on the grapevine and Kurt was obliged to give a party in the mess to formally introduce Fraü Sasha. He also sent sufficient wines and beer to the other messes. He was very happy, 'the best thing I have ever done.'

Towards the end of May the High Command issued its restricted 'Guidelines for the conduct of the army in Russia' to be seen and discussed down to regiment and junior commanders only. At a regimental meeting, Kurt and other battalion and company commanders were lectured by the intelligence officer. Broadly, he said that the coming war was a preventative strike against Bolshevism, an unholy alliance of Jews and reactionaries which threatened the Fatherland. Hitler's new order could only be achieved by the destruction of the Jews, the Bolshevik élite and the decimation of the decadent Russian people. This was not entirely a matter for the SS units, the army also had a role in this essential purification.

'Our object is to fight a war for strategic, economic and political ends. Russia is a prize worth winning, with its manufacturing production, oil and mineral wealth, all of which we need. Stalin, by carrying out his extensive purges, had in fact helped us.'

Some 10 per cent of the Soviets were in vast concentration camps in Siberia. The purges removed many essential managers and skilled workers and dislocated production of essential materials for the armaments' industry.

The intelligence officer went on to outline information about Soviet weaponry and the state of their armed forces.

'In spite of Stalin purges, the armaments' industry has produced some excellent modern weapons, but fortunately, on a small scale.'

He outlined briefly the principle arms likely to be

encountered: the T34 tank, well-armoured, fast and with a gun perhaps better than the Mark IV 75 millimetre, not to be underrated, but, fortunately, few in number, around 1,000 compared to nearly 3,000 Mark IIIs and IVs.

'They have several good fighter aircraft, YAK 1 and MIG 3 and LAGG 3, none as capable as our Messerschmitt 109 and fewer in numbers. However, they have the advantage of being closer to the action and thereby having more time at the point of engagement. The YAK 2 Stormovik fighter-bomber you can expect to encounter and the PL 2 bomber, but they are in very short supply. The same 76.2 millimetre gun on the T34 is also mounted on a wheeled chassis as an anti-tank gun. It is easily concealed and should be treated with respect. A new weapon is named the Stalin Organ, a multiple rocket or mortar bomb launcher whose missiles cause an organ-like note passing through the air, more disturbing than dangerous.'

The regimental colonel gave a talk on the state and disposition of the Red Army.

'Following the Red Army's unsatisfactory performance in Finland,' the colonel said, 'the Soviet Union have more or less been obliged to sign a peace treaty with Finland. The only gain to Stalin was to strengthen the defences of Leningrad.' He went on to describe the purges of the officer corps and the political commissars attached to the army units, following the débâcle in Finland. Marshal Vorishilov was now head of defence, solely because he had defended Stalingrad, or Tsaritsyn as it was then known, in the Russian Civil War in 1920 against the Whites. Stalin considered himself to be an expert on military affairs and despatched anyone who opposed his ideas to the gulags. 'Although Stalin is aware of our probable intentions, he apparently hopes to maintain his alliance with us. It is obviously impossible for the Red Army to guard the enormous frontier and we are aware that their army groups are concentrated well behind, guarding Moscow, Leningrad, Kiev and the war industrial zones. Our initial moves will see us well on the way to Moscow before we meet serious resistance.'

Kurt decided that it was time to send Sasha away. She was showing a bit, but it would be safe for her to travel. Karl and

Emma had been most considerate and understanding in their letters and Sasha would be more than welcome. Elsa von Schramm, Kurt's erstwhile fiancée was, of course, very upset but wrote that she was very glad that they had not anticipated the wedding. She was still pure. The general, as he had promised, provided the necessary documentation and all was ready for Sacha's departure. Sasha had few possessions, nothing that could not travel with her as baggage. Their parting was very sad. They were so suited to each other that it was like surgically dividing a body into two pieces.

Kurt said, 'It will soon be over and we shall be together again for ever.'

At the same time he thought, it is more likely to be a long war. We have so many enemies and now it seems that America is not very friendly.

The colonel, now a brigadier, gave the promised information session on the order of battle.

He began, 'The *Erst Panzer* Division, as you are aware, comprises two armoured regiments of which I command one. Each regiment has three battalions of three Panzer companies, all now with Mark IV Panzers. In addition, there is one reconnaissance battalion, one Panzer Grenadier regiment and an artillery regiment. These supporting units are distributed among the battalions, down to company level in the case of the Grenadiers.'

The division, he explained, was one of five Panzer divisions, forming the second Panzer Group, commanded by General Guderian, 'Whom many of you will have served under in France?' He went on, 'Guderian's Second Panzer Group is part of the Army Group Centre commanded by General von Bock. Army Group Centre comprises, in addition to the second, three other groups, the total amounting to nine divisions and 42 infantry and other divisions. In addition to army Group Centre, there is Army Group North, aimed at Leningrad, and Army Group South to take care of the industrial sector towards Kiev and beyond.' The brigadier ordered a covering sheet to be removed from a large blackboard. On the blackboard was a map of Western Russia with the principle cities and the planned movements of the three Army Groups. 'You will study this and note that our objective is Moscow, the principal target of Operation Barbarossa. We could be there in August.'

The intelligence officer addressed the orders group.

'You already know about the Russian weapons you will be encountering. The largest formation you will possibly find confronting our advance will be a tank brigade, part of a large corps formation. The brigade, equivalent to our regiment, comprises two tank battalions, each of three squadrons, all equipped with T34 tanks. In addition, there's a reconnaissance battalion, two regiments of self-propelled guns and two anti-tank regiments distributed among the battalions. Each brigade has a strength of 100 tanks. The armoured corps is closely supported by motorised infantry. You will see from the diagram that our forces comprise 19 Panzer divisions and 143 infantry and other divisions, a total of some two million men, far more men than Napoleon's *Grande Armée* of 1812. Our Panzers outnumber the Russian tanks by three to one. There will be no element of surprise. The Russians are very well aware of our intentions and only have sufficient resources to try to protect their major cities and industrial areas.'

By mid-June, the units had moved up to their start points, concentrated on the border with Soviet-occupied Poland. On 21 June 1941, Hitler gave the orders and the massive formation swept forward. Operation Barbarossa was on the move, into the fine summer weather. The High Command had mentioned to Hitler that the troops were all in summer dress, no provision had been made for the winter.

Hitler retorted, 'Winter. It will all be over before then.'

23

Objective Moscow

The *Erst Panzer* Division led Guderian's Group crossing the Soviet/Polish border en route for Bialystok, a former Polish provincial capital near the Soviet border in Belorussia. The leading regiment, spearheaded by Kurt's battalion, met with no resistance. The Soviets on 21 June 1941 were undecided. Stalin could not believe that Russia was being attacked and diplomatic overtures continued. Molotov, the Soviet foreign minister was eventually handed a formal declaration of war by Ribbentrop, Hitler's foreign minister, with the German army already on its way.

Two days later, Guderian was over the border and on the way to Baranovich and Minsk, following, in fact, the route of Napoleon in the former war. Kurt led his company up to the outskirts of Baranovich. The Hussaren were in fine spirits, the long weeks of waiting over, the Panzers well-stocked with supplies and the commissariat operating smoothly. As the Panzers approached the city, Kurt was startled by the sharp crack of a high-velocity shell, followed by the thump of the gun. Immediately, this was followed by a fusillade of armour-piercing shells coming from a battery of anti-tank guns. Kurt led his company to the right to outflank the guns, but not before three Mark IVs were hit. One was stopped with a track blown off, another disabled by a shell through the driver's compartment, killing the two occupants and setting fire to the reserve ammunition bins. The turret crew managed to bale out and seconds later the exploding ammunition blew the turret off vertically into the air, to crash back alongside the flaming Panzer.

The third took a projectile into the turret which virtually exploded. None got out. The battalion laid a concentrated high-explosive barrage on the enemy battery and Stuka dive-bombers, alerted by radio, finished them off. Since the beginning of Barbarossa, the Luftwaffe had destroyed hundreds of Soviet aircraft on the ground and were constantly bombing the rear areas and lines of communication.

The following night when they laagered, forming a rough circle, guns facing outwards, no lights, the Grenadiers dug in round the perimeter, Kurt spoke to the Panzer commanders.

He pointed out, 'We were caught out today. We must be much more vigilant and quicker to respond. In spite of what we have been led to expect, Ivan is not to be dismissed lightly. We must be prepared for stiff opposition.' The night was dead quiet except for the distant crump of bombs on the rear areas.

'Poor Ruskies, they are getting stick.'

Inside the turrets, coffee was being brewed on the field petrol cookers and mess tins handed out with cold stew and black bread. Before dawn they were ready to move out and Kurt received three replacement Mark IVs with crews.

The division moved on towards Minsk, an important city which could be anticipated to be defended. The going over the high grass or wheat-covered steppe was good and visibility such that there was little chance of being ambushed. Minsk was in sight at the beginning of July, Barbarossa was going well.

Army Groups North and South were thrusting deep into Russia. In the north, Leningrad was already threatened. Von Kloist and von Runstedt in the south were moving across the Ukraine and in sight of Kiev. Further south, the Black Sea coast and the Crimea were occupied. However in the Ukraine the Red Army had skilfully avoided encirclement and had securely withdrawn to fight another day.

One morning, pushing on towards Minsk, Kurt saw with astonishment flames pouring from the turret hatch of a nearby Panzer. Three scrambled out and fell to the ground, uniforms on fire, and soon after the turret blew off. The driver and co-driver got out unhurt. Kurt realised at once they had been using the petrol pressure stove, strictly forbidden on the move. Well, they had learnt their lesson the hard way and warned others not to be foolish. Punishment – already received.

Regimental reconnaissance patrols had penetrated towards the approaches to Minsk and reported units of at least divisional strength dug in. T34 tanks were sunk into the earth with only turrets visible, a formidable situation. Air reconnaissance confirmed this and aerial photographs revealed tanks, guns and support infantry in a very strong defensive position. At last the Red Army was showing itself, standing firm.

'Well, we will smash them, no doubt, poor Ivan.'

Guderian ordered the *Erst Panzer* division to take up positions for a frontal assault and two other divisions to carry out pincer-flanking attacks, the classical horns of the bull manoeuvre. Kurt's company was in the centre and he could see the Panzers of the division, nearly 1,000 stretched out across the steppe, line abreast, an inspiring sight, and in front a very dangerous situation: dug-in tanks, all the advantage with them firing from static positions. Not like France, he thought, that was a piece of cake. Stukas dive-bombed and all the artillery of the three Panzer divisions pounded the Russian position. Surely nothing could survive such a storm of fire.

The curt order came over the radio, 'Advance', and the long line moved towards the Russian positions, the flanking Panzer divisions were already on the way. As soon as they were within gun range of the T34s, they opened fire, a murderous hail of armour-piercing shells, delivered with accuracy from fixed positions. All along the German line Panzers burst into flames, some fortunate *Hussaren* scrambling out and running for cover. It was as though the terrific bombardment by bomb and shell amounted to nothing. Still the Panzers advanced, there was nowhere else to go. To hesitate would have been fatal. The order came, 'Speed up', and the Panzers roared on, now firing back as fast as the guns could be loaded. Kurt ordered half the company to concentrate on the nearest T34s to the right and the other half on the left and work towards each other. Firing on the move is a hit-and-miss affair, but they had some success and knocked out several tanks. Meanwhile, the Panzer divisions on the flank were in position to take the enemy from the rear. Kurt's company, or what was left of it, were right on top of the Russian tanks and after a furious fight all along the front, the T34 crews remaining alive baled out, arms above head in surrender. The booty was considerable: many T34s, self-propelled guns and anti-tank pieces. The Russian infantry, who had taken no part in the action, gave up disconsolately, throwing away their weapons, a miserable bunch.

It was a costly victory. A third of the Panzers of the First Panzer Division were knocked out. Never again, prayed Kurt, a frontal attack on dug-in tanks: suicide. His company was reduced to half-strength, good men gone. Those who survived unwounded would return with new Panzers. There was, fortunately, no shortage of Mark IVs. The armaments' industry was in top gear and replacement crews were constantly being turned out from the depots. In a few days all was brought up to strength and ready for the next round, hopefully less boisterous than Minsk.

Having been on the go for nearly two weeks without proper rest, the *Hussaren* welcomed the respite: first sleep, then a good wash down over a bucket and a shave. Kurt's crews were becoming accomplished cooks and produced some acceptable meals. The quartermaster's department had functioned splendidly so far. Ammunition, fuels, food and water had been readily available. As the lines of communication became stretched, supplies would not be so easy to deliver. There was, however, the Russian railway which went as far as Borodino, nearly to Moscow, a narrower gauge than the European system, but the engineers would cope with the problem. The railway was a boon which Napoleon did not have.

The battalion colonel told Kurt that he had done well at Minsk, handling his company with dash and efficiency.

'Who knows,' he said, 'you may even get your own battalion command?'

It was not to be, as we shall see. The brigadier called an order group of senior officers, down to company commanders.

He said, 'We did well at Minsk, although our casualties were heavy. We must not underrate the Red Army, as the intelligence officer will tell you. They have very quickly reorganised under new commanders. Also, they are rapidly building up their armaments' industry, harnessing all the resources of their almost limitless labour and raw materials. Our next objective will be Smolensk. We can expect it to be heavily defended. No more frontal assaults. Our tactic is to surround them from the flanks, encirclement without the possibility of a safe withdrawal. So far, although Stalin ordered a scorched earth policy, the Red Army had avoided destroying bridges over the rivers and the roads, such as they are, very poor indeed, were no hindrance. Probably the Russian field commanders reasoned that they will be needing them soon, when they advance. One very heartening piece of news was that the much improved Panzer, the Mark V, is in production. Whatever, we will smash them at Smolensk and then on to the final obstacle before Moscow, the Vyaz'ma Line.'

The I.O. outlined the changes that had very quickly taken place in view of the success story so far of the German Army. Like Hitler, Stalin was now in charge, defence commissar and commander-in-chief. Following the purges of the generals, the command structure was in the hands of old and trusted cronies of the dictator. Timoshenko was chief-of-staff and army groups were headed by tough, experienced old soldiers: Zhukov, Budenny, a tank commander probably the equal of Guderian, and Voreshilov and Rokossovsky.

'Smolensk is heavily defended,' he told them, 'and we shall have to concentrate on encirclement, armoured thrusts followed up by infantry. Once surrounded, the Red Army surrenders, as we have already seen at Minsk, with the gain to us of thousands of men and much material.'

The 200 miles of steppe from Minsk to Smolensk was without incident, no enemy air activity. The Red Army Airforce had not recovered from the hammering on the ground at the start of Barbarossa. Occasionally dust clouds away from the route indicated shadowing armoured cars. In a few days the advance guard were in sight of the city and recce units reported at least three armoured divisions and several infantry divisions with supporting artillery. T34 tanks were dug in on the perimeter in front of the infantry; not a good move always, as mobility was denied. The battle opened with saturation bombing and shelling by a thousand massed guns and Guderian's Panzers and their stalwart Grenadiers moved out under the cover of the inferno falling on the enemy. The regiment moved towards the right flank, battalions and companies in line ahead, followed by other regiments. The Panzer divisions aimed at both flanks. When in gun range the formidable army could shell at will. As soon as Kurt's company was in range, he opened fire, a signal to the rest to commence firing. The result was a barrage of armour-piercing high explosive and, just to confuse things, a few smoke shells. Hundreds of Spandau machine-guns chattered away, marked by deceptively slow-moving tracer bullets, quite ineffective but adding to the unearthly din. Very little fire came back at first as the T34 tanks could not bring their guns to bear. Then the Russians moved in their self-propelled guns and some Panzers were hit and erupted in flaming funeral pyres. Only a few of the crews ever got out. So it went on throughout the long hot July day, the Panzer crews battling away inside amid smoke and cordite fumes. All were heartily relieved to see the sun go down, but with chilling thoughts. What will the dawn bring?

There was little rest for anyone, only snatched impromptu meals and replenishment of fuels and ammunition. The supply lorries went round with great courage right up to the firing line, even at night, when too much noise would bring a hail of fire from zealous enemy gunners. The very inflammable and explosive contents of the lorries made the job unenviable. Kurt, like everyone else, wondered what tomorrow would bring, perhaps the end. The Russians were very restless, firing flares which illuminated the scene. The sound of tank engines went on through the night, the T34s being extricated from their pits for redeployment, a hopeless task in the dark. Kurt thought, they are unlikely to be in position at first light and we can hammer them before they are ready.

At first light the Panzers were manned; no coffee, no time, a drink of water from the canteen, most likely mixed with a little cognac, Kurt's certainly was: no harm; in the tense situation, alcohol had little effect. The Panzers moved forward, firing ceaselessly as they went, curving in behind the rear of the enemy. Individual duels occurred with the odd T34 which appeared opposite. Casualties were remarkably light. The Panzers were not a good target when moving, but their sheer volume of fire power was most effective. They were winning the fight.

So it went on all day, the battle raging and the Panzer divisions getting further round the Russians to complete the encirclement. Kurt had a personal fight with a T34 which emerged from the smoke and dust only 100 or so metres away. They both fired simultaneously. Kurt's gunner hit a track and the T34 slewed helplessly round. The T34 gunner got off a round which missed the Panzer turret, but ploughed through the storage box behind, destroying the crews' precious blankets and packs. A further direct hit on the T34 penetrated the hull and the tank exploded spectacularly. None got out, for sure.

The night was a repeat of the one before. The din of conflict stilled, there was a chance to rest nervously and eat a cold mess of food. There was no replenishment of fuel and ammunition and no mechanics to work on the Panzers. The trucks could not reach them in the dark. Never mind, thought Kurt, tomorrow we shall finish it. He sat alone in the closed turret having a drink of cognac and a smoke. By the dim interior light he took Sasha's photograph from his wallet and wondered if he would ever see her again. After Minsk he had received a letter from her, posted at Tilsit. She was well and Kurt's parents were very kind and had made her more than welcome. She was growing big and the little one was kicking around in her womb.

At first light they were off. The situation had miraculously changed and it was very quiet after the turmoil of the day before. Then they realised they were approaching the infantry to the rear, probably not of the best quality. There was desultory shooting by a few anti-tank guns, quickly dealt with. By midday they had met up with the Panzers coming from the left flank. It was over. All around the Russians were surrendering, throwing away their weapons.

'Comrade,' they were crying, hands on their heads, 'don't shoot.'

The booty was enormous, more then 300,000 prisoners, 500 tanks and 1,000 guns, the miserable dejected prisoners destined for camps where few would survive from starvation and disease. For the victors there was a welcome break for men and vehicles.

The Mark IVs were now subject to breakdowns. It had been a long hard drive over rough ground. They were complicated machines, operated by hydraulically driven systems, subject to irritating faults, which, with all the expertise of the fitters from the mobile workshops, gave frequent problems, such as failing to traverse the turret or elevate/depress the gun. Examination of the Russian T34 revealed that it was more basic. For hydraulics, man-draulics. It was simply an engine, a chassis on tracks, and a very good gun, no frills, simple to maintain. Only the tanks at company command level and upwards were equipped with radio. There was rumour of a new and better tank in production, the KV85, a heavy, the Russian answer to the Mark V Panther.

The *Wehrmacht* established a base at Smolensk, building up reserves before pushing on to Moscow. Kurt reasoned, are we anticipating a not-so-quick-as-planned victory? Hospitals and even brothels for the soldiers' comfort were provided, the latter with carefully screened, choice Russian women. There were also officers' brothels, but Kurt abstained, true to the one love of his life, darling Sasha. Letters were now fairly frequent and up-to-date from Sasha, his parents and, above all, his grandfather, General Brausch. Kurt considered that there might well be censorship of incoming mail, although he had so far not detected any sign of letters being opened. Outgoing letters were very definitely censored and must not contain any mention of places, movement, or anything military.

Although Smolensk was taken by mid-July, it was well into August before a move began against the Vyaz'ma defensive line in front of Moscow, 100 miles to the west and about the same from Smolensk. Kurt and his fellow company commanders queried the apparently unnecessary delay.

Has Barbarossa run out of steam? Surely we should be well on the way by now.

They were not to know that Hitler, as commander-in-chief, was undecided. Was the drive across the Ukraine to seize the riches of the Ukraine and the Caucasus not more important than taking the capital? Finally, Hitler ordered half of the two Panzer Groups of Army Group Centre, under the command of General Heinz Guderian, to proceed south to join Army Group South, von Runstedt in the battle for Kiev. The *Erst Panzer* division regrouped, with the newly-formed corps under General Hoth.

At the orders group, the brigadier told them that the next objective was to crush to Vyaz'ma defensive line. The line, some 20 miles long, guarded the approaches to Moscow and was manned by no fewer than one million men, up to two thousand tanks and thousands of guns and anti-tank guns.

'It is a formidable fortification, but we shall roll it up from both ends. Our plan is to attack on both flanks, each prong consisting of two Panzer divisions and ten infantry divisions. The other Panzer division, the *Erst*, will have an independent role in front of the line, along with another ten infantry divisions, to prevent a break out back towards Smolensk. We cannot expect a quick victory. It is a hard nut to crack and we shall miss General Guderian and his four divisions. In strict confidence, not to go beyond this room, it must be assumed that Operation Barbarossa has run out of steam and Moscow is no longer the prime target. We must, therefore, be prepared to face the winter. As someone wrote, "Moscow, the city of a thousand freezing snows and ice-laden air that defeated Napoleon Bonaparte and his *Grande Armée.*" So the sooner we are there the better it will be for us.'

It was mid-August before the battle commenced. The two prongs poised ready for the off were preceded by the usual intensive artillery and air assault. The *Luftwaffe*, which had always provided invaluable support, was hampered by constantly increasing demands and by the huge proportions of the vast land battle. In addition, the Red Air Force had quickly recovered from its initial defeats and was now back in action with the latest fighters and fighter bombers. The low-flying Stuka dive-bombers, the artillery of the air, had now to be protected by fighters, an enormous strain on the *Luftwaffe*.

The regiment took up position strung out on a line out of anti-tank gun range, by battalions and companies. They attracted some heavy artillery fire, a nuisance to the infantry divisions deployed to the rear who suffered not a few casualties. The sounds of the battles raging on the flanks could be clearly heard: the crump of bombs and thump of shells and the crack of the Panzer cannons; evidently a furious fight was in progress. All day they watched for movement from the front but, apart from the shelling, all was quiet. Kurt got his wireless operator to tune in to *Rundfunk Berlin* for the news and inevitably the soldier's song, Lala Anders singing 'Lili Marlene' in her husky, inviting voice:

> *Vor den Kaserne, Vor der Grosse Tur,*
> *Stedt da ein Machen, wie heist Lili Marlene . . .*

Very nostalgic and the soldiers loved it, and not only the Germans. Forces of all nations listened on their radios, when they should have been concentrating on more important frequencies. So they passed a quiet day, eating, smoking and, perhaps, a suck of the cognac bottle. They were well supplied by loot from the occupied countries of Europe, even British cigarettes, inevitably Woodbines, and sometimes Scotch whisky, from the vast stocks of the NAAFI, liberated in France. At nightfall, the Panzers pulled back into laager, guarded against enemy infantry attack by the faithful Panzer grandeur. The Panzers were completely vulnerable to infantry at night. All they could do was to start up and move, very dodgy in the dark, with inevitable collisions and not without loss to persistent foot soldiers. A grenade lobbed in a turret hatch was deadly. Moreover, the commanders' head sticking out above the hatch made a good target, silhouetted against the night sky, either by pistol, rifle or the increasingly available sub-machine pistols. However, it was a quiet night, the sky lit up by the occasional brilliant parachute flares, blue German ones and white Russian.

Before dawn, the Panzers were back in position and as the light grew stronger they could see in the pre-sunrise to the east, two columns of T34 tanks emerge from the Russian positions, well supported by infantry. Kurt estimated two brigades, perhaps 200 tanks, which he observed to spread out into line-abreast formations, steadily moving forward. The regiment was ordered forward to meet the breakout on both sides and cut it off. The infantry and guns would block any who got through. The battalion colonel ordered the Mark IV companies to act independently as soon as they were in range. A Panzer versus tank dogfight ensued. Kurt ordered his company to form line ahead and fire broadsides, not terribly effective on the move. As the T34s turned to meet the threat, Kurt, over the radio, changed his formation to meet the tanks head on.

'Stick close together. Don't break up. Follow my moves.'

Very soon, they were in among the T34s. At short range it was impossible to miss. Very quickly, the fight became a cauldron of flaming vehicles, dust clouds and confusion. Kurt kept his Panzers in a tight group. Some were hit. Crews baled out and gallant attempts were made to get them to comparative safety. So it went on all day and at dusk Kurt ordered the company to withdraw for the night. By a miracle, some of their own Panzer Grenadiers reached them and gave Kurt a respite, to take stock. About one third of the company was missing, ammunition was perilously low and fuels nearly exhausted. They settled down to an uneasy night: no sleep, collecting the wounded wherever the Grenadiers could find them; in everyone's mind, what of tomorrow? What on earth will happen? Shall we survive? In extremity, men offered up silent prayers to a God they hardly believed in, 'God get us out of this and I will be good for evermore.' Quite absurd, and those who so prayed perhaps felt very sheepish afterwards.

Before dawn, they were mounted and ready for whatever was to be. As the light grew, they were astonished to find themselves alone. The Russians had pulled back. The anxiety of the night vanished like early morning mist. Maybe God had heard their cries. Orders came from the colonel: reform by companies on the previous start line and dig-in. The batteries of medium artillery were brought up so that, if necessary, they could fire over open sights. A message from the brigadier told them to sit tight and contain the enemy.

'Our pincer movement is going well and in a day or so it will be over.'

The Russians continued the assault, determined to break out. Tank battalions stormed the lines and again the area became a shambles of burning tanks. The fight went on endlessly, the Russians throwing in more and more tanks and men, always to be repelled with great loss. The Panzers suffered also, and the unprotected artillery. The line became stretched but held.

So it went on: no respite, no let-up for several days; almost no sleep; constant vigilance. The men were becoming exhausted automatons: load and fire the guns almost without stop; at night fill the bins with replacement ammunition; change worn out machine-gun barrels, the fitters repairing broken down parts. Then one morning, there was no renewed attack, no sally from the enemy. The news came from Army Group that the encircling of the Vyaz'ma line was complete. The entrapped Russians, communications severed, had no choice but to surrender. As the day wore on, vast columns of men, hands on head, moved towards the German lines. The victors were swamped under the deluge and literally bogged down for several days in order to cope. None must be allowed to escape to fight another day. The collection of the material abandoned on the field would be carried out by others.

German High Command, based at Smolensk, estimated that some 700,000 prisoners were taken, over 1,000 tanks and more than 5,000 guns of all kinds. Never before had such a huge amount fallen into the hands of the army. It also revealed that to date, on all fronts, the Russian losses were estimated to amount to 2,500,000 dead or wounded, or taken prisoner, 18,000 tanks and 14,000 aircraft either destroyed on the ground or in aerial combat. Unbelievable, such losses on so vast a scale. The *Wehrmacht,* in its great sustained offensive, had also suffered terrible losses. At Vyaz'ma the *Erst Panzer* Division had lost two thirds of its strength. Army Group Centre had lost nearly half of its infantry strength. Moscow was no longer a priority so it was late September before the group was re-equipped to return to the offensive.

Early autumn was too late. The rains came and the Panzer advance was choked in a sea of mud soon after they set out on the final stage. Kurt, who had so far escaped unharmed, became exhausted in the struggle to extricate bogged-down Panzers and at the same time beat off attacks by small groups of T34s which, with foresight, were equipped with broad tracks. It was a nightmare, added to which the lines of communication were becoming over-stretched and the forward units were living on a hand-to-mouth basis. In the north, Leningrad was under seige but showed no sign of breaking. Army Group South at Kiev and further south, on its way to Rostov on the inland sea of Azovskoya, was making little progress. The Black Sea region, including the Crimea, was in German hands, but not a particularly advantageous gain.

Stalin, meanwhile, had entrusted the defence of Moscow to Zhukov, a ruthlessly tough general who had already performed miracles in the defence of Leningrad. Zhukov immediately set about marshalling all available reserves. Among other measures, he created the Moscow Volunteer Corps in which many intellectuals and Jews served, many of whom did not know how to use their weapons but, nevertheless, swelled the ranks: cannon fodder. Later on, during the *Wehrmacht* push, they were strongly mauled and captured Jews suffered a terrible fate.

The Panzers edged their way on to the capital against heroic opposition by the Soviets. The rains eased off and some days the sky was an inverted bowl of blue, the sun still warm enough to take the chill out of the air, for with the presage of winter there were frosts at night. At the beginning of December, the main body of the *Wehrmacht* was only 20 miles from Moscow. Reconnaissance units were already in the suburbs. Kurt's company of Panzers, sadly depleted, were right behind and he was astonished to see across the Moskova River the gleaming onion domes of the Kremlin, Cathedral of St Basil's. Few others were to get such a glimpse. Kurt's reaction was joyful.

'Look,' he exclaimed to his crew, 'there is the prize. The war will soon be over.'

But it was not to be.

The skies turned leaden and heavy snow fell, blotting out all around. Temperatures fell well below zero. The men were not equipped for such conditions, neither were the Panzers, being in many cases immobilised for lack of winter-grade engine oils. Turrets, gun movements and controls operated hydraulically, were sluggish or froze up altogether. Then General, now Marshal Zhukov, hurled his acclimatised Siberian divisions into a fierce counter-attack. The High Command ordered the Panzers to withdraw and refit, the infantry to hold the line. Unbelievably, the German army was on the defensive, not only in the centre, but all along the front. Stalin had ordered an all-out offensive. Many of the Panzers in front of Moscow had to be abandoned. With the few remaining in Kurt's company, he pulled back with a feeling of utter despair.

'At so great a cost in lives, to be forced to turn back from our goal.'

Grounded crews rode on the outside of the Panzers in freezing conditions. Such cold was unimaginable. Freezing wind-blown snow lashing around them, many men succumbed and simply lay down to perish in the snow.

To add to the misery, Zhukov mounted an offensive from the north and south of Moscow. The tanks and infantry were adapted to the terrible conditions. After all, it occurred every year. The *Wehrmacht* centre was driven back some 200 miles, leaving very much of their strength in men and machines behind, the dead and abandoned. The same was happening on all fronts and there was a general withdrawal, in spite of Hitler's insistence that the lines must be held. Hitler turned his fury on the generals. Von Runstedt, Guderian and others, all the best ones, were sacked; placed on the retired list for daring to give ground and not to hold on at all costs, a foolish error by the *Führer*.

Back at the Vyaz'ma position, by the beginning of 1942, occupying the ground which they had previously captured with such gallantry and loss of life, the army was given a short respite to rebuild itself.

The Soviet offensive had run out of steam. At great cost they had turned the tables and almost certainly saved Russia for the time being, anyway. With the Japanese pre-emptive strike on Pearl Harbour, America was now in the war and there was a new dimension added. America, with its enormous resources of men and materials, joined the Allies and declared war on Germany.

24

Vorwärts Wir Gehen Zurück

Old sweats probably recalled 1918, the end of the Great War and a somewhat sick-joking expression, a cry of 'forwards, we are going back'. It was to revive during the vicissitudes of the war against Russia which, with Barbarossa having failed to achieve a swift defeat, could drag on for years. Kurt had done his best to keep the remaining *Hussaren* of his company in good heart. The retreat or, more diplomatically, the withdrawal from Moscow, was hell on earth. Frequently, the Panzers bogged down in deep snow, packed under the belly so that the tracks could not grip and simply turned idly. To get the Panzer going again, it had to be cleared of snow under the belly and from in front: a nigh impossible task. The poor half-frozen men, inadequately clothed, were likely to freeze to death, as some did. But there was no alternative. Roving small packs of T34s were deployed to close in and destroy the Panzers. So, immobilised, the only chance to survive was to keep moving and fight. Sometimes a Panzer could be extricated by towing with another Panzer, using the heavy steel tow rope which they all carried. Under the enormous strain, even these would snap and the loose ends whip back with great force, causing deadly injury or instant death to any unfortunate in the way. Following two fatalities the *Hussaren* learnt to keep well out of the way.

One day there was a letter for Kurt, not unusually tattered, sender General Brausch, written in accordance with postal regulations, inscribed:

Major Kurt von Ritter
First Panzer Hussaren
Fieldpost 3679

It probably had been opened. The general's letters usually appeared to be. It began:

Mein Leibe Kurt,
Der Krieg ist Verloren . . .

Kurt was horrified. To put such sentiments on paper was courting disaster, to state bluntly that the war was lost. Kurt and many others were indeed beginning to have the same thoughts, since the obvious failure of Operation Barbarossa, but did not dare to express them. The *Gestapo* was everywhere, watching and listening. Long after, Kurt learnt that the general had been taken away and had disappeared without trace. It might also have happened to Kurt, as the recipient of such traitorous correspondence, but someone begged that he be left alone. Major von Ritter was a very experienced Panzer company commander, one of the few originals remaining alive. He deserved promotion but to forfeit it would be sufficient punishment. As time went by and he remained a company commander, he realised that the fatal letter was to blame. Nevertheless, he resolved, 'I will show them, I will be the best.'

In January, good news came from Sasha. They had a fine son. 'He already looks just like his Daddy.'

Kurt was very happy. Following his grandfather's letter, this was indeed welcome news, but there was little chance that he would get to see his son for a long time, or, sombre thought, if ever.

The way back was pure torture. The enemy harassment was to be accepted, but the climate was far more punishment and the cause of more casualties. Many were literally frozen to death and frostbitten fingers and toes were common. If they did not fall off, amputation was often necessary. The infantry were worse of; transport inadequate and unreliable, the verges of the highway were strewn with broken-down vehicles, lorries, Volkswagen runabouts and useless motorcycles. At least in the Panzers there was shelter from the endless blizzards but touching the armour plate with bare hands caused the skin to adhere and be torn away. Food was a problem for all: nothing hot and only cold water to drink, the petrol cooking stoves, not very reliable at the best of times, mostly gave up. 'Indeed we are going forwards to the rear.'

The Russian offensive slowed down. They had saved Moscow, Leningrad held firm and the Germans were halted or pushed back on all fronts. As the remnants of Army Group Centre reached a line near the depot at Smolensk, the weary disheartened soldiers gained some respite. At least they could halt and supplies of food and winter clothing were coming up and, blissfully, a ration of cognac. Spirits rose somewhat and the men soon recovered and the re-equipping of the tattered army began. The *Erst Panzer* Division, reduced to a few Panzers and crews, was withdrawn further back towards Smolensk to reform, hopefully, with the rumoured Mark V Panther, which would even the odds against the Russian T34s. They were to be disappointed. As Kurt had anticipated, although others junior to him had been promoted, he remained a company commander.

The Mark IV Panzer was destined to remain in service until the forseeable future. The Panther had encountered technical problems and was not to be ready for service for another year, a major influence on current events. Another Panzer was already in production, the Mark VI Tiger, a massive 56 tons of thick armour plate and mounting the excellent 88mm gun, a very formidable weapon. The Russians were working on the Joseph Stalin to counter the Tiger, equally heavy and well-armed. Neither of these were to play a great part in the war.

The *Erst Panzers* were brought up to strength and ready for combat. However, neither side showed much activity as the icy winter continued. Spring would see a reawakening of the conflict. The division, along with other élite units, was given a new role, to become independent under direct High Command, OKH control, to be used as and when emergencies occurred on any part of the front; a sort of fire brigade. This meant that much of the time they were in reserve, ready for instant movement, or that was the plan.

The High Command had realised that the Russian T34 tank

could not be bettered unless the Mark V Panther would be shortly available, and in quantity, which it was not. The combat generals at the front, in despair, advocated the production of the T34 as the principal battle Panzer for the *Wehrmacht*. This was turned down by the armaments industry; too difficult to cope with the technicalities of production changes. There was, in any case, the political factor and the final veto from Hitler.

'The war will be over soon and certainly before our T34 version would be ready.'

None believed him. It was going to be a long war, not like France in 1940.

The *Erst Panzer* Division was ready again for action. The replacement crews were well-trained by the Panzer training regiments but, of course, 'not like the ones that had gone before them.' In early spring, the long, hard winter coming to an end, Hitler ordered an offensive in the south, continuing the occupation of the vital Ukraine. Moscow and Leningrad could wait. Contained, their turn would have to come later.

Orders came through for the division to move to the south, to spearhead General von Kleist's First Panzer Army of five Panzer divisions and nine infantry divisions, with support units of artillery, anti-tank and mortars, mostly self-propelled. In addition, they had their own *Luftwaffe* Air Corps, consisting of fighters and fighter-bombers with a radio link. General von Kleist, one of the generals not purged, had been very successful the previous year with Army Groups South under the overall command of the now departed von Rundstedt. They had taken the vital city of Kiev, on the River Dnieper, in a fiercely contested battle in which some 20 million Russians were killed, mostly civilians. The Group had pushed on across the Donetz Basin, taking Kharkov, another important centre, and down to Rostov on the Black Sea. They had been halted by communication problems, and the winter, which was however not too devastating in the south, and also the Red Army counter-offensive.

The division set off in fine spirits, glad to be on the move, after the stagnation of the unforgettable winter's miseries. An 800-mile journey through the steppes with abandoned maize and wheat fields: the Russians had fled or been transported by the SS for slave labour in Germany. Kurt was elated. News from home kept him informed of his son's progress: little Karl, named after Kurt's father. He was very fortunate in having the same crew, who left Poland on Operation Barbarossa: all very good at their jobs. The gunner and driver, the key men, would have been hard to replace. The company would shake down on the long journey and be fit to go into battle. Well, he said to himself, it is not so bad. Although I have missed promotion, I am lucky to be alive and, after all, life goes on.

The *Erst* joined up with the 1st Panzer Army at Rostov, after a considerable journey on tracks, which caused few serious problems to them as the going was good. General von Kleist welcomed them by speaking to the senior officers of each regiment in turn. He said that the operation was, firstly, to seize Stavropol and then to advance around the Causasus mountains to Grozny, on the Caspian Sea, the objective being to capture the oil fields in the region. This was the Russians' main fuel supply, without which they would be unable to continue the war. In addition, the oil supplies would enable the Germans to continue the war, indefinitely, if it should be necessary.

Von Kleist pointed out that, 'The opposition comprised the 1st Guards Army and the 46 Army, commanded by Malinorsky, nothing we can't handle. In addition, Timoshenko to the north was attempting to regain Kharkov, so that will keep the Red Army to our flank, well-occupied.'

He spoke of a new Russian land-mine, 'A wooden box mine, cheap and easy to produce, but powerful enough to stop a Panzer. They are buried flush with the surface and the gauze metal cover, sprinkled with dust, is difficult to detect. So, *Achtung Minen.*'

25

Stalingrad

Stavropol, 200 miles from Rostov across the steppes, and it was anticipated that the Panzer army, even with the expected delaying tactics, would reach there by the end of April. The army set off on a bright spring morning, full of beans. 'Let's have at them. Look out, Ivan, here we come,' was the sentiment. The recce regiment of the *Erst* went in front, the armoured cars keeping away from roads or tracks which might have been mined, the Panzers followed close behind with Kurt as senior company commander, leading. All went without incident until in the late afternoon, with the sun behind them in the west, two armoured cars were blown up by mines; badly damaged, but the crews escaped. This was immediately followed by anti-tank guns firing from close range. Two of Kurt's Panzers were hit and destroyed, exploding spectacularly. To halt would have been suicidal, so Kurt ordered his Panzers literally to charge the guns. Followed by the rest of the battalion, they reached the battery in a matter of minutes, losing several more Panzers. The Russian gunners attempted to flee but were all machine-gunned down. Kurt pressed on through the battery to where a battalion of infantry were deployed, obviously uncertain whether to stand or flee. Faced with the steel wall advancing on them, Kurt gave the nearest no chance to decide, ordering the company to open up with every machine-gun, even the Panzer commander's own weapon mounted on top of the turret. The fire fight was amazing, multiple streams of bullets, marked by tracers, cutting down the helpless Ivans. The rest of the battalion joined in and in a matter of minutes the field was clear. Only the dead and dying remained, the wounded who would soon die anyway, left behind on the steppes.

Similar harassment by the Red Army continued and delayed the Germans from reaching sight of Stravropol until later than planned. One day, recce regiment reported that they had reached sight of the city which was heavily defended from the western approaches and inside the suburbs. *Erst Panzer* were ordered, in the planned general pincer attack, to get into the city on the right flank, to cause havoc among the units of the Red Army inside. Following a day of shelling and intensive bombing, they set off at first light, the *Erst* racing to the chosen point. They encountered little opposition and soon the Panzers, closely supported, as always, by the Panzer Grenadiers, were in among the houses. Battalion ordered Kurt to penetrate on a main street as far as he could, the company, in two lines, proceeding down the road, turrets traversing to cover buildings as they went. Suddenly, all hell broke loose from both sides and from the front, a hail of machine-gun bullets which cut down the two leading Panzer commanders. Head and shoulders out of the turret, as they were obliged to, the drivers kept going and the gunners fighting. Then three Panzers burst into flames, hit by infantry, hand-held anti-tank weapons, similar to the German *Panzerfaust*. The projectiles, launched at close range, were designed literally to drill a hole in the armour plate and explode inside with an intense flame, igniting the stored ammunition. None of the crews survived. Kurt rallied the rest and hammered the buildings with a hail of armour-piercing and high-explosive shells and machine-gun fire. Behind the Panzers, the Grenadiers were infiltrating the side passages, cleaning out pockets of riflemen, losing not a few men in the process. By nightfall the company halted, joined by the rest of the battalion. There was no sleep for anyone, the Grenadiers particularly alert on the perimeter against infantry night attack, when the Panzers were defenceless.

The battle for Stravropol continued for three more days. Casualties were heavy on both sides, particularly among the *Erst* fighting inside the city. Finally, the pincer closed and the Russians gave up. There followed a halt of two weeks, whilst units were made up to strength, delayed by the replacement Panzers coming the long way forward. Meanwhile, the Red Army to the north had mounted an offensive to recapture Kharkov which had been in the *Wehrmacht* hands since the previous year. Timoshenko, Stalin's old comrade, had practically enveloped the important city using the 9th Guards Tank Army and the 57th Guards Army. The German defenders, von Paulus's 6th Army, took a tremendous beating, but managed to hold on as Timoshenko was slow in exploiting his initial gains. The Germans consolidated their position and held on until further units arrived.

Back outside Stravropol, von Kleist sent for the *Erst Panzer* Division to proceed to cut off Timoshenko's forces around Kharkov, from the rear, breaking his lines of communication. The division, re-equipped, set off on the 500-mile journey, via Rostov, bound for a position to the east of Kharkov, between that city and Volchansk, Timoshenko's sole supply route. Time was vital and the division moved without stopping from before dawn until after dusk and in less than a week were in sight of the objective.

Timoshenko, faced by a furious counter-attack, had urged Stalin to authorise reinforcements and in response, units of the 11th Guards tank army were on their way. As the Panzer division reached the area of the road, which they were ordered to cut, they could see the guards' tanks moving down the highway from the east to Kharkov. The strength of the Soviets was estimated to be two divisions. The *Erst* general ordered an immediate attack to straddle the road and split the enemy in two. Kurt's battalion was ordered to spear the advance.

'What, us again, why not choose someone else?'

They drove a wedge between the column of tanks, the Panzers firing on the move. The weight of the unexpected onslaught caused the Guards to hesitate and the Panzer division was deployed over the vital area. Now to hold their advantageous position.

The Guards' tanks spread out on both sides of the Panzers and in the ensuing fight the division was attacked from the front and rear by forces twice the size. All day the Panzers fought like demons, back to back, and were still, the following day, undefeated. Timoshenko was screaming for his reinforcements, which could not break off the engagement with the Panzers, who were fighting as though they were possessed by the devil. The German 6th Army, led by von Paulus, encircled Timoshenko's forces who in attempting to fight their way out, were slaughtered by endless assaults which broke on the German massed artillery. The attempt on Kharkov failed. A quarter of a million were taken prisoners and the guards' tanks, severely mauled, gave up, leaving *Erst* Division once again seriously depleted but victorious. For his outstanding bravery, Kurt von Ritter was awarded the highest decoration, the Knights Cross. He was now a much decorated major, destined to remain in that rank.

The division was reduced to half strength and, before it could return to the fray, needed replacement crews and Panzers and would remain at Kharkov until that was complete. It was a period in which to repair tired body and mind. They were well-supplied with food and tobacco and welcome cognac and beer. The brigadier gave a dinner for all the regiment's officers to celebrate Kurt's decoration. Letters were written and a back-up of mail and parcels from home arrived. In a month, they were ready to go and were ordered back to von Kleist, the 1st Panzer army which was still battling its way to the Caspian Sea. They found the Panzers still not much further on beyond Stravropol and it was already September. They were now in sight of the Caucasus mountains and the Russians, with one flank secure against this barrier, were resisting stubbornly. Stalin had ordered the Germans to be stopped at all costs and his generals were fully aware that to fail meant death or disgrace and Siberia. Equally, Hitler was adamant. He was right in assessing the strategic importance of the objective, but he should have left the tactical handling in the field to the High Command and the general on the spot. Far away in Berlin, he commanded the whole Russian front by radio. The generals were far from happy. Of course, they knew best.

The *Erst* were welcomed back by von Kleist, who told them he was preparing for an all-out offensive to take Grozny, less than 100 miles from the Caspian Sea and the way to Baku and the oilfields. The *Erst* resumed their role in the lead with, of course, Kurt's battalion out front. The Russians fought very skilfully. Delaying actions and minefields were employed extensively to halt von Kleist in a virtual ambush. Grozny was reached in late September, where the Red Army was deployed in force and well dug in. Stalin echoed Clemenceaux, 'the tiger', at Verdun in the previous war: 'they shall not pass.'

The ensuing battle was horrendous, the *Erst* and two other Panzer divisions were ordered to attack on the flank, which they found heavily defended and failed to pass. The Russian tanks came out in strength and the ensuing dogfight on the move resulted in the Panzers being compelled to withdraw or possibly face surrender. Kurt had ordered his Panzers to keep together, not to break formation, and lost only a few. The frontal attack was also repulsed with very heavy losses and the lines of communication so overextended that von Kleist was obliged to break off the engagement, causing Hitler to rage at the delay. Meanwhile, Grozny remained secure in Russian hands. In the coming weeks, the Germans were driven back the way they had come and only managed to hold outside Rostov. The *Erst Panzer* Division had already gone off on the next special assignment, to Stalingrad.

Stalingrad was an important city on the River Volga and early in the spring offensive the Germans were in sight of the very desirable occupation of it and the gateway to the industrial areas beyond. Originally called Tzaritzsin, during the Russian Civil War in the early 1920s it was defended against the Whites by Stalin and his comrades, Timoshenko and Voroshilov, presently generals in the Red Army. To take the city would, therefore, be a humiliation for Stalin, whom Hitler hated with a personal vindictiveness. Stalin was determined to defend Stalingrad at all costs.

In September 1942, the 6th Army, comprising six infantry divisions commanded by General von Paulus, was detailed to assault Stalingrad. Stalin entrusted the defence to Marshal Zhukov, to hold Stalingrad at all costs. With considerable skill, von Paulus smashed the defenders on the approaches and established a bridgehead over the Volga River. Some of the divisions were in the suburbs before the end of September. Stalin refused to evacuate the civilian population of some 200,000, as this would be tantamount to surrender. Von Paulus's flanks were increasingly exposed and in October Zhukov launched a counter-offensive aimed at cutting off the bridgehead. The German troops were fighting a terrible battle in the streets from house to house. Hitler, furious at the slow progress and convinced that the defenders were on the point of collapse, ordered the 4th Panzer Army to join in the battle and to prevent Zhukov from closing the gap round the bridgehead.

The *Erst Panzer* Division had already joined the 4th Panzer Army and was already on the move, painfully slowed down by tenacious attacks by the Russians. By the time they reached the bridgehead, Zhukov was positioned to close the gap with pincer thrusts along the Volga from the north and south. The *Erst* led, of course, by Kurt's company, fought their way in, with considerable losses. They were followed by two other Panzer divisions and the remainder of the 4th were denied access. Zhukov, with suicidal assaults, had completed the encirclement of Stalingrad.

The Panzers were deployed, among the by now ruined buildings, supporting the infantry in a virtually static role, shelling positions hampering the infantry advance: a slow thankless task, not a proper role for the Panzers.

At the end of the month they learned that the British had decisively defeated Rommel's *Afrika Korps* in North Africa at Alamein and it was only a matter of months before the Germans would be forced out altogether, The first defeat of the *Wehrmacht* so far since 1939, some saw it as the writing on the wall.

At Stalingrad the Red Army held on desperately, clinging to an area on the west bank of the Volga. Von Paulus's troops launched a massive attack and with enormous casualties reached the river, then frozen over. It was mid-November and the dreaded winter added to the misery of his army, trapped in the city, growing short of ammunition. There was no possibility of crossing the Volga on the ice. There was no cover and it would have been suicidal. The 6th Army was at a standstill. The men had winter clothing, but rations were cut to a minimum, the awful snow fell ceaselessly and the eternal frost and ice created pure hell. Outside Stalingrad, General Manstein was ordered to mount a counter-attack to relieve the beseiged army, in spite of High Command's entreaty that von Paulus should fight his way out. Hitler insisted that von Paulus under no circumstances should retreat and the *Luftwaffe* had assured him that they could deliver sufficient supplies to keep the entrapped force to hold on at least until the spring. Manstein's counter-offensive bogged down, defeated by the appalling weather and the fierce resistance of the Red Army who, after all, were accustomed to the harsh winter conditions. So there were some 250,000 German troops, Panzers, reduced to a mere 100 in service, around 2,000 guns, short of shells and a vast array of trucks with nowhere to go, locked up in the city.

Kurt's few remaining Panzers were scattered in pockets separated by city streets. Several had been lost by anti-tank projectiles at close range by courageous soldiers. Several of his commanders had been hit in the head by marksmen and killed outright or seriously wounded. To make a daily visit to the sections involved a deadly desperate journey among the ruins, often under fire. The rations were brought up nightly by the Panzer Grenadiers from a comparatively safe position to the rear, the only chance to have hot food and drink. There was no cognac and tobacco was running out.

Reversing his Panzer one evening at dusk into the comparative shelter of some ruins, a Russian shell struck the wall above, causing a shower of heavy masonry to fall. Kurt was hit on the head by a large lump and knocked unconscious to the floor of the turret. His crew could do little but bandage his head, which was bleeding profusely, and manhandle his body out of the turret to the ground and carry him down to the advanced dressing station to the rear. From there he was taken by ambulance to the airfield and flown out by a tri-motor Fokker transport plane with other wounded. He was lucky. Shortly afterwards the airfield was captured by the Red Army and any further supplies were by parachute drop; no more evacuation of the wounded, many of whom were to die of their injuries. The plane landed at Brest Litovsk, near Warsaw, where there was a fully equipped military hospital. Kurt was in a bad way and it was some days before he opened his eyes, unable to move his limbs or body. His skull had been crushed, the bone pressing down on the area of the brain controlling movement. After some days, when Kurt had recovered from his ordeal, the surgeons carried out a trepanning operation, removing a linear section of the bone from the damaged area. He slowly recovered, pain diminished and he was able to move his body very slightly at first and then fingers and toes.

News came in frequent letters. His father, Karl, who had kept up the old boy network with comrades in the *Kreigsampt,* expected to be able to travel to see him very shortly.

Kurt made remarkable progress, aided by a very competent physiotherapist, but as the physiotherapist told him, 'You must learn to walk before you can run. Fortunately, you are very fit and strong, but you must be patient, the treatment will take a long time.'

Kurt suffered from occasional severe headaches. The area of the trepanning had been covered by a steel plate and the scalp sewn back over it. His head, completely shaven, was itching abominably as the hair sprouted under the bandages. He was horrified when he saw his face in a mirror, barely recognisable from the old handsome Kurt, ravaged by the strains and terrors of the war, so long in close combat, the eyes particularly reflecting the internal unquiet.

His father Karl came at last bringing gifts: a new uniform and shirts, underclothes and toilet articles. Many things were now in short supply but they managed very well in Prussia, having foodstuffs to use for barter. Kurt enjoyed the many photographs of his son and Sasha.

'I hope I get some convalescent leave when I am well enough and then I shall see them in the flesh.'

Karl told him the bad news.

'At the end of January, Stalingrad fell to the Russians, all of the 6th Army remaining was captured, nearly 300,000 men. Von Paulus, newly promoted to field marshal in order to stiffen his resolve to fight and win, was also a prisoner.'

Few survivors emerged from the dreadful camps when the war was over. Hitler was enraged but unable to take it out on the generals, who were either prisoners or dead.

Karl continued with the bad news.

'Your grandfather, the general, has disappeared, we believe spirited away by the *Gestapo*, but I cannot find out for sure. I believe he has been executed.'

Kurt told his father about the letter.

'After the dreadful business at Moscow in the winter of 1941, the general wrote me a letter in which he expressed the opinion that Germany had lost the war. I suspect that the letter had been opened.' He went on, 'After Moscow I was led to believe that I would be promoted, but in spite of the opportunities caused by the casualties, I remain a major, company commander. It is thought I am tainted by the general's views. Probably I also would have been liquidated, but experienced front-line officers are too valuable. Let them die in action. So there it is.'

His father agreed, 'Yes, I am sure you are right. These days we can trust no-one. Be very careful with our comments and certainly beware of what we write in letters.'

Whilst Kurt was slowly recovering, well taken care of (after all he was a hero), the Russians, soon after Stalingrad, opened up a winter offensive along the whole front. Unhindered by the bitter weather conditions, the Red Army relentlessly pushed forward two or three hundred miles and, even worse, von Kleist, near his goal, the Caspian Sea, was driven back to Rostov and the sea of Azov, inland from the Black Sea, hundreds of miles, to where they started in the spring of 1942; all had been in vain. The Germans floundered in deep snow and failed to hold back the Soviets until the weather eased off and even a few miles to the west conditions were better.

At the beginning of May, Kurt was declared fit enough to go on convalescent leave. His body movements were almost normal, having responded to the rigorous and often painful physiotherapy. The journey back was very slow along the main railway line to Dresden, the principle rail junction and marshalling yards for traffic bound for the front. Frequently the train was stopped in sidings for several hours to allow seemingly endless trains to pass: troops and supplies, frequently flat-bed trucks with Panzers, guns and trucks, draining away the resources of the *Reich* and the occupied territories. After Dresden things were better but Kurt arrived home very weary indeed. Sasha was overjoyed to see him after such a long absence, although she did not display her dismay, horrified by his changed appearance, still haggard and wan, his cropped head still only sprouting a covering of hair and practically bald over the area of the wound. Nevertheless, Kurt enjoyed the best of treatment, in the marital bed, slow at first and then recovering his sexual vigour. Even baby Karl, now a year old, gurgled and blew bubbles at his father.

The month's leave passed all too soon and he was ordered to report to a medical board in Berlin.

The board, consisting of three medical services colonels, were quite astonished when Kurt said, 'Gentlemen, I can save your time. I am quite fit and looking forward to returning to my unit.'

The president of the board remarked, 'Well, that is a change. Mostly we get endless excuses for not being sent back. Good luck, major.'

So Kurt returned to Tilsit and prepared to leave.

Karl understood but Sasha and his mother exclaimed, 'Why always you? Haven't you done enough?'

His leave-taking was painful. He thought, it is causing so much sorrow, I hope this is the last time and the war will be over.

The return journey was little delayed and all too soon Kurt was at Smolensk from where he was sent to Bryansk, about 200 miles to the south on another railway reopened by the engineers. The *Erst Panzer* Division was being rebuilt there. The division, or what was left of it, was captured at Stalingrad. He reported to the battalion and found only a few officers whom he knew, returned wounded like himself. The new colonel welcomed him warmly.

'Von Ritter, I am very pleased to see you back, we certainly will need officers of your calibre. I suppose that in truth you should be in my place, but there it is. Shall we say bad luck?' The colonel continued, 'We are attached to the 2nd Panzer Army which is part of Army Groups Centre, commanded by General Kluge. We expect to receive the new Mark V Panthers. There are not very many ready for service yet so we are the chosen fortunates. The division will also be having some Mark VI Tigers and the very new Ferdinand, nicknamed the *"Elefant"*. The Ferdinand is a rather lumbering self-propelled anti-tank vehicle, but armed with an even more powerful 88 millimetre gun, weighing 65 tons due to the frontal armour being 20 centimetres thick and a consequent speed of only 12 miles per hour. As you will realise, a big operation is planned. We shall know the details very soon I expect.'

Kurt went to his old company. Only one officer remained from the original ones who left Poland two years ago. His old crew were either dead or, less fortunately, prisoners of war in the indescribable hell of a Soviet camp, where they were likely to die anyway, a slow death from exposure to the climate and starvation. In mid-June the Panthers arrived, they were a great improvement over the old Mark IV which, however, remained the main battle tank of the Panzer Korps. The 'Panther' had sleek lines designed to deflect armour-piercing projectiles and was armed with a 76.2 millimetre gun, a copy of the very successful Russian weapon, with thicker armour and faster than the Mark IV. They were very pleased. A new expensive toy to beat the Russian T34s with. At the same time, a regimental orders group informed them that the operation was against the great salient established around Kursk during the winter campaign.

26

Kursk

The Russian front had been stable for some weeks and Hitler, known then as the *Gröfaz*, the greatest general of all time, decided, against the advice of his generals, that a massive assault should be mounted against the salient at Kursk, using the full weight of the Panzers. General Heinz Guderian had been brought back from retirement and given overall command of the Panzer Korps, with equivalent powers of an army group commander. He told Hitler that the Panzer divisions were exhausted and needed more time for recovery. Hitler dismissed this plea and pointed out that with the new Panthers, Tigers, and increased thickness of armour on the Mark IVs, the time was ripe for a blow which could finish the Russians off. He pointed out that the Allies would soon be landing in Europe and that an all-out offensive was therefore essential to bring Stalin to his knees.

The bulge was some 300 miles deep and 500 miles long, cutting the German front in the centre and threatening the north and south. The basic plan was to drive a wedge in the centre, a *Panzer Keil*, a battering ram, the spearhead of which was to employ the Tigers and lumbering Ferdinands in front with the Panthers and Mark IVs on the flanks. Simultaneously, attacks would be mounted on the north and south of the salient. The operation would deploy nearly all of the armour. Stalin, unbeknown to Hitler, had full details of the German build-up from a spy network code-named Lucy based in Switzerland and from the British 'Ultra' decrypts of German High Command signals and messages. As a result, Stalin strengthened the defences in the salient. When the battle opened the forces employed were of great magnitude. The Germans had nearly 3,000 Panzers against 2,500 Russian tanks. The Red Army had 20,000 artillery pieces and the *Wehrmacht* half that number. German strength in men 900,000 against 1,300,000 Russian. Supporting aircraft were over 2,000 on each side. Mind-boggling numbers.

The attack was launched on 5 July 1943, opening what was later described as the most decisive battle of the Second World War and the *Todesritt*, death ride of the Panzers, the greatest tank battle of all time. The Army Group Centre headed by the 4th Panzer Army attacked with the Tigers leading flanked by the Panthers. They immediately ran up against carefully prepared positions. Stalin, forewarned, had ordered a fortress to be established round the perimeter and in depth. Kurt's company was leading the *Erst Panzer Hussaren* on the left flank of the Tigers in close support. Zhokov was ready and immediately the Germans ran up against fierce resistance from anti-tank guns. There began an appalling bloodbath, the most brutal engagement of the war. The Panzer Grenadiers in the centre were subjected to a decimating bombardment from the ground and air which continued in depth to the advancing troops behind.

Kurt lost several Panzers right away, the shells penetrating the thinner armour of the hulls which were broadside on to the enemy guns. The Panthers did not come up to expectations, being easily set in flames because the petrol supply systems, tanks and lines were inadequately protected. The Panzers on the flanks traversed their turrets to open up a defensive fire, inaccurately from the moving vehicles. The fire from the heavy guns of the Tigers was more successful and the thick armour saved them from easy destruction. To makes things worse, the Panzers were now in the grasp of dense minefields and soon tracks were shattered by enormous explosions. From these the crews were able to bale out only to be gunned down on the ground. None escaped from the blazing Panthers. They went up too quickly and in the following explosion were blown to pieces. Soon the field was obscured by smoke and dust and burning debris. With the gain of only a few miles, the slaughter continued all that day.

At nightfall the fighting died down and the Panzers were able to sort out their units, which were sadly mauled and reduced to an unbelievable few in number. A night of feverish activity followed. Kurt had lost half of his company and there were no replacement Panthers, so they were supplied with the old Mark IVs, familiar friends, safer than the Panthers, if any Panzer could be in the inferno of fire. The *Panzer Keil*, the wedge, was severely blunted. It was a dreadful night: refuelling and no replenishment of ammunition, scanty meals and overall anxiety of being attacked by infantry, who if they broke through the Grenadiers, would pounce upon the defenceless Panzers. The only possibility under such an attack was for the Panzers to move with all speed, with the dire event in the darkness of crushing their own troops in their slit trenches and of damaging collisions among themselves. To add to the misery, occasional heavy shells fell among the closely packed units and more nerve-racking mortar bombs with the eerie approach noise and flat resounding thump when they hit the ground, spraying the area with deadly shrapnel. A horrible night, one of the many similar ones to come.

Before dawn they were ready, tired but eager to get on with it and break out of the iron ring of the Soviet defences. So off they went, the Ferdinands up with the Tigers on the flanks. The slow moving *Elefants* would not delay the action, which was hardly likely to move forward at other than a snail's pace. Hopes were high for a breakthrough. The Tigers and Ferdinands, with their heavy armour and armament which out-gunned the Russian tanks, were practically unstoppable. However, the crews of the Ferdinands were exposed from the top and the rear, vulnerable to attack from the air or from infantry. As soon as they got in among the Russian positions, infantrymen in concealed weapon pits, very courageous soldiers, armed with anti-tank projectiles, popped up and, launching the missiles at the vulnerable sides of the Tigers, succeeded in destroying several. Some Ferdinands were similarly treated by hand grenades tossed into the open crew operating space, killing the men and sometimes blowing up the ammunition with devastating results, bits of *Elefants* all over the place. With the sheer weight of armour, fresh Panzer divisions pressing on from behind forced the *Keil* slowly forward.

Kurt, with his company, repeatedly exhorted them over the radio to keep together in formation. As soon as they came under attack from the T34s they turned to face them and closed sufficiently to beat them off from the immediate vicinity. They succeeded in destroying several tanks, with equally a few Panzers in flames. All day the horrific fight went on, the Germans moving inexorably forward, nevertheless, with terrible losses of armour and men. By the end of the awful day they were out of the tangle of minefields and defence lines and could fan out on the open steppes. At nightfall they formed battalion laager and the company commanders reported the state of their units to the colonel.

The night was a repeat of the previous one, a furious replacement of lost Panzers and crews re-fuelling and restocking with ammunition. One company commander had been killed, so the colonel ordered Kurt to command the two companies combined as one unit. Well, Kurt thought to himself, promotion of a kind at last, without the rank and pay.

The colonel, sensing Kurt's reaction, said, 'You have done well, as always. I shall see what I can do for you when it is over.'

They both knew, however, from the rejection of previous recommendations, that there would be no successful response from higher up, it would be blocked. Shades of the fateful letter from his grandfather, seemingly aeons ago, *'Der Kreig ist Verloren.'* Again the following day the Panzers were engaged in close combat with swarms of T34s. The Tigers and Ferdinands were no more, all knocked out or broken down with mechanical faults. As the day wore on, seemingly endless, praying for the sun to go down, Kurt had lost half of his combined companies, himself engaged often in close combat, in the confusion of burning, smoking vehicles and exploding ammunition. At the end of the engagement he came out unscathed; with good fortune, skill and experience as a commander and the Lord's help. God with us.

The tattered remnants pulled back into a regimental laager to work feverishly, reorganising, replenishing and receiving new Panzers. In the middle of all this, brilliant parachute flares lit the area like day, and night-operating fighter bombers literally swarmed overhead, squadron after squadron. The scene in the laager was horrific. *Hussaren* crawled under the Panzers for shelter only to be destroyed when the vehicle received a direct hit. All things come to an end and when the bombing was over they set about picking up the pieces, a nigh hopeless task. The regimental doctor issued Benzedrine tablets, which prevented sleep, for those who wished to take them. There were likely to be more days and nights without any rest.

So it went on, day after day of savage combat, the Panzers taking a terrible mauling, but there was no question of giving up. Both sides fought with indescribably savage bravery, determined not to give in, the pride of the *Panzer Korps* at stake against the dogged resistance of the Guards Tank Army.

On 13 July, after a week of desperate combat, the remnants of the Panzer Army, only 600 in number out of 3,000 which had set out seemingly ages ago, formed up for the final *Todesritt*, the death ride. In the battle that followed, by the end of the day only 200 Panzers remained and the battle of Kursk was lost at enormous cost. The *Wehrmacht*'s élite armoured corps, equipped with the latest Panzers, designed and built by superior German technological skill, manned by carefully screened troops, had been defeated at the *blitzkrieg* operation they had excelled in. Stalin had won the strategic initiative. This was to prove the turning point of the war.

The infantry, who had barely taken part, now were left to stem the tide, the onslaught which would follow, Zhukov pressing on all along the front. The pincer movements against the Kursk salient had also ended disastrously with the destruction of all but a few of their Panzers. All for nothing, a miserable gain of 20 miles in the centre. Kurt was one of the few survivors and, incredibly, still in the Panther he set out in long ago. It seemed an age. A survivor, through luck combined with experience and the quick unhesitating responses of his driver and gunner following his cool, clear commands, keeping his head in spite of the furore of the combat. The Panzer divisions would rebuild but would never be the same again.

The *Erst* was practically wiped out and in the battalion the colonel, a handful of officers and fewer than 50 *Hussaren* remained unharmed. There were a few wounded who lived. Those who had got out of the blazing Panzers were cut down on the ground in the awful carnage of shot and shell. The *Erst* pulled back, or rather limped, to an area outside Bransk, conveniently situated on the railway from Smolensk to Kharkov. Very soon Panthers were rolling in, the latest models with the fuel system adequately protected. The recruits were younger, only partly trained, but promising material, willing, keen, intelligent, specially earmarked for the élite *Erst* division. And that was a new start, the rebirth of the division, to rise from the ashes. Some of the new officers, all Prussian sons of families Kurt knew well, would fit in admirably, if they survived the first battle.

27

Nocheinmal Vorwärts Wir Gehen Zurück

Zhukov went on the offensive and the Red Army steamroller moved inexorably forward, eventually to arrive at Berlin and end the war, no more retreats. The previous two severe winters and the ferocious tenacity of the Russian soldiers, fighting on their native soil, had defeated Hitler's strategies and he was now on the defensive. The reversals of Stalingrad, and particularly Kursk, had changed the war on the eastern front. The long-awaited attack by the Allies in the west had not yet begun. Stalin was angrily urging Roosevelt and Churchill to get on with it. Now was the time, with the Germans reeling in Russia. There was no quick response from the Allies. They were not yet ready. For the Germans, once again advance to the rear.

The Soviet autumn of 1943 offensive was concentrated along the Baltic Sea at Azov. The Red Army crossed the Dnieper River, trapping the German forces in the Crimea. Hitler was still obsessed by the opening of the route to the precious oil region and the defence of the mineral ore deposits already in German hands. The general's protests were ignored and the OKH was ordered to mount the counter-attack. Units from Army Group Centre were detached including the *Erst Panzer* Division which had reverted to its independent role under the High Command. The newly formed division with the latest equipment was ready and the newcomers anxious to get at them. The weak areas would quickly be weeded out in the first engagement. Inexperienced troops were completely lost when first coming under fire, disoriented, and that was when the weaknesses were eliminated and the survivors left to carry on.

Kurt had been elevated to second-in-command of the battalion, a sinecure, of course, but no advancement in rank or pay. In the unlikely event of the colonel being killed or wounded, he would take over. The division travelled over the same route south that they had taken last year on the way to Rostov now in Russian hands. As an armoured division, their role was not to support infantry in the attack, so they were ordered to mount a push along the Caucasus mountains, in front of Odessa, and open the trap from the south, whilst the main frontal assault was proceeding in the Kharkov region against the Donetsk basin.

The division, elated at being in cavalry role, set off in high spirits, the *Erst Panzer Hussaren* in its usual place out front. The leading company of Panzer Grenadiers set off at a cracking pace behind a few recce armoured cars. Aerial photos had revealed little resistance. The battalion and the regiment followed some way behind, spearheading the division. Without warning, the advancing company was fired on from the rear and immediately they spotted T34s to the flank and were trapped by a force of unknown strength. The company commander took advantage of a declivity in the hills and faced his Panthers outwards, protected at the rear and both sides. They reported their dilemma to battalion over the radio and were ordered to sit tight, not try to break out, which might have entailed destruction of the whole unit.

The colonel ordered Kurt to take the remaining companies and drive a wedge through to the beleagured company.

'I will follow with the rest of the regiment. Be careful, it looks as if it may develop into a full-scale battle. The enemy are a stronger formation than our intelligence indicated.'

Kurt set off once again to the fray, glad to be on the move with his Panzers. They soon encountered the Russian tanks, which fired on them too soon, out of range and warning the oncoming Panthers. Kurt's companies, in vee formation, swept on firing furiously, a storm of shells, armour-piercing and high explosive. The Panther, unlike the old Mark IV, was equal to the T34s in armament and armour. Several Russian tanks went up in flames and the rest broke away. Very soon Kurt reached the trapped company and together they formed up on the steppe and cautiously advanced, ordered over the radio to halt if they met with strong opposition.

After a few miles with the armoured cars scouting ahead, they were attacked from the air by fighter-bombers, with little effect. Soon after they came under shelling from heavy artillery and Kurt decided to halt and wait for the regiment to arrive. It looked as if a full-scale battle was developing. Division's orders were to consolidate until all the units were in position, prepared for divisional action the following day. At dawn the leading regiment moved out of laager into the relatively unknown situation which resolved itself very soon when encountering a large group of tanks on the steppes, blocking their path. Orders came to close battle and the Panthers swept forward, guns ready for instant action. When both contestants were in range, some Panthers and T34s were soon ablaze. Kurt thought, here we go, Kursk all over again. Holder of the highest award for bravery, the coveted Knights Cross, and only those who were there at the time knew at what cost of daring it was won, and few survived to tell the story, by rights I should not be here and probably shan't be for long.

A good scrap emerged when the *Erst* and a Red Army Guards Tank Division were engaging with the clash of the Titans, an armoured fight Panzer versus tank, almost man to man. Kurt, back with battalion as second-in-command, watched the companies' progress. Soon they were in close combat, well matched and only the individual skill of the commanders decided who was the victor. One company was hemmed in by T34s and, fired from all sides, faced destruction. The colonel ordered Kurt to take the reserve company and rescue them. The T34s were taken by surprise when Kurt's Panthers engaged them from the rear, sending several up in flames, with subsequent spectacular explosions, bits and pieces flying and no survivors. All day the battle continued and at dusk they pulled back, licking their wounds. Casualties were fewer than anticipated, but they were too far away from base to receive replacements.

During the night orders came for the division to pull back. The attack to their north had failed. The Russians had carried out a lightning strike over the Dnieper and thus might well isolate the Germans in the Crimea. In addition, on the Ukranian front, Kiev was threatened. The division was ordered north to join the fight to save the very important city from reverting to the rightful owners, the Russians. With hardly time to pick up replacements they were off.

On arrival in front of Kiev, the *Erst* was at once committed to the battle, their role to harass the southern flank of Marshal Rokossovsky's Ukranian army. In spite of a fierce fight, the Germans were beaten back by overwhelming force from a very determined foe. Kurt's battalion, along with the rest, were hammering away at the flank which was heavily defended by self-propelled anti-tank guns, their attacks made futile as the Panzers moved into range. The scene was indescribable, artillery on both sides pounding away, often over open sights. Overhead, fighters, protecting the fighter-bombers, were locked in aerial duels, the sky filled with vapour trails.

Inexorably, the Red Army stormed forward, heedless of casualties, and Kiev was lost. Moreover, their drive was of such impetus that it was 100 miles before it ran out of steam and Army Group Centre could pause and recover.

Stalin ordered a winter offensive from Leningrad to the Black Sea. Unlike Hitler, he did not command, but left the details to his generals. The third dreaded winter was upon them, the Russians coped but the Germans staggered, reeling from savage attacks, as though paralysed by the endless snows and the blinding whiteness. *'Gott Hilfe Uns.'* The main attack came against Army Group Centre pushing towards the Soviet frontiers. The other groups were obliged to send all the Panzer divisions to help out, the *Erst* among them, struggling along the roads enveloped in deep snow, often bogged down in drifts, slow to arrive, too late to stem the advance of the Soviets.

By the end of 1943, the siege of Leningrad was ended, the Germans pushed back towards the borders of Finland. The front at the new year stretched from outside Leningrad, just before Smolensk, to Bryansk and to the Black Sea, threatening Odessa. The OKH High Command ominously pulled out of Smolensk and moved to Brest-Litovsk in Poland with an advanced headquarters at Minsk.

Hitler raged at his generals, 'Idiots, are you children? Odessa and Smolensk will not fall or I shall have some of your heads.'

The *Erst*, relatively whole after supporting the Army Group Centre by fruitless efforts to stem the Russian advance on the flanks, were ordered urgently to Smolensk, which was threatened and if lost would seriously affect railway communications. After a hard journey through the snow, the tired engines of the Panthers sometimes giving up altogether, the division arrived at Smolensk. They were detailed to dig in on the open ground outside the city, along with other Panzer units to form a fortress of steel. At dawn the next day the T34s appeared, a swarm of tanks, unhampered by the snow due to their broad tracks. As soon as they were within range, the Panthers began picking them off and soon the front was littered with burning tanks. Still they came, seemingly endless numbers, until, in spite of heavy losses, they were on top of the Panthers, which, unable to manoeuvre, were virtually sitting ducks. The Panthers could only extricate themselves by reversing along their tracks, firing as they went. Kurt, taking stock when night fell and the battle died down, found that one third of their battalion was wiped out. In the morning, the Germans evacuated Smolensk, taking the road to Minsk, over the ground which was the scene of the victorious *Wehrmacht* advance of two years previously.

By now Odessa was threatened also and Hitler ordered the city, doorway to the Balkans, and the countries of his Allies, Hungary, Bulgaria and Rumania, to be held at all costs. Off went the overworked *Erst* division once more, the long trek south, warmer weather ahead but the going hard on the Panzers. The regimental fitters' group were hard-pressed carrying out repairs under freezing conditions, mainly worn out tracks and faulty engines.

The battle to hold Odessa was fought for several weeks, made more desperate due to the threat of entrapment from the great bulge the Red Army had driven above Odessa in the centre. Day after day the Panzers slogged it out on the steppes facing the city; no respite, no retreat, death or glory. The battalion fought well, sticking together and holding on. The colonel used Kurt, as before, to go to the rescue with the reserve company to plug the front when threatened to break. A very desperate encounter, Kurt thought it the worst he had so far experienced.

In spite of all the blood and sweat, eventually the *Wehrmacht* was beaten to its knees. In April 1944 Odessa finally fell to the victorious Red Army. It was mainly won because the defenders were drastically short of men, equipment and supplies of all kinds. Then, providentially, the thaw set in and the whole Russian front became a sea of mud. Operations were brought to a halt until mid-May when the Red Army moved swiftly in an offensive at Minsk, ever nearer to Berlin, the ultimate goal; far away but miraculously in sight.

The *Erst* was, of course, ordered to the next trouble spot, the battle for Minsk. Hitler did not need to threaten the generals on this occasion, they knew it was vital to hold the Red Army there, or be forced to move back the whole front. The division, during the pause in the mud, had refitted and replenished Panzers and *Hussaren*. The new men were by this stage of the war from the bottom of the barrel. Nevertheless, they were all young, perhaps too young, but very keen to fight for the Fatherland and its glorious champion Adolf Hitler. The Army Group Centre was threatened with destruction, so the OKH moved the troops from Army Group North in an attempt to save a desperate situation. It transpired that the remaining forces in the north were then cut off, with the loss of some 350,000 men, the most serious defeat of the war.

At Minsk the *Erst*, along with many other armoured divisions, was deployed on the plain before the city to meet and hopefully bar the advance of the Soviets. Kurt's battalion probed forward with others to meet the oncoming Guards tanks which they encountered moving in great force towards them, T34s with the infantry riding on them or moving behind under cover of the armour. The Panzers closed to within gun range but could not hope to stem the advance. It did not develop into a full-scale encounter. The Panzers steadily withdrew until they reached the main body and prepared to stand.

Kurt considered that the clash of armour that followed was the worst he had experienced, the most savage. Regardless of their enormous losses from the Panzers and the formidable 88 millimetre anti-tank guns, still the Russians came on. The *Erst* were once more reduced to a few fighting units and after a few days were pulled out of the battle to re-equip once more.

Before the *Erst* was ready to go back to the battle which was raging at Minsk, there was some momentous news. The Allies had landed in France. The colonel returned from division where the general told the commanding officers the news.

'We are already withdrawing from Minsk,' he told them, 'and we are ordered to Normandy along with the SS *Totenkopf* Panzer Division. The SS are a tough, hard-bitten bunch, who like ourselves have seen much action. We leave at once. It is urgent that we arrive as soon as possible. Hopefully the poor tracks will make it?'

Stalin, following the long-delayed Allied invasion of Europe, assured of victory, decided that the Red Army could take its time and the summer offensive was restricted to large-scale partisan activities, disrupting communications and army operations against strong points. The Baltic Coast was reached and the front line, by the time the *Erst* left, stretched down to the Black Sea close to the Rumanian border.

The colonel called all the officers to an orders Group. His opening remark was a great surprise, 'Gentlemen, we are going to France to fight the Americans.'

They were excited, so much to talk about, above all to be away from the damned Ruskies and the terrible climate, to a friendly atmosphere and only the stupid Americans to contend with.

28

The Western Front

The *Erst Panzer* Division set off on the long march out of Russia and across Europe, strung out over many miles of roads. Halts were only allowed for replenishment of the vehicles, any rest being taken on the move, with two drivers changing over, scanty meals without hot drinks. From Warsaw on the going was good, the roads and bridges in good repair, slave labour plentiful and expendable. From Warsaw the division pressed on to Prague, thence the long haul to Cologne and over the border of France to Lille and they were soon in Normandy, the journey accomplished in the incredibly short time of just over a week. On arrival outside Caen, they were deployed for action with barely a pause. The British had taken Bayeux and were pressing on to capture Caen and its vital airfield, Carpiquet, in use by the *Luftwaffe*. Overlooking the airfield some miles away, the Hill 112 dominated the area. This was the division's job, to get there and block the British advance. The Americans were moving down the Cherbourg Peninsular, aiming to join up with the British and cut the Germans off from escape to Paris.

The division reached Hill 112 before the British, who were reported to be approaching from the north-west, an armoured division in strength. The regiment was deployed along the edge of a copse on top of the hill with open ground in front, waiting for the British tanks. The weather was warm and sunny and the early morning sun brilliant, which would blind the enemy and aid the Panthers. The Panthers had been joined by some Tigers of the 21st Panzer division, which had served with distinction in

North Africa with Field Marshal Rommel. Kurt was tucked securely behind a thick hedge, intrigued at being once again in the country of his paternal ancestors. He watched the first British tanks emerge from the long, steep climb up from the plain below and spread out on the open area in front and waited for orders before opening fire. The tanks were Shermans supplied by America. They were known to have inadequate armour plating, but a good all round 75mm gun. The latest model, the Firefly, had an improved weapon, a 17-pounder which was equal to the Panther's 76.2 millimetre cannon.

The Panthers waited until the Shermans were on the hill, about brigade strength, and then opened a murderous onslaught of armour-piercing shells. In minutes the Shermans were reeling, many in flames and exploding. Those crews who got out were machine-gunned. Those left withdrew out of range and, to Kurt's astonishment, fired bright yellow-coloured smoke in the direction of the Germans. A squadron of Typhoon rocket-armed fighter-bombers flying cover over, discharged their 60-pound rockets right on the target. The effect was awful, a nightmare of thunderous explosions, the ground shaking. Kurt thought it was comparable to the discharge of a battle cruiser of the *Kriegsmarin* which he had once witnessed in the Baltic. The first squadron was followed by others, but to little effect. Few Panthers were actually hit and destroyed and none of those in the front line.

At dusk a small group of Shermans crawled forward with their infantry close behind and approached the Panthers after nightfall. The Panthers fired randomly at the Shermans and illuminated the ground with star shells, to little effect. Then the British infantry were in among the Panthers using infantry hand-held projectiles with devastating effect. In the light from the burning Panzers the commander could see the infantry at close range and, following Kurt's example, fired bursts from the machine-pistols which were carried in all the turrets. The Panzer Grenadiers had been driven back by the Typhoons. Some of the Tigers were also destroyed.

After a sleepless night they waited ready before dawn for the next onslaught by the British tanks. Again the Shermans were decimated, moving up in great numbers and losing more and more, until at the end of the day they were forced to give up. The following day the Shermans stayed away and the Panzers consolidated a position with the Grenadiers securely dug in amongst them. Before sunset, Kurt was astonished to hear the faint drone of bagpipes and to see emerging onto the open ground a great line of infantry. Under a dense smoke screen the enemy advanced with great courage and determination, in spite of fierce machine-gun fire from the whole German position. By nightfall the infantry were in among the Panzers, only to be slaughtered. A whole division had probably lost half its strength in a futile attack.

The next day was quiet on Hill 112 and they were treated to a grandstand view of a great clash of armour, over the plain to the north of the River Orne. Two British armoured divisions, each stiffened by units which had fought so well and defeated Rommel in Africa, advanced across the plain, their objective to cross the Orne and enter Caen. They were very effectively stopped by two Panzer divisions, the *Panzer Lehr*, comprising troops from the Panzer Schools and the Hitler *Jugend* division, both relatively untried but well-equipped fanatical fighters. The British were repulsed with terrible losses, the plain littered with destroyed, burnt-out Shermans.

Further fruitless attacks on Hill 112 were subsequently repelled by the Panthers and eventually the British commander, Field Marshal Montgomery, gave up the apparently hopeless attempts to secure Caen, and laid on a massive, saturation bombing raid to flatten the city. Caen was destroyed pointlessly, as German infantry remained securely among the ruins. The second week in July, Montgomery mounted an all-out infantry offensive to cross the Orne and take Caen. With very costly losses of up to half the infantry involved, Caen was taken. Below Hill 112, British Sherman tanks, with great persistence and a terrible battering, took Carpiquet airfield. The German defenders of Hill 112 were obliged to withdraw or be trapped.

Even though the Germans knew that the Sherman tank was inferior to the Panzers, even the old Mark IV, they realised that sheer weight of numbers would tell. The *Erst* moved down from the infamous Hill 112, the way the British had come, with little effort of the enemy to impede them, they were busy elsewhere, and then turned towards the Bocage country, an area of high hedgerows and narrow winding roads. They halted at the village of Bray where the Bocage began and with an open flat plain to the north where the British tanks would come from. It also was the gateway to Falaise and the good tank country beyond.

Reconnaissance warned of the approach of a British armoured division and a build-up of artillery units facing towards Bray. The Panthers were securely dug in, only the turrets exposed above ground, a barrier of steel. The battle opened with a dawn raid by 1,000 bombers. The earth boiled under the hail of 2,000-pound bombs. The crews of the Panthers closed the hatches and were secure, except against an unlucky direct hit. Nevertheless, the devilish inferno was unnerving and some suffered from uncontrollable shell-shock and were unable to carry on. The bombing was followed by an equally terrible barrage of medium and heavy artillery shells. Then the massed field artillery 25-pounders laid down a creeping barrage behind which the Panzers could observe an estimated brigade of Shermans coming forward slowly. In spite of the heavy bombardments, most of the Panthers were fit for action. The order came to hold fire until the Shermans were in comfortable range. On they came, confident that there would be little opposition. Kurt, from his now open turret, anticipated with glee the order to open fire.

'Come on, you bastards, we've got you now.'

The salvos from the Panthers ripped through the oncoming Shermans and in no time the field was littered with flaming tanks. Still the remnants came on, followed by another brigade. The slaughter of the enemy was terrible to witness. After several hours of just sitting tight in their holes in the ground and firing away with everything, the opposition ceased. Hundreds of Shermans had been destroyed. The *Erst* were justifiably elated by a glorious victory.

To their astonishment, they were ordered to withdraw into the Bocage and to operate in small groups, ambushing the British tanks as they came on, as inevitably they would. The Americans were coming fast down the Peninsular and would trap the

Germans inside the Bocage, with no escape route. Kurt took half of the battalion and moved down a sunken road between high hedges and outside a small hamlet called Beni-Bocage pulled his Panzers off the road at a junction with signposts to Vire and Mortaigne, deploying them in a large orchard. They spent a restful couple of days, helping themselves at the inn and the few shops. The civilians had fled and only a man and a woman remained, the innkeeper and his wife. Kurt told them that when the British came, to tell them that there were no Germans in or around the village, they had all gone some days previously.

Kurt had sent a lookout in his *Kriegswagen* to watch the road for advancing British forces. They came back around noon the next day and reported that a column of Shermans was coming down the road. From the lookout's vantage point they counted about 80 tanks, a battalion strength. Kurt waited until the leading squadron was past the crossroads and was halted. He observed an officer go into the inn, leaving after a few minutes, quite unperturbed. Obviously the innkeeper had told him that there were no Germans in the area. As the officer climbed back on to his tank and the column started to move, Kurt opened fire, followed by the others. The British could barely retaliate and were shot to pieces, Shermans blazing and exploding up and down the road. Before he died in his Sherman, Kurt saw the same officer put two shells at close range into the inn, practically demolishing the small building. The friendly innkeeper and his wife were surely killed. A few only of the British tanks managed to escape, reversing down the road. It was a considerable victory for the Panthers. Kurt could see from the medal ribbons on the prisoners' tunics of a few that got out alive, that they were veterans of the North Africa Campaign. An added bonus.

The *Wehrmacht* withdrew out of the Bocage through the Falaise Gap to the open country which eventually led to the River Seine and Paris. General von Kluge, realising that, squeezed between the British and Americans, they were doomed to failure, requested permission from Hitler to retire beyond the Seine. Hitler refused and ordered an immediate counter-attack. By this time several generals had been wounded, among them Rommel and von Rundstedt; others had committed suicide following the reversals due to Hitler's mismanagement of the situation. Von Kluge, practically isolated with 200,000 men in what was to become known as the Killing Ground, eventually also committed suicide.

The *Wehrmacht* fought furiously for several days to prevent the British and Americans from closing the Falaise Gap, but eventually the Allies succeeded and there was now only one way out, towards the Seine. In spite of stubborn resistance, fighting every inch of the way, the Germans were slowly driven inwards. Von Kluge ordered the *Erst* Panzers to keep the way to Paris open at all costs. The colonel of the battalion was severely wounded during a massive bomber strike, so Kurt took over command. He thought, well, I have got the job at last. Maybe this time I shall be promoted. After all, suitable replacements are getting thin on the ground.

It was fated not to be.

The division divided at the escape route, literally back to back. Kurt found himself for the first time facing south from where the Americans could be expected.

'We shall soon see what the Yanks are made of,' he remarked.

The battle in the Killing Ground raged on for several days before the Allies turned their attention to the gateway out, determined to close the trap. Kurt was alerted by the reconnaissance patrols that a large force of Sherman tanks was approaching. He ordered the battalion to sit tight and wait until they could see 'the whites of their eyes', to fire when he did. On the Shermans came and they were met by a murderous hail of anti-tank shells. Just like Bray, the *Hussaren* thought, like sitting ducks. So it went on for, it seemed to the defenders, endless days and still the Americans came on in spite of the enormous losses, the ground littered with the smoking ruins of burned-out tanks. Von Kluge realised that the end was in sight and took the only possible decision, to pull out and be damned to Hitler. Save what could be saved to fight another day.

Troops weary from battle struggled back towards the protection of the Seine. At the end of the battle of the Killing Ground, 10,000 were dead and 50,000 prisoners taken. The Allies fought hard to close the passage, held open by an exhausted Panzer division. The *Erst* had suffered heavy casualties, down to less than half strength. When the general saw the end was in sight, he ordered the Panzer regiments to advance and attack the enemy with a last supreme effort. Kurt set off at the head of the battalion on the Ride of the Valkries, hurling the Panthers at the group of Shermans nearest. In the mêlée that followed, a Sherman fired at Kurt's Panther at close range, the shell passing through the thinner armour plating on the side of the turret and smashing Kurt almost in half.

Poor brave Kurt, at 28 years old, did not deserve to die. Perhaps he was chosen by the Valkyrie warrior maidens and carried off to Valhalla, the Hall of Heroes, by Brunhilde the warrior chieftainess herself. At least he was spared the ignominy of the long withdrawal to the *Reich*; the joining up of the victorious Allies and Russians in Berlin and along the river Elbe and the suicide of Adolf Hitler.

Farewell to Kurt, last of a line of gallant soldiers.